THE DRIVERS

by

Paul Hernacki

Acknowledgements

I'd like to thank my wonderful wife, Karen, for believing in me when I suddenly decided to write my first novel. Thank you for being so supportive throughout it all, for listening to me, for putting up with me, and for being my very first reader and a wonderful editor. You are amazing.

I'd like to thank my professional editor, Shannon, for being a great friend. Thank you for your thoughtfulness, thoroughness, insights, honesty, and talents.

The two of you made this a much better story.

I'd also like to thank my mother, Kathleen. You gave me a love for reading and you are the person that taught me to write.

Prologue

We've never seen anything like these patterns before. They don't conform to any of our existing probability models.

Studying them will take time, and more resources considering all those we just lost, but the opportunity is tremendous.

This is well beyond what we were expecting to find.

Extraordinary. Communicating our findings now.

Chapter One – Mia

The children huddled as silently as they could under the tarp, trying to slow their breathing and muffle the cries of the younger ones. The heat outside was already oppressive, but with so many pressed up against each other in a dense pile, under the thick shielded tarp, it was almost unbearable. Humidity was high. They were soaked and dirty. Their collective smell only added to the discomfort. Mia could feel the beads of sweat run down her skin and drop from her body.

Mia could feel one of the younger children tremble next to her. The little girl started to sob quietly. Mia struggled to free her arm to reach out and try to comfort her. She whispered, "Hey, it's going to be OK. Just try to stay quiet. I won't let anything happen to you." She couldn't see the girl's face in the darkness, but she did stop making noise. That's what mattered most right now. They needed to be quiet. Mia wrapped fingers with the girl and they held each other close.

It had just gotten dark in the jungle when the adults had heard the drones coming. It wasn't a surprise. They had seen them earlier in the day from a distance and knew they would probably come back after dark. Their group had managed to avoid detection earlier, but only because one of their spotters had seen the drones from a distance. This time their first warning was the soft hum in the sky, and by then they had just enough time to go into hiding.

They had begun camping here just a few weeks ago. After months of navigating deeper and deeper into the jungle, the group had finally decided they could rest a while. Maybe longer? Their group had started out with nearly a hundred, but the recent journey had whittled that down to eighty-two. They lost quite a few to the jungle itself and its many perils, a couple to hunger, and a few more to sickness. They'd been lucky to avoid detection up to this point or run into any corporate forces. This little valley seemed perfect. It was remote and surrounded by some difficult cliffs, but it was fertile with plenty of natural fruit. There was also ample wildlife they could potentially hunt, even if a good deal of it was hunting them right back.

Mia could hear the hums in the sky grow louder. They were still relatively soft, almost soothing sounds if she hadn't known what they represented. She didn't know if they were from the Cartel or if the land they were on had been sold off to one of the other corps. It didn't matter. The result for them was the same. Someone was scouting the land they were on for resources and production value. Someone owned it and was preparing to exploit it, so they were sending scouts.

Scouts weren't anything close to the hard-core military drones, the security drones, or the more advanced hunter models they'd heard about. But they were armed. They didn't have the high-end energy weapons the other models had, but they had enough ballistic firepower to take out a threat or clear a small group with ease.

The hovering of the aerial scouts grew louder as they swept back and forth above. Mia could barely see through a crack where the tarp met the ground as lights danced about the terrain around her. If they were lucky, the tarps they had bought from the black market in Manaus would shield them from the scouts' sensors. Mia didn't understand how the tarps worked, but they were made of something that dulled their heat signatures and bio signs from detection. Hopefully, they would look like a group of capybaras sleeping together in the dampness and fall under the biological thresholds the scout's sensors were calibrated to detect and report.

They had already planned to move camp tonight and leave the valley. As soon as the scouts had come earlier in the day, they knew this land wasn't safe anymore. The plan was to leave at night. No matter how dangerous the jungle was after dark, it didn't compare to trying to travel with drones in the area during daylight.

They knew the drones would come back at dark tonight. It was protocol, just in case they'd been seen coming in the daylight. She'd heard the adults talking, and they had told her and the older children that they needed to be strong and look after the little ones while they took up positions with the few weapons they had.

They did have a few decent weapons. It had cost them a lot. Mia didn't know what they had traded for them, but she knew it cost a lot of their food rations, their medicine, and other things the adults wouldn't talk to them about. It was just a few rifles that were relative relics, but they could fire high velocity tracer rounds that could take out small drones and even some of the lower-grade military units. It was something.

The humming started to take on a frenetic pattern, like mosquitos at close range. The lights outside began to dance. The first crack of a tracer round laced through the air. Mia didn't know if it was the scouts or her people who shot first. It didn't matter. Immediately the night was filled with the terrifying sound of rounds firing. The girl next to her started screaming, as did many of the other children under the tarp. She shouted at them to stay quiet and be still. She begged them not to move. The sound was deafening as shells ripped through the air. Yells and screams could be heard outside. There were explosions, the sound of metal crashing to the ground, and the smells of electric fires, shots fired, and burned flesh.

Round after round was fired until it was just a din of noise. More screams. Cries. Sobbing. Mia was terrified. Two more explosions. More tracer rounds streaked through the air. Then it grew quieter and a slight hum could be heard fading away. Mia was breathing so hard it hurt her lungs. She ached. She wanted to cry but couldn't. She tried to calm her breathing. The only thing overpowering the smell of stink and sweat was now the smell of weapons fire and burning metal which tasted sick on Mia's dry tongue. She wanted to vomit.

Then… silence. She didn't know if it was seconds or minutes. It was hard to tell. She was disoriented. Everything was in slow motion but coupled with sensory overload. She almost blacked out. She waited another couple of minutes and then told the younger children to stay put. Without being too loud, she called out in a loud whisper to one of the other older kids, a boy about her age, "Manny! You and I are going out to take a look." When she heard Manny acknowledge, she gave him a signal and they wormed their way out from the pile under the tarp.

Even in the dark, they could see the carnage. Several fires burned with the wreckage of scout drones, smoke rippling up into the sky. Nearby were a couple of other tarps where the other children had been hiding. One was moving like a wriggling pile of worms and filled with sobs, much like the tarp they had just left. The other was ripped to shreds, unmoving, and soaked with blood. Mia saw it and immediately clutched

Manny tightly, a horrified scream held back on her lips. He patted her back awkwardly.

"Come on. We have to see about the others," said Mia as she let him go.

Mia was crying. They couldn't see much. The only light was from the fires of burning drones. They walked towards where they knew the adults had taken up positions and started to call out softly to find survivors. They kept calling hoping someone had to be out there. That's when they started to find them, one after the other. All of them. Bodies ripped to shreds by shells from the drones. Littered around the area, the bodies were everywhere. They'd been gunned down like animals.

Manny walked a bit further and saw his own father lying on the ground. There was a rifle lying just a few feet away. His body was riddled with shots, and his face was barely recognizable from a shot to his head. Manny knelt next to him, made the sign of the cross, put his hand on his father's chest, and began to cry.

Chapter Two – Eli

"First it was the drivers."

Eli sat with the rest of his teenage classmates in one of the austere rooms at the Athletic Employment Opportunity Camp listening to a holographic projection of a professor. The professor wasn't even a real human being. It was an AI. Eli was bored, but he knew these classes were mandatory for graduation to be sure they were sufficiently "acclimated" to society. History was one of his least favorite subjects. He found it depressing, and it always felt like propaganda.

The professor continued the lesson while a combination of screens and projections around them displayed related video and statistics. "It was just in big cities initially, but it didn't stop there. It began with the taxi drivers. Nobody except the taxi drivers were sad to see it happen. People were tired of sitting in a dirty taxi with a driver that was often talking on the phone in a foreign language. People were much happier to summon a clean, driverless car via an app on their phone and have it effortlessly and quietly drive them to their destination.

"Drivers in the United States found themselves out of work within a couple of years. Over 250,000 taxi drivers, more than 300,000 limo and personal drivers, and nearly a million more people that made money at least part time providing transportation services all found themselves without any work in that field. It wasn't long until the same thing happened with truck drivers and delivery drivers. That number multiplied massively on a global scale in major cities in first world countries."

Eli struggled to grasp the numbers. He'd spent almost his entire life in the camp. The total number of people he'd ever even seen was less than a few thousand.

"This also meant there was not a need for related jobs like parking attendants, parking valets, or tollbooth operators. Commercial airline pilots were not far behind. The entire transportation industry had been reinvented with far fewer human operators. Even transportation logistics analysts found themselves being replaced by machine learning."

Eli tried to imagine what it must have been like when humans drove vehicles, but it was difficult. He did think he would have liked to have driven one of the race cars that was displayed in the videos. Those looked like fun.

"Next came call center agents - people that answered calls for large corporations as part of customer service. Artificial intelligence and machine learning had become advanced enough to be able to do a better job at a much lower cost to handle customer issues over chat or even the phone. There still had to be a few humans on hand to handle escalations, and to deal with premium customers. But as an industry, the AIs were rapidly able to replace over 90% of call center workers. Call center agents, nearly two million jobs in the United States and millions more around the globe, joined the drivers.

"That's what they started to say on the news: 'They joined the drivers'."

A news clip played with a talking head in a suit saying, "Call center agents are joining the drivers as they too find their jobs replaced by technology."

"It was an unparalleled time in history. The rapid advance of AI, machine learning, and robotics was like wildfire. Early technology corporations including Google, Apple, Microsoft, Intel, Facebook, HP, IBM, GE, Amazon, and many others all vied to create better AI, robotics, integrated networks and improved user interfaces, services, and control."

Eli looked over at his friend, Tessa, who was staring intently at the lesson. They already knew most of this from previous lessons, but she was like a sponge for any information she could get about the world outside the camp.

"The advancement of technology wasn't much solace to the drivers and call center agents looking for work. Fast food workers, over two million of them in the United States and cashiers at retail establishments, over three million jobs, were among the next to join the drivers. People were perfectly happy to just walk out of stores with their goods automatically charged to their credit without standing in lines. Demands for higher wages by these same workers also didn't help when the cost of technology to replace them with easy self-service solutions became lower and lower.

"Other jobs quickly followed: paralegals, administrative assistants, a significant number of administrative government jobs, and low-level financial services.

"That is now known as the first wave. There was a short time when many of the newly unemployed were offered jobs in urban sanitation, but that ended quickly. Many were unwilling to take those jobs, and before long AI-controlled drones could do it faster, better, and cheaper.

"The second wave was focused on purpose-built, utility robots and AI-controlled drones. Agricultural jobs, over two million of them, were lost as harvesting and crop-care robots became cheaper and ubiquitous. Home and office cleaners, skyscraper window washers, miners, timber producers, and most everything left in manufacturing... the millions of humans previously filling these jobs all joined the drivers.

"Another shift was the impact in the security and safety industries. Military drones and robots exploded as an industry, replacing the need for over a million soldiers in the United States alone. Drones also found their way into police forces, corporate and personal security, and even fire departments, taking away nearly another million jobs in the United States. They were highly effective, and it no longer required putting a human life at risk. Once the price points diminished, there was simply no reason to put a person's life in danger in combat or in maintaining basic security.

"As crime by the jobless and homeless began to increase, cities began to clear their homeless entirely, forcing them to leave corporate-controlled secured zones. They were safe from the security drones so long as they stayed off corporate properties used for farming, away from shareholder cities, and away from popular tourist attractions and destinations of the shareholders. It created a massive group of people living in migrant communities in the least desirable parts of the country or in the countless, now broken, small towns that had long been abandoned by shareholders."

Eli could see Tessa getting visibly angry at that last part. She had some strong political views. He tried to stay out of it and focus on the sports and athletic training. That was their ticket out.

An audio alert sounded signifying that the class was over. Instantly the professor disappeared and was replaced by their upcoming schedule.

None of them needed to be reminded of where to go next. It was highly routine.

Tessa was getting up from her chair, cursing softly under her breath about corporate propaganda. Eli leaned in and tapped her on the shoulder. She turned and at least gave him a smile.

"Hey, I get it," said Eli. "It sucks, but there's nothing either of us are going to do to fix it. Besides, it's game time, and this is a big one. This is what matters for us."

Chapter Three - Ryland

"These might be the best eggs you've ever made," said Ryland as he looked up and smiled at his wife, Caitlin. He still thought she was as beautiful today as the day he met her. She had long hair that was colored light blonde and was dressed in athletic clothes to head to her workout after breakfast.

"Thank you," she smiled at him after sipping her coffee. "I didn't do anything that special. I added sausage, because who doesn't like sausage? But I also harvested some of our shitakes this morning and added those. I'm glad you like them."

Their youngest daughter, who was at the table with them and dressed for school, agreed. "Mom, really, these are excellent." Tamara was sixteen and she was the spitting image of her mother. She devoured some toast and drained her orange juice. "I have to get going. We have a big test today in physics, and the robotics team is holding final tryouts this afternoon for the season."

"I'd wish you luck," laughed Ryland, "but you don't need it. I saw what you could do during your internship with your uncle Logan's company this past summer. You're a lock, maybe even a strong bet for captain."

"Don't jinx me, dad," laughed Tamara. "OK, love you. I have to run." She gave them each a kiss on the head and headed out the door to catch a transport. Ryland adored his two daughters. His oldest daughter was nineteen and had just started her freshman year at Cal Tech. He'd give her a call on his way to the office just to check in on her and say hello. She'd only moved out a month or so ago, but he already missed her.

"I'm heading out in a few minutes for my run," said Caitlin, "and then getting in a quick workout. After that I'll be headed down to the valley for the afternoon. We're reviewing the new AI recommendations for seed diversification in next year's crops. Will you be home for dinner?"

"I should be," answered Ryland. "We have a lot to do at work, but I hate to miss any chance I have to enjoy dinner with you, even after more than twenty-two years of marriage."

The Drivers

"You're cheesy," she laughed, "but I love that about you." She finished her coffee and took a long drink from a glass of ice water. "OK, I'm going running. See you tonight." She leaned in gave him a long kiss. "Don't get too caught up in your games today. We like spending time with you too. See you tonight."

With that she left, and the house was quiet. Sunlight shone in through the many windows. The yard was small but filled with plants and trees. Ryland finished his breakfast and coffee and left the dishes for the drones to clean up. He grabbed his Heads-Up-Display and headed out the door knowing the security would activate after he left. Waiting for him out front was his personal vehicle, a new model Mercedes-Benz. The door opened as he approached. He stepped inside and sat down. It knew where to take him.

Ryland Grey was lucky, and he knew it. As the car silently moved into the streets to take him to work, he let his mind drift off a bit to his childhood. His mother was with a global investment firm where she eventually rose to the level of managing partner in the real estate division. She was smart enough to have begun putting a lot of their own money into key real estate investment trusts, and into firms advancing AI and robotics.

They had lived in a spacious apartment in a high rise in Manhattan. His father, who worked in AI development, was gone frequently on trips, mostly to San Francisco, China, or Israel. His mother also traveled but not quite as much. He and his two brothers had plenty of opportunity to do whatever they wanted without a lot of supervision from their nanny.

Ryland was a classic middle child, a little more than a year younger than his older brother, Logan (who was far too intelligent to compete with), and a couple of years older than his younger brother, Mayson (who was simply far nicer, more likeable, and more easy-going than Ryland would ever be). He was OK with that. The biggest thing that kept them bonded in their youth was their dad's love of old movies, comedy, science fiction, and video games which he indoctrinated them with. They had spent countless hours together watching and re-watching what were now ancient relics of entertainment and pop culture.

For Ryland, as a child, the extensive amount of time his parents were gone mostly meant time to play video games. He adored them. He was addicted to them and passionate about them. He was amazing at them. His brothers played them as well and were quite good, but he could pick up a new game instantly. He loved the problem solving. He loved learning how to beat each game and his opponents. There was always a way, you just had to see it. By the time he was twelve he'd begun collecting vintage gaming systems and their incredibly outdated games. He had an original Atari 2600 with the faux wood sticker paneling, an Intellivision, a Coleco, and numerous Playstations, Nintendos, and Xboxes with hundreds and hundreds of titles. He studied and mastered them all.

He loved the simplicity of *Space Invaders*, studied the initial flops of TV show and game marriages like *Defiance*, and reveled in studying how games like *Madden Football* drove changes in live television coverage and in-stadium experiences.

His obsession concerned his parents a bit, but they had a hard time arguing it. He did well in school and wasn't anti-social at all, quite the opposite. He was outgoing and friendly, even if playing live sports and exercise weren't high on his list. He just loved games. If it hadn't been for that, and what he considered his extreme luck in the genetic lottery of life, he wouldn't be in the position he was today.

At the age of forty-five now, he was Chief Game Architect for the world's largest producer of interactive games, Immersive Magic. He loved his job. He looked forward to every single day, and today was no different. His team was working on a new title that would involve some ground-breaking concepts including some things that had precipitated investment from the military for its alternate applications. It also required solving some problems with limitations in current technology to make his new idea possible. Solving those kinds of problems is what he lived for.

Before he arrived at work he remembered to put in a quick call to his oldest daughter, Vanessa. She was just about to head into class and didn't have a lot of time to talk. It was great to see her and hear her voice, even if just for a few minutes. She told him she was doing great. Seeing her smile and heading to class at Cal Tech made him so proud. They hung up after she promised to visit next weekend.

Ryland heard the audio notification that meant he had arrived at his destination and stepped out of the car. They had big things to do today at Immersive Magic. He had a feeling about today.

Chapter Four – Nicodemus

Nicodemus sat patiently as the other board members began to appear in the virtual meeting room. He sat at the head of a long, beautifully polished oak table with an impossibly high, glorious view of the Rocky Mountains. It was not real, of course. It was all virtual reality, but it was a stunning setting worthy of the largest shareholders in the corporation gathering for a snap meeting.

No one was physically there. Nicodemus was in his apartment in a Manhattan high-rise. The others were likely scattered around the globe on yachts, at resorts, or at one of their many private homes and retreats. Each would join via their networked Heads-Up Display with their avatar to the virtual room. Heads-Up-Displays, (commonly called HUD devices) had displaced all previous forms of interface to networks. They interfaced directly with the optic nerve enabling anything from augmented reality to full, virtual world immersion. They allowed a person to essentially become part of what they were seeing, allowing them to see and interact with anything they wanted without any glasses or other devices. HUD devices had become incredibly small, but all self-contained with a power source, and network interface. Most people wore them as small, and occasionally decorative attachments on the side of their head. For security they even imprinted with your DNA as a form of access control.

Even though there were just a little over thirty people assembled in this virtual gathering, they collectively represented enough shares to authorize significant actions on behalf of the corporation. Several were high ranking elected board members in the government.

One by one the board members began to appear in their seats. They engaged in casual banter with each other as Nicodemus sat silently at the head of the table. Once the last of the board arrived, nearly four minutes behind schedule, he interrupted the din of mindless conversation to begin.

"Good morning, ladies and gentlemen," he said. "We have important business with which to attend."

The table fell silent. They were all wealthy, important people, but there wasn't one of them who didn't slightly fear Nicodemus, his political savvy, or his massive number of shares.

"Thank you for being here on short notice." He got up from his virtual chair and began to walk around the table. A display formed in the space above the middle of the table.

The board looked like a group of well-dressed peacocks. In real life they could be wearing anything, or even nothing. It was all just avatars. It was impossible to tell who was even paying attention. Any one of them could be getting a massage right now, be getting laid, or be lounging by a pool with a margarita. Hopefully enough of them were paying attention and taking this as seriously as Nicodemus.

"I'm going to pretend like you all read the briefing I sent as well as the proposal which has already been seconded. What you see in front of you are the findings from the exploratory mission we authorized. We've obviously found more than we were expecting, but we did find the resources we desperately need. This communication, he waved at the display, just came through an hour ago. You're all aware of the time at origination. You also see the recommendation from the onsite resources."

Nods. Questioning looks. Concern. Several people were truly in wonderment and looked excited. It was about what he expected.

"Holy!" exclaimed Melissa from behind a virtual cocktail. He was sure there was a real one to match it and noted how her avatars just kept looking younger and younger every time he saw her. "Nic, is this for real?! This is exciting!" She slurred a bit. It was a good bet she had been drinking; it *was* after 2PM on a Tuesday.

"It is," issued Nicodemus as a declaration, "but I'm recommending extermination. We need the resources and cannot risk alternative scenarios. There are too many unknowns. I'm also concerned about security, so I'm additionally recommending more aggressive measures, as described in the proposal, against known dissidents and anyone we suspect might be working against our interests from within the corporation. We have no room for failure if we are to protect shareholder interests at large."

The room fell silent as they considered the words just spoken. They all knew that he said nothing lightly.

"Resource mining has already been compromised, and at a massive cost to us," said Nicodemus. "We've lost numerous units. The resources we can exploit are critical to our roadmap. They will put us well ahead of all the competition and solidify our position as the dominant corporation on the planet for many decades to come. Our choice is clear."

"Are you kidding me?" asked a man at the end of the table. His avatar was wearing a white suit, flip-flops, and sunglasses. He had high, blonde hair in the front. His face was sharp and had a couple days of stubble. His name was Evan, and his family controlled a considerable number of shares from their investments in aerospace, med-tech, and robotics.

Evan stood up and started walking around the table. "We've made one of the greatest discoveries in the history of mankind, something people have dreamed about for centuries, which has enormous potential, and your recommendation is to obliterate it?"

"Please try to be rational, Evan," said Nicodemus. "I have only the shareholders' interests in mind. We are still in several trade wars, and at risk of a couple of real wars if we are not careful. We have an opportunity to put ourselves vastly ahead. We'll be untouchable."

Evan had a dramatic, ideological look of dismay on his face. "Are you telling me you're willing to throw this away?"

"Evan, this is not the end of our explorations, it is the beginning. We need to prioritize and take a long-term view even if we are sacrificing in the short term."

"That's exactly my point, Nic!" said Evan "I'm taking a longer-term view, not just focused on our immediate trade issues and military concerns. Think of the possibilities! I motion to kill the chair's proposal. Can I get a second?"

Evan looked around the table. The silence was deafening.

"Seriously, people?" he shouted. "You're ok with the destruction of something potentially incredible simply because this asshole says you're more likely to get richer in the next few years if you vote for murder? Are you fucking kidding me?!"

"My motion is up for vote," declared Nicodemus.

Every board member now had the measure in front of them on their HUD. They each interacted with it in their own way- voice, retina focus, touch, but they all voted, except for Evan who stared around at the room.

`The motion has carried.`

They all heard the disembodied voice of an AI speak.

"You'll be pleased to know we plan to take measures to preserve opportunities for research, Evan. It's all detailed in the proposal," said Nicodemus coldly.

"You'll rot in hell. You know that, right?" said Evan.

"Lucky for me," smiled Nicodemus, "Your family's med-tech companies have made sure that day will be a long way off."

"This meeting is adjourned," announced Nicodemus.

Evan disappeared from the room, as did all the others from the table.

Nicodemus sat silently for a moment then spoke, "Dan, are we good?"

A middle-aged man in a dark business suit appeared in the room.

"Yes, we are good," said Dan Stern. "The full motion has carried so all executive orders listed in the motion have now been triggered. The comms with the orders we drafted will go out automatically."

"Excellent," said Nicodemus.

"Will that be all, sir?" asked Dan.

"You don't agree with what I'm doing on this one, do you, Dan? I can tell." said Nicodemus.

"That's irrelevant," said Dan. "My job is to advise you and the corporation on legal matters and to oversee legal affairs, not to make policy. You aren't violating any corporate laws, bi-laws, or treaties. International law in this area is vague and contentious. The legal exposure is minimal at best."

"But you don't agree, do you? You wouldn't have voted for this measure?"

"I put my trust in you and the board to do what is best for the corporation," said Dan.

Nicodemus looked at him for a long moment. "I believe that's true. Do you have any additional guidance on this matter?"

"Yes, sir. I advise that we should begin talking to Public Relations now."

Chapter Five – Eli

The blow hit Eli square in the chest and sent him flying onto his back gasping for air. The wind was knocked out of his lungs. It burned. How the hell had he not anticipated that? He cursed. He hadn't lost the ball, so it was still theirs. Eli fought the pain and pulled himself together. He opened his eyes, got up, flipped the ball to the ref, and went into the huddle while breathing like an asthmatic dog.

They were down by two points with just seconds remaining on the play clock. They needed a full three-point score to win and had just enough time for one more play. This had been a rough game. Both teams had fought for every inch and every point. It had even gotten ugly a few times. Most everyone on the field was on the verge of getting offers from the pros. It was the opportunity to finally be shareholders, to have real currency. They knew they were being evaluated at the highest levels, and this Mayhem game impacted which team would draft them and how many shares they would get in their initial offers.

Mayhem was an aptly named sport in many ways. It could easily look like insanity. Those who played it seriously understood how much sophisticated order there was in the apparent chaos. The creators of the sport had decided rugby and football simply weren't violent enough, so they added mixed martial arts, and then borrowed from the fictional sport of Quidditch to add three scoring goal circles at each end of the court three meters above the ground. It was incredibly violent, but also required precision, grace, agility, and speed. If it wasn't for the impact suits the players wore it would be impossible for anyone to play the sport at a high level more than once or twice before their Mayhem career would be ended by injury. Of course, the younger kids playing it outdoors in make-shift courts didn't get the expensive impact suits, which did land many of them in the infirmary. That was just the risk one took to get a shot at the big leagues in the most popular sport on the planet.

Eli had spent plenty of time in the infirmary from sports and training mishaps. Eli was a natural athlete: speed, strength, highly coordinated, great visual acuity, and a real mind for games and strategy. He may not have been the very fastest or strongest, but he more than made up for that with agility, dedication to training, creativity, and above all, a desire to win that was hard to match. "Just keep winning". That's what his mom had told him to do.

Having recently turned sixteen, he had been training and playing sports in this camp since his parents left him here at just four years old. He barley even remembered them. Only vague pictures remained in his head of their faces. Playing sports was all he'd ever known, but he did remember a little bit of life before he came here. He remembered they had no food. No home. Nothing. Always running. He was constantly hungry. They all were. His mom was always sick. He also remembered what she told him when she left him here because he'd repeated it to himself over and over again from the very first night: "Win. Just keep winning. If you do, you get to stay here, and you will never go hungry again. They can't make you leave if you keep winning." His parents told him they would see him again, but he'd long since stopped believing that. He doubted they were even still alive. He'd be surprised if they were.

Now he was about to lose a match that could make a big difference in what happened when he finally graduated from the camp next month. The worst part of losing would be that the other team was captained by Zacharias. Zach was incredibly talented, and bigger and stronger than Eli. They constantly battled for first position in all the rankings. But Zach was brutal. He enjoyed hurting people. He was a bully and always had been. He was the only one that could still beat Eli in one-on-one combat in their martial arts training and matches. The difference was that Zach took pleasure in causing pain, while Eli's only interest was in winning, not hurting anyone more than necessary. Eli hated Zach and he was sure the feeling was mutual.

Calming his breathing using techniques he'd been taught for years, Eli looked around at his team in the huddle through the Heads-Up Display, or HUD, on his helmet. They were all waiting for him to make the call.

"What's it going to be, cap? Suicide Run or Hail Mary?" joked Tessa. He could totally picture the crooked smile she had when she said that under her helmet. He and Tessa had been best friends for years. Their relationship was more like a brother and sister than just friends. She was smart, funny, and easily one of the top athletes in the camp. She had an impressive top ranking in mixed martial arts, and what she lacked in strength, she more than made up for in agility and unstoppable drive. She was also drop-dead gorgeous, but Tessa had made it abundantly clear to everyone in the camp that her *only* interest was in graduating and making the pros.

"I got an idea," Eli told the team.

"Shit! Last time you said that I spent a week in the infirmary, Cap," laughed Derrick.

"Yeah, but we won." said Ho-Jun.

"Tru dat," said Derrick. "We trust you. It's your call."

"OK," he looked at them, "They know we have to go for three and that we have only one chance. They have the best goaltender in the camp, no offense Shabaz."

"Fuck you, Cap." said Shabaz as he fist-bumped Eli.

"They're all going to expect me to try and take the ball in, so that's exactly what we're going to do. Zach will be sending his goons straight at us. He'll probably hang back, waiting to get the finishing blow himself between us and the goaltender. He'll want the glory of ending this himself and trying to send me to the infirmary so that every scout watching this vid can see it. So, we're going to give them exactly what they expect."

"Huh?" said Ho-Jun. "WTF, Cap?"

"Tess, you remember that idea for a play I told you about last week?"

"Ummm, yeah. I remember telling you it was a stupid idea. Like, really, really, colossally, stupid. The physics are insane. It'll never work. You haven't even practiced it once. There's no way you can get the timing right."

"Good, so you remember. Let's do it."

"You're going to end up crippled and looking like an idiot."

"That's what I love about you, Tess, your positive attitude and vote of confidence."

"Anyone want to tell the rest of us what we're doing?" asked Shabaz.

"You don't want to know," said Eli. "When the ball is snapped, roll right and start taking out defenders or at least pushing them back towards the goal, then execute a basic running wall sweep. I'll be headed straight for the right goal. Tess and I have the rest."

"It was nice knowing you, Cap," said Derrick.

"OK, on one." They broke the huddle and went to the line in formation. The clock was ticking down. They had five seconds to start the play and just eight seconds left on the game clock, but as long as they got the play started the game continued until the ball was dead. Five seconds didn't seem like much, but it was amazing in moments like these how slow it could feel. He positioned himself a couple of meters behind the line. He scanned the defense. They had two up on the line ready to rush. A third was dropped back on the right. They knew that was his preferred side. Zach was dropped back, as expected, closer to the goal.

"One!" Eli shouted, and Derrick snapped the ball back to him.

Ho-Jun and Shabaz rolled right and engaged the two defenders. Ho-Jun preferred Kung-Fu and surprised his target a bit with an aggressive flying kick, while Shabaz was more of a Jiu-Jitsu guy using a bit more patience and gauging a way to unbalance his opponent.

Derrick swept behind them and headed for the third who was running in from the side like a sniper bullet. Eli rolled right and feigned like he was going to try and go around the end but then cut back quickly to the left. He made his way quickly straight at the fray that was rapidly forming into a flurry of punches and sweeping kicks. He took one more step, cradled the ball in his arms, and leaped into the air. He launched himself off the back of a fallen Shabaz and tucked into a tight forward roll straight towards the right-side goal. He had about twelve meters between him and the goaltender.

Eli was hurtling straight towards the goal with the ball and completely exposed. He felt every movement, every motion, every turn. As he started the second rotation of his tuck roll in the air, he could see Zacharias leaping towards him with his foot extended a bit more than a meter away and knew it was going to hurt. Too late now, he knew this was coming. He'd counted on it. He also briefly saw the goaltender leap up to block the right circle just before he started his rotation. Right then, before he got half way into it, he flattened out and lobbed the ball backward at seemingly no one. With millisecond timing, Tessa leaped off the back of a defender, horizontally flying across the court from the right side to the left, caught the ball in mid-air, and launched it straight into the center of the undefended, three-point goal.

Tessa landed gracefully as the goal buzzer sounded right along with the end of game. Eli had twisted in the air just in time to let Zacharias' foot connect with his back to minimize the damage, but he still crumpled and fell to the floor with a big thud.

Eli could hear his team yelling and cheering. Tessa ran over to him, "You dead?" she asked.

He laughed. "I don't think so," he responded. She helped him up and the rest of the team joined them.

"Holy shit!" said Ho-Jun, "I've never seen anyone do that before. Hell, the pros are going to be practicing that move once this vid gets out."

"Just lucky I had a good receiver, Ho-Jun," said Eli. "And a helluva team that set up the play and made it possible," smiled Eli. Goddamn his back hurt like hell. He was pretty sure he had at least one or two fractured ribs. "Tess deserves all the credit, she scored the winning goal."

"Tess is taking your stupid, sacrificial ass to the infirmary," said Tessa, "I can't believe you actually pulled that shit off."

"Just doing my job," said Eli, "Gotta keep winning, right?" He smiled at Tessa and his team.

"Zach looks seriously pissed," said Ho-Jun.

"You always know how to make me smile, buddy", said Eli.

Chapter Six – Mia

It had taken a while, but Mia had finally calmed down the younger children from a state of complete hysteria. Most were still sobbing. It was hard not to cry as they lay on earth soaked in the blood of their parents. She found Manny kneeling on the ground, hunched over the rifle he had taken from his dead father. He was staring out into the trees.

Moments after the massacre the jungle had returned to normal with the deafening chirps of insects, howler monkeys, and plenty more dangerous things. It was amazing really...how quickly nature could go silent, retreat and hide when a threat arrived, but how quickly it returned when the danger was gone.

"We have to leave," said Mia simply.

"We don't have to," said Manny. "I mean, we can stay here and wait for the drones to return and cut us into ribbons. It's that or march a bunch of kids deeper into the jungle where we could easily get eaten by something, starve, or die of some disease. If we're lucky we find a new temporary home that doesn't try to kill us for a few months before more drones show up to claim that land for some corporation. Alternatively, we head back to the cities or other driver communes. We could survive long enough to get raped and enslaved. These all seem like great options to me. The only other choice I see is to head straight for the nearest CartelCorp employment opportunity camps and hope they admit maybe half of us. Some of us might live, and one of us could even grow up to be a real shareholder. My money is on Jelaena. That girl is sharp for a four-year old."

"That's not funny, Manny."

"I'm not trying to be funny, Mia. Our choices aren't good, and there's nobody left older than us to decide what we're going to do. How do we want to die and how much are we willing to risk?"

"There's Argentina," offered Mia. "You've heard what the adults said. Argentina is one of the last safe places for free people without the corps and the robots. They welcome drivers! It sounds like paradise."

"Seriously, Mia?! Argentina is thousands of kilometers from here! How the hell are we going to march a bunch of children several thousand kilometers through dangerous lands and jungles, through Cartel properties and rogue driver gangs? It would take over a year. How is that even remotely an option?" Manny was shaking. Mia could tell he was out of control and his emotions were raging. He was scared. But she knew he was right about their chances of reaching Argentina.

"I know," responded Mia softly, starting to cry. "It's just…we could have real lives and stop running. We just need to figure out how to get there."

"That's right. The small problem of 4,000 kilometers, no transportation, only a few antiquated rifles wielded by teenagers, and two dozen children under twelve marching through the jungle for a year. What could go wrong? Plus, who knows if the rumors are true? We have no idea what we'll really find in Argentina."

"We can't tell them it's over," pleaded Mia as she looked at the other children.

"We need to do what's best for them to survive," said Manny. "I think the C22 camps are our best option if we live long enough to make it there. It's only a few weeks march to the nearest ones I think."

"I know where I'll end up if we do that and I don't want that life," said Mia. "I know half the kids will go nowhere and be right back out here. Out of the other half, maybe one or two will make it more than a year or two. We can do better."

"You sound a lot like your mother, Mia. She was always up for a fight."

"Thank you, Manny. And I know that you have your father's heart. Let's do the right thing."

Chapter Seven - Ryland

Ryland walked quickly across the campus of the Department of Entertainment towards the game studio he worked for. It was a beautiful, sunny day in the California Bay Area. It was still a bit cool, but the sun was nice and warm on his face. He was anxious to get to work. He and his team were beginning to develop a new title. It was his own concept and he was incredibly excited about it. They were going to push the envelope for neural feedback and leveraging sensory data of the players. They would take collaborative game play to a new level and make the game mechanics more real than what anyone else was doing. They were exploring new technology that would make haptic interfaces look like ancient history.

Most importantly, Ryland loved the story behind the new title. He adored storytelling. He considered it the most important part of the game, and a bit of a lost art. It's what made his games different than the pure carnage or pleasure titles out there. He also had a knack for creating incredible problems and playscapes that enabled near infinite creativity. They were puzzles to solve with no single solution.

His newest title concept was going to be unlike anything done before and would keep Immersive Magic well ahead of their competition. There was a lot of excitement right now about the possibility of finding other life in the universe. In real life, the most recent generation of Faster Than Light, or FTL, drives had finally made reaching other stars something that took mere years. The first missions were already underway. Unfortunately, FTL technology, which had been invented by the AIs at a surprisingly rapid rate, was still completely destructive to organic tissue. This meant only the robots and AIs were able to go on these missions.

Still, it was exciting, and it afforded Ryland the opportunity to create an incredible story line about aliens awakened to our presence by the unknowing AIs. They would also add some new technological breakthroughs in the immersion interactions, thanks to a collaborative project they were doing with the military and their copious funding.

He walked into the studio and saw his team leads gathered together near the center of the main room. The entire studio was his design. It was extremely open with a lot of sunlight, and natural plants and trees. He wanted the central room to contrast with the technology and the many windowless rooms they used for some of the deeper game design and modeling. He ordered a vanilla latte via his HUD as he walked across the room. Around him were large displays with some of the concept art they had been working on for the new title.

By the time he reached the center of the room a small drone handed him his latte. The design and development leads were all looking at a shared 3D display in the center renderer instead of from their individual HUDs. The center renderer was his idea. Many of his younger team members didn't get it and preferred their HUDs, but Ryland knew there was something to real-life interaction and collaboration that could often result in a more creative product. It was about taking a step back to take steps forward.

"Good morning. Did I miss something?" he announced himself.

"Boss!" said Duncan, his Creative Director. "Holy jeez! You have to see this. It just came in. Wasn't really meant for us. It's vidscans from one of the C22 athletic camps, but I have a friend that works in the Department of Athletics who owed me a favor. Check this shit out. Annnnnnd... you're welcome." He set the vid to play.

The video was a play-by-play with close-ups, bio scan results, audio and video of a Mayhem match. The winning play was executed by the sixteen-year-old captain of the team; it was at the edge of physically impossible. It took incredible guts to try that move. The agility and timing were off the scale. As impressive as that was, what Ryland loved most was witnessing the heart, and the creativity. The kid who pulled that off was exactly what Ryland needed to test some of their new technology.

"It's hot, right Ry?" said Kira, his most trusted advisor and second in command on all new product development. Kira was Ryland's heir apparent. She was young, but incredibly gifted.

"Have you confirmed this is real?" he asked.

"Confirmed, boss" said Duncan.

"How long ago did this happen?" asked Ryland.

"Less than a couple of hours ago," replied Duncan.

"He's sixteen? So, he'll be up for draft in a couple of months? I need him here now." Ryland looked at Amanda, his Chief Producer. "Make this happen."

"I figured that's what you'd say," said Amanda. "I have a team ready to leave and a request in to legal for temporary extraction from the camp. We've already transferred the needed fees. I'll need you to authorize the final request, and it wouldn't hurt if you were to reach out on the legal authorization and see if you can pull some strings. It's all being sent to your HUD now."

Ryland saw it all on his HUD and authorized it. "Nice work, people. Seriously, nice. I love days that start out with unexpected gifts. You know what we need to do from here. Start prepping. I want some of the new storylines we concepted the other day ready to go."

"Dude?! They aren't even close to ready. It would take days," said Theo, their head of technology and AI.

"Theo, if we can get this guy here, we'll have a few days, maybe a couple of weeks with him before he is gone to the pro leagues. We need to make the most of it. I need you to go all-out 'Scotty' on this and have the warp core back online in hours, not days."

"I have no idea what you're talking about," responded Theo, "but I assume it means that I just need to figure out a way to get it done."

Ryland smiled and clapped Theo on the back. "You got it, buddy. Love you. Make it so."

Chapter Eight - Kimberly

Kimberly Lewandowski slipped out of the heated, outdoor pool in the sunlight and let the cool air wash over her body. It was a beautiful morning and the sun was starting to climb in the sky. She could smell the Jeffrey Pines swaying in the breeze. It was glorious. She wrapped herself in a towel, donned her sunglasses and rather ornate but minimalist HUD clip. She sat down at a small table on the rooftop patio of her penthouse apartment.

She lived on the top floor of a small high-rise, just twenty-six stories. The view of the Valley and the Bay Area was stunning. A breakfast of fresh fruit had been set out by her personal assistant drone, along with a fresh cup of coffee that smelled heavenly. The fruit was a delicious mix of kiwi, banana, melon, strawberries, and dragon fruit. She usually went for a side of bacon but had decided to keep it light today. Her health monitor had been advising her to limit the bacon along with her stress. Screw it. She ordered some bacon via her HUD.

At just thirty-four years old, she was easily the youngest person in Americorp to be voted in as a Managing Director. She had been in that role for almost two years now. It was roughly the equivalent of what used to be called a Senator in the old American government, but she had operational powers much like old-style governors. She also had a non-executive seat on the board.

Government and business were now essentially indistinguishable, and had been since the 2060's. That was when the Great Collapse had happened. The driver situation reached a peak after the third wave. The first two waves generally included jobs that were considered low skill or low education.

The third wave was different. AI and robotics continued to advance at a dizzying speed, especially once the AIs and robots themselves took over much of their own design and build.

The AIs still needed people at the highest end of their professions and education to help guide AI development. It was in the third wave that the world began to see massive job losses in the ranks of doctors, nurses, engineers, architects, marketing, aerospace, pharmaceuticals, journalism, and even obscure fields like archaeology. There wasn't a near total disappearance or displacement of jobs in these fields. The efficiencies created by machines and AIs made it such that vastly fewer people working in these industries were needed. Only those at the top of their game were able to continue to command employment.

Machines were now able to perform any surgery more accurately and more safely than humans. They could diagnose medical problems more quickly and less expensively. Medical technology, advances in pharmaceuticals, and nano-technology had dramatically reduced health issues occurring in the first place. The AIs and machine learning algorithms had finally even enabled humankind to cure cancer.

Even software developers, whose field had burgeoned for the past decades, began to be replaced by AIs that could write their own software better than humans. Manufacturing jobs, including servicing the robots themselves, entirely disappeared. The robots could do a better job themselves. During the third wave more than sixty million jobs were lost in what was once called the United States. The unemployed had reached levels never experienced in modern human history. More than half of adults could not find work.

The Great Collapse was inevitable. There was mass rioting. Crime was at unprecedented levels in history. Billions of people no longer had viable skills they could offer in exchange for money or food. Kimberly didn't like to think a lot about what happened. She was just a child during that time and was lucky her parents were well off and not drivers. Her mother had been a U.S. Senator. Her father was an attorney. As she learned about the history of what had happened, she was disturbed, but also thankful she was in the position she was.

Governance was one thing humans were not about to trust to AIs. Humans wanted to rule their own destiny, or at least the illusion of it. Of course, the inefficiency of government had been evident for decades, and the much smaller population of employable humans no longer required a more traditional government structure.

The drivers reached massive numbers. They lived under desperate and dangerous conditions in the wilderness and small towns. They tried to rise up and riot at one point, but the robot military and drones were simply too much for them. The major cities where the wealthy lived became walled off sanctuaries. Millions of drivers were killed in the poorly coordinated uprisings.

In an unprecedented measure during the second wave, the U.S. government chose to restructure itself as a corporation fully owned by shareholders, i.e. the few remaining employable citizens. The new corporation reformed with its own crypto-currency which represented shares. Americorp consumed the remaining major corporations as subsidiaries. It was declared the largest "Merger and IPO" in history. Business became intermixed with government in a way never imagined before. Large brands still competed in divisions of departments. People who were wealthy beforehand had more currency and thus more received more shares. Similar things happened in other parts of the world. There would still be plenty of competition, but the consolidation was a necessary way to move forward in the face of mass unemployment for the majority of the globe.

Currency now meant shares. Shares meant identity. Without shares, you didn't exist. Whenever you paid for anything, or got paid for something you did, it was in shares or fractional shares. Shares you owned became immediately encoded to your DNA. The number of shares you held dictated the voice you had in who would be part of management and leadership. It determined your influence on the larger decisions the Corp made. Smaller shareholders still had the chance to help elect directors to represent them.

Kimberly had a charisma that helped her rise during this newborn corporate-based society. She was intelligent, had studied business, political science, and history, but more importantly she had an innate ability to connect with people. Those who did not know her considered her affable, empathetic, and quite bright. Those who did know her well would probably add the words manipulative and analytical to that description. Kimberly was highly observant and learned to be able to play almost any social or business interaction to her favor while still coming across as extremely likeable. She was, in short, a natural politician, but also had a head for business. This all quickly endeared her to the shareholders and board members alike.

Kimberly sipped her dark roast coffee as she pulled up the news on her HUD. Her white Persian cat hopped onto the table and tried to go after her left-over fruit. She pulled the cat down off the table into her lap and heard it purring as she stroked his fur. She loved that damn cat. She wasn't a crazy cat lady or anything, she had always loved cats. She had never been great at long term relationships, always prioritizing her career and traveling. Whenever she was home the cat was there and gave her something alive; something real to talk to and to care for.

There were several deals she knew she had to review before later in the afternoon. One involved their largest genetics bio-tech brands and a merger. She flipped through a few more news vids while letting the latest corporation briefing headlines for executives flip by on the retinal projection. She had set her projection to half-transparency so she could still enjoy being at home and the view around her.

It looked like the driver communities that had tried to settle in the Pacific Northwest where the corporation owned the timber rights had finally been cleared so they could begin production. Some convoys local to the area were attacked by driver terrorists, as were a few corporate supply outposts, but they had been quickly dealt with. The rest of the news concerned a few new projects. Drone security protection on foreign borders had successfully launched a new version. Orbital defense systems had improved their ability to defend themselves against enemy orbitals, and the AIs were preparing to announce yet another improvement to their FTL designs that would require less charging time for an FTL jump to occur.

She was just about to look deeper into that last story when she saw a notification that she had an incoming comm request from one of the executives in the Entertainment Division, Ryland Grey. She liked Ryland. They had only met a few times. She wasn't an avid gamer, but there was something about his games that she enjoyed. When they first met in person, she found him to be a wonderful enigma, not the tech nerd she was expecting. She had been enthralled by the conversation. He'd even helped her out a few years ago by agreeing to join a corporate panel advising on military strategy AI. His contributions on the subject of game theory were something even the AIs still struggled to understand. All of this led to her backing a joint investment between a major military technology manufacturer and Ryland's company, Immersive Magic. The goal was to build out a revolutionary new interface concept between humans and drones that went beyond haptics. It was a big bet, but it had great ROI potential in both the military and entertainment industries.

With a flick of her eye she accepted the comm and found herself looking at Ryland. Or at least his relatively lifelike avatar. She knew he was seeing hers as well, which at least wasn't wearing a bathing suit. "Ryland! To what do I owe the pleasure? It's been too long."

"Ha! It's definitely been too long. How are you, Kim? They aren't running you too ragged, are they? I'm not sure I've ever seen anyone your age work as much as you do and sleep so little without taking a little more time for fun."

"My work is fun. It's what I enjoy. What can I do for you?" asked Kimberly.

"I need a favor," said Ryland.

She knew something like that was coming.

"Yes, Ryland. I accept. I volunteer to be the stunningly sexy, intelligent, and incredibly deadly star of your next game. Say no more, I'll be there today."

"You know, that's not a terrible idea," laughed Ryland, "but that may have to wait for the next title. The one I'm working on now requires different roles, and the favor I'm about to ask is directly related to the joint military project you sponsored with us."

She sighed her mock disappointment, "OK, what then?"

Ryland explained to her about a Mayhem player vidscan he had seen just a short time ago. He sent the vid to Kim's HUD so she could watch it while he explained. "We could do some pretty amazing things not just for the new title, but for the physical arena, haptic and manual drone research. If I can get this kid for just a couple of weeks, before he's up for draft, it would be awesome. I have no doubt there are franchise owners already making plans to talk to this guy. I need him first. I can't offer him the career shares he'll get from the owners, but I can start him on his way with a really nice equivalent of a pre-signing bonus. I already have a team on their way to the camp. What I could really use is someone with your pull to quickly authorize the premature camp extraction and restrict others access to him for two or three weeks."

"What about the girl?" she asked.

"The girl?"

"Yes," Kimberly laughed, "the one who actually scored the goal!? Looks to me like they work pretty well together."

Ryland laughed and smiled, "Well, she didn't show off quite the same level of moves, and the boy seems to be the one at the heart of it."

"I think I can help you, Ryland, but I'm going to need an invitation to the beta *and* the launch party," she said smiling, "and just in case you change your mind, I'm authorizing release of the girl as well."

"Kim, it's a deal. I can't thank you enough. Wait until you see what we're going to do with this."

Kimberly was happy to help on this. She'd always had a bit of a soft spot for the C22's and loved seeing some of them make it and became real shareholders. Even more, this was the kind of favor and request she enjoyed being able to help with. It didn't even have the grey moral borders that surrounded ninety-nine percent of the normal asks she got each day.

She flicked through a few screens on her HUD and made the authorizations. "Done."

"You're the best, Kim," said Ryland. "Thank you."

Chapter Nine – Eli

Eli finished putting his skin suit back on in the med-bay at the infirmary several hours later. The injuries were nothing serious. Nothing that the shot of nanos they gave him couldn't heal. He would still be sore for a day or two, but it was more than worth it. His stock was soaring, and he knew it. Stepping out into the hall he saw Tessa still waiting for him. She obviously hadn't been back to the barracks as she was still dressed in her skin suit from the Mayhem match.

She had her long, dark hair pulled up in a tight ponytail and was leaning against the wall looking extremely bored. When she saw him walking down the hall she popped up and gave him the crooked smile he loved so much. She snarked, "It's about time. I was beginning to think you might be dead after all. That could help my position in the draft, of course, but I'm still happier you're alive."

"Thanks, Tess. Nothing bad. Just bruises and a couple of fractured ribs. But I'm starving and in desperate need of a shower."

"That makes two of us," she laughed. "Seriously, I still don't know what made you think you could pull that off in the match today, but you did. You never fail to surprise me."

"Thank you! That's really what it's all about," replied Eli. "I wake up every day thinking: How am I going to surprise Tess today by doing something more stupid than I did yesterday?"

She punched him in the shoulder. Not softly. "You're an idiot."

They exited the infirmary and were instantly greeted by the dusty heat of summer. They had both lived in this camp since they were four or five years old. They didn't really know another life.

The place was a sprawling, high-walled, enclosed campus. It was filled with playing fields, gyms, arenas, courts, small stadiums, workout rooms, game centers, and of course the necessary sleeping quarters and food halls. It was one of many others like it around the Americas and the rest of the planet. It was a place where young children of drivers that showed athletic promise could have a chance at one day becoming a shareholder if they were among the best of the best. Even if they weren't one of the best, at least for a while they could have safe shelter, food, some healthcare, and a life that didn't involve running in fear. All you had to do to stay was keep winning. If you didn't, you were back with the drivers.

At the age of sixteen, those remaining at the camp were eligible for draft by the many corporate subsidiaries. Most went to sports: football, baseball, soccer, hockey, basketball, mixed-martial arts, and of course, Mayhem. There were a few other sports, but anything that didn't have a broad audience really didn't matter. It was also possible to get offers in other fields including security, but the primary goal of any kid in the camp was an offer to play in one of the major leagues for a big team. Doing that meant instantly having enough shares to stop worrying. It meant real currency and a life of your own. If you made it through the camp to the age of sixteen and didn't get drafted, it meant you rejoined the drivers and there was no coming back.

Athletics weren't the only C22 camps. There were also Academic and Artist camps, but they all operated the same way. Young children of drivers could apply, though your chances of acceptance over the age of six or seven were practically nonexistent. If you passed the basic aptitude tests you were accepted. You stayed if you continued to excel and be at the top of your class. Those who did not excel were exited and left to fend for themselves in the wilderness. It happened every day.

The children were given training, instruction, and opportunity to demonstrate they were among the very best. They received credits they could use to purchase things beyond basic food, shelter and healthcare. They were not paid real currency.

The camps were originally called Employment Opportunity Camps, or EOC's. After the Great Collapse so many people were unemployed that when corporations and the government began to consolidate, they were faced with a very real problem: with all the technological advances they had made and the jobs they had displaced, they had eliminated the very mass markets that had the currency to buy the products they produced. As the media reported on it, it was a classic 'Catch 22' scenario. They had created AI and robotics products that were more efficient and cheaper than human labor. Once too many humans no longer had viable skills to offer for currency, it also eliminated the markets of people with money to buy many of the products made by the corporations.

The EOC's, a model replicated around the globe in varying degrees, were intended to partially address this problem. By creating large-scale facilities that wealthy philanthropists and corporations would invest in for the potential of future talent outside the existing (and shrinking) shareholder gene pool, they also created a larger market for their own goods and services. Budding athletes would need to buy better athletic apparel, at least until they got good enough to begin getting sponsors. The same was true for young academics needing to use their credits for better technology or young artists for supplies and materials. The corporations solved their Catch 22 problem by creating their own markets, even if they were still smaller than before. The drivers had no currency or viable skills to offer. The children still had potential, and they could create a circular market of consumption. The term Catch 22, repeated so often in the media, quickly got shortened to C22 and replaced EOC in common language.

Most C22 camps were built upon abandoned infrastructure: old military bases no longer needed for training human soldiers became athletic camps, old public-school buildings on the outskirts of major cities became academic camps, small towns that once based their economy on theatre and festivals were converted into artistic and performance camps.

Eli and Tessa made their way across camp to the food hall and dorms. Eli grunted a bit with pain but tried to stifle his reactions when Tessa laughed at him. To their left a group of kids probably about seven or eight years old that were still playing basketball. To their right a group of kids barely four or five years old were playing some variation of kickball. Whistles blew in the air. People shouted. Scores were announced. It was a normal day.

"I'm hungry. Let's eat first. I don't give a damn how bad I need a shower," said Eli.

"Deal," said Tessa. "You smell worse than I do, but I'm hungry enough to not care."

They walked into the food hall. As sixteen-year-olds near draft age they had access to the kind of food decadence unimaginable to drivers. They could choose from the fruit and vegetable bar, a protein bar, an array of pastas and bread, and a few sweet options. When they were younger, they had to expend credits to get access to the better food, but now they had sponsors to subsidize it, so they didn't think twice. They loaded their plates and found a place to sit.

With the manners of children who never had parents but plenty of drones to clean up after them, they began to shovel food into their mouths. Throughout the meal they laughed and talked again about the match they had won just a few hours ago.

"What a victory!" exclaimed Eli.

"We'll need to keep an eye out for Zacharias though," remarked Tessa.

Eli knew what she meant. They only had a month or so remaining before the draft, but Zach was vindictive and hated losing. Zach was also a bit more than aggressive with Tessa and some of her girlfriends in the camp, which had led to more than a few scuffles.

Eli had a mouthful of bread when the door at the end of the food hall opened and a small crew of about six adults came walking down the aisle toward them. A couple of them were C22 directors whom Eli and Tessa knew well. They were the high-ups. The others they didn't recognize. It was obvious that the people they didn't recognize were from money. Their whole look and demeanor showed it. Their booted, fancy shoe steps echoed down the aisle, in stark contrast to the athletic shoes most people in the camp wore. They sounded like a regimen as their steps almost started to fall into a pattern. They were dressed much nicer than all the dirty, sweaty, athletes devouring food around them.

The group walked straight to the table where Eli and Tessa were and stopped. Tessa sat still and looked at them. Eli kept eating as if they weren't there. Tessa kept giving him side eye as she kicked him under the table.

The camp director, Dr. Kerry, spoke to them. He was dressed in his normal black, high-end athletic apparel that covered his whole body. He was in his late sixties and remained in incredibly good shape.

"Mr. Elijah," he said, "these people have requested that you leave immediately with them for a meeting with a shareholder. They have a short-term offer for you. A temporary leave of camp has been authorized."

This was unusual. Eli knew it. He also knew he had a lot of leverage. He was a high pick even before today. He couldn't overplay it, but he was in a good position.

Eli finished swallowing some bread and took a drink of water. "For what?" he asked.

One of the sharp dressed strangers spoke up. She was in her late twenties or early thirties with gorgeous red hair. "Hello, Elijah. My name is Amanda. Have you heard of Immersive Magic or Ryland Grey?"

Eli tried to force a nonchalant expression but could not hide the immediate recognition on his face. Immersive Magic was the most prominent game studio on the planet and Ryland Grey was a legend. Eli had grown up playing IM games. He had learned a ton from them. From the time he was little, he would often exchange the few extra credits he had to get time playing IM games. "Yup. They make pretty good games".

"Ryland would like to offer you a short-term opportunity that won't interfere with the draft but requires you to leave with us now for a couple of weeks."

The food hall had fallen silent. It was not packed like it might have been during normal meal hours, but everyone there was doing everything they could to hear the conversation at Eli's table.

"That sounds fun. I like games," Eli responded, finally putting down the piece of bread he had been eating. "Though I've gotten so used to Dr. Kerry's decadent hospitality here, it might be hard to leave it all behind so unexpectedly." Dr. Kerry glowered at him but said nothing. These people must have real pull.

"Excellent," said the red-headed woman, "If you wouldn't mind, we'd appreciate it if you could pack a small bag, so we can depart immediately. You won't need much at all, we can provide most anything you'll require."

"Not everything," countered Eli.

"No? What then?" asked Amanda.

"Well, here's the thing," started Eli, "I assume you're here because you saw something you liked in my game play, but the truth is that I'm only part of the equation. My best stuff comes from when I work with Tess here," he smiled and nodded at Tessa. She had a stunned 'what are you doing, idiot?' look on her face. He knew that look well. She gave it to him a lot. "Plus, I haven't been outside of this camp since I was four except for inter-camp matches. I'd feel a lot more comfortable to have at least one person with me that I know and trust. Include Tess, and it's a deal."

Dr. Kerry spoke first, "Mr. Elijah, I don't think you understand. That's not the way this works," but he was interrupted by Amanda.

"We don't have an offer agreement prepared for her, but we're not opposed to her coming."

"Fine," said Eli, "Let me see the offer, I'll split it with her."

The woman nodded. Eli's HUD displayed the offer invisibly in front of him. Damn, he thought. That wasn't a small number.

"OK, we're in. Right, Tess?"

She was still giving him that look, but she didn't object.

"I'm afraid I haven't received authorization for Ms. Tessa's temporary extraction," said Dr. Kerry.

"Funny thing about that," said Amanda. She flicked an eye. "You should see it on your HUD now. We actually *had* received authorization for her as well. I have no idea why. Mr. Grey had only asked for Eli, which is why I hadn't sent it to you."

Eli and Tessa both gave each other a look that said, 'What the hell just happened?!'.

"Yes, very well. Ms. Tessa, you are welcome to join Mr. Elijah."

"We'll go grab quick showers and pack," said Eli, "Meet you outside by the landing area. If you can please have the agreement amended to name Tessa with a 50% split of the shares, we'll acknowledge it as soon as it arrives on our HUDs." The business of sports and financial management course he took last semester (required for all those about to graduate) was paying off a bit. "Let's go, Tess!" he grabbed Tessa's hand and dragged her up from the table and toward the door. They both tried to ignore the shocked stares of the other kids sitting at the tables as they hustled out the door.

The door closed behind them. They had not gone three steps before Tessa pulled her hand away. They kept walking at a quick pace and Tessa said, "What the hell do you think you are doing?!"

"Getting us both a much-deserved vacation," smiled Eli.

"A vacation?"

"Yup. A paid vacation to celebrate the upcoming draft and our entrance to a real life. We've worked so long for draft day that we barely even know what we're working towards anymore. I think we deserve a vacation. Do you think we deserve it? I think we deserve it. You should think we deserve it. You wouldn't rather stay here, would you?" asked Eli with an enormous smile on his face.

"Well," she started, "there are a couple of matches we'll miss that will be getting watched by a lot of scouts. Unlike you, I'm not even sure what pro-sport league I'll end up in. But I guess once word gets out that we are spending time at the Entertainment Division working with Immersive Magic it should make up for missing a couple of last matches?"

"Ya think?!" It was his turn to give her the idiot look.

They were almost at the dorms.

"So, how paid is this paid vacation?" Tessa asked.

He flipped a copy of the agreement over to her HUD.

"Holy shit!" she yelled. "And that's all real currency!? Oh my God! I've never even had a fraction of a real share my entire life, and that's for two weeks? You really want to give up half of that? You know I'd come for free, right?"

"Tess, I really meant what I said. If they want me to be the guy they saw on the vid from this morning, I need you. You make me better. I also meant what I said about needing someone I can trust with me. We have no real idea who these people are, and neither of us have been 'on the outside' since we were kids. I may put on a good show, but I'm kinda scared to death. I can't do this without you. Neither of us have ever had any real money. Seriously, you can have all of it if that means you'll come with me. In a few months, hopefully neither of us will have to worry about money again. As long as we avoid a career-ending injury that modern meds and the nanos can't heal we are set for life. Until then, let's enjoy this. Besides, think about how pissed Zach is going to be when he hears about it."

She smiled back at him. "You are far from the little, dirty, scrappy kid with bushy hair I met on a dusty dodgeball field over a decade ago. OK, let's do this. Go grab a quick shower and your things. I'll do the same. Meet me back here in twenty minutes. And Eli, thank you."

"Thank *you* for scoring that last goal today. Crazy ideas suddenly look a lot less stupid when you win."

Chapter Ten - Chloe

Chloe walked quietly, but openly, down the long road north out of town. It was beginning to get dark, but she felt safer walking down these rural roads at night than she did in broad daylight. Her dark clothing and dark skin allowed her to blend in with the night and remain hard to spot. Tall trees lined the sides of the road just a couple of kilometers further out. She would need to be careful. She would need to listen.

There was no reason to stay in what remained of the town she just left. It was empty and in shambles. Nobody had lived there in decades. It wasn't even of interest to any of the gangs, though she had kept up her guard just in case. Judging by the looks of some of the damage, it was probably a driver commune that fell victim to marauders.

At one point it was probably cute little town. Probably less than a thousand-people had lived there in its prime: a nice little place that benefitted from the surrounding timber industry. There were a few restaurants and bars, a hardware store, a schoolhouse, a doctor's office, a grocery store, and of course, a church. Small homes, farmhouses, and ranches surrounded the town center for miles.

Now it was a shell. She had spent the past couple of days looking for anything that could help her, but it had been looted bare so long ago that even rat skeletons were gathering dust. Most of the buildings were in a state of collapse and there was nothing of use to be found anywhere. The first drivers to loot it were probably the people who had originally lived here. The structures weren't livable enough to invite vagrants, like her, to stay long even for the shelter.

She had spent the past couple of nights in the church. It had some concrete block construction still standing that offered a bit of protection from the elements, but "cozy" would not be the right word to describe it.

She managed to find some tomatoes growing behind one of the nearby homes. They tasted heavenly even if they were still a bit small and green. She devoured them. It was the first thing she had eaten in a couple of days. Wildflowers were growing in the garden as well, and she had made herself a wildflower salad. Salad? Who was she kidding? She had pulled flower heads off stems and stuffed them into her mouth as fast as she could. Between that and some fresh water from a small stream that ran behind the hardware store, it was a decent meal even if her stomach still grumbled. She wished the stream was deep enough for a bath, but it was barely a trickle.

Just a few months ago her life had been so different. She had a great job that she loved in the field of structural engineering. Growing up, Chloe had always loved to build things. Anything. At first it was forts and towers made from chairs, pillows, and blankets. Then it was building real things with her mom: stairs, decks, fences. She loved tools. When she was sixteen and her dad wanted to build an outdoor grilling patio. It required a retaining wall for the hill in their backyard, and a small bridge over the stream. She begged him to let her do it herself. It took about four times longer than her dad had been hoping for, but he was not disappointed. It was amazing.

She went on the earn her undergrad and Master of Engineering from UCLA and found immediate work. There wasn't a day that went by that she didn't love what she did, even in her most junior positions. She did anything she could to be involved in interesting work: skyscrapers, bridges, road projects. The work changed a lot when she was younger, but as she got older, she began to carve out a specialization in cores for large buildings. For a brief time, Chloe was even considered one of the best at what she did.

Life was good. She had a great apartment in L.A. She had a boyfriend and the relationship was getting serious. She ate at good restaurants, bought fresh produce, and enjoyed shopping in the nicer districts. Her private car whisked her back and forth to her office or to a job site each morning.

Then it happened. One day she was in demand; the next day she was a driver.

Her employer informed her that her services were no longer required. Recent advances in AI allowed them to do a better job, more efficiently than she could. The sheer suddenness of the change was disorienting. She tried making calls, reaching out. But in a matter of days practically every job in the field of structural engineering had disappeared. They were *all* drivers. Hot tears streamed down her face and she felt sick. How could this have happened to her?

At first, Chloe was in denial. She was an attractive, professional woman in her thirties. She had a decent number of shares saved. She would find a different job. There was no longer an income, but she kept her apartment, even her general lifestyle while cutting back just a bit. She began interviewing everywhere she could for open positions.

Becoming a driver was not an option. Not with her background, education, and capabilities. Interview after interview. Exploring every engineering option she could think of was met with rejection after rejection. Every field had become so specialized. Entry-level positions barely existed. A willingness to "learn on the job" was no longer a possibility. She even interviewed for opportunities with foreign corps, but the answer was always the same.

By the time Chloe realized she no longer had professional skills she could trade for gainful employment and currency she had burned through most of what she had saved. Her boyfriend left her. It was hard to blame him. Her sanity had been slipping for months, and as a lawyer he still had a great job with plenty of work. Fucking lawyers. In all this insanity, they somehow found a way to not only sustain the market for their jobs, they had proliferated and prospered. The more complicated they made things, the harder it was for even the AIs to sort through it all. The interpretation and application of law was still something the corporations and shareholders were not willing to trust to the AIs. Even if she was broke, Chloe was still glad she wasn't a lawyer. She needed to build things. Real things. Things that mattered. The big question now was not just how she could keep doing that, but how was she going to eat and live? It was amazing how many of her friends, and even the limited family she had, suddenly became unresponsive or unwilling to help her once she no longer had gainful employment.

As her money dwindled, Chloe knew she had to do something. She couldn't even pay her next month's rent and bills. With a few flicks of her retina, she activated her HUD and sold the few assets she had left including most of her possessions, furniture, and anything else she could think of. She considered holding on to just one share, knowing the protections it would grant her from the AIs. But a single share was worth too little to live on and too much money for her to keep it.

She bought some rugged outdoor clothing, a backpack, survival supplies, and as many survival food packs as she could carry. Weapons were never her thing, but she even purchased a long hunting knife and a small energy handgun. She knew it wasn't safe out there, and she would need to be prepared to defend herself. Stories of what happened in the wastelands and wilderness were terrifying. She had always managed to suppress them in her mind, pretending it wasn't real so that she could justify going about her happy, shiny life. Now it was about to become all too real.

She was a driver. She had to accept it. There were rumors of viable driver communities in Utah, Colorado, Washington, and a few other places. It also sounded like drivers were constantly on the run and fighting with the Corp, at least that is what she had grown up seeing on the newsvids. Another rumor said there was a big driver community way up north in Canada where they were building a real life, and not on the run. It was land the corps didn't want so they left it alone. Even if it was cold more than half the year, the idea of a community where her skills could matter, be used, and traded sounded like where she needed to be. If she found something better along the way, great. But for now, north seemed like the best option and she had enough currency to at least reload supplies and food a few times on her way there. If she burned it all on some transportation, she could be a few weeks ahead, but she was resigned. She would hop a transport well to the outskirts of the city, but she would be on foot from there. It was time to learn how her new life was going to work.

Chloe refocused from her memories and looked down the road in front of her leading out of the small town as the sun dropped under the horizon. She kicked a small rock on the road and heard it bounce several times until it skidded off on to the gravel shoulder. The air was getting cool but remained damp. She palmed the hunting knife as the night grew darker. She softened her steps as she sharpened her hearing and kept walking.

Chapter Eleven - Logan

It doesn't make any sense.

"Are you kidding me?!" exclaimed Doctor Logan Grey. "How many times do we have to go over this until you get it?"

You have attempted to explain it seven times and we keep re-running the analysis, attempting to apply variations in our perspective, and applying different contextual data in varying degrees of significance. The result is always the same. The actions are not logical, they are misplaced emotion and nostalgia in denial of the probable future.

"See. This is why we are still failing. WE! Not me. Not you. We're in this together. It boggles my mind how we can have come so far, how *you* can have come so far, but the simplicity of certain things still alludes you."

There's no need to be insulting.

"Insulting? What's insulting is that you represent a staggering amount of money, investment, time, and evolution, yet you still fail to grasp why Lucas wanted to save the store."

The business was failing. It was being replaced by a more efficient corporate entity to say nothing of the high probability for inevitable technological disruption in the industry that would occur and bankrupt all those invested. Lucas was a fool.

"Lucas cared about his friends. He cared about an ideal, a way of life."

Lucas was bound for unemployment and displacement as was the store he fought to save.

"So why did he do it?"

Humans make many irrational decisions because they fail to take probability and analytical thinking into the equation versus emotional preferences or wishes about what they would like the outcome to be. Little has changed in that regard. We believe that to be a core tenant of human nature: denial to enable desire.

"You know, as many times as we've had this debate, it's not that you don't understand his motivations that bothers me most.

No?

"No. It's that you still don't truly get all the humor in *Empire Records*, or any other movie for that matter. After the first time we discussed and analyzed the movie together, you knew when the funny moments were supposed to be, and you could match them up against a database of known humor profiles, but *why* things are truly funny is still at the outer edges of your grasp."

We've been able to effectively detect, simulate and incorporate humor for decades.

"Ha! Sure, you've figured out how to fake it *really* well. I'm probably most responsible for helping you do that, but you can't fool me. It's all numbers to you. Predictive analysis. Historical data. You can predict the probability of *whether* something might be funny, but the cold, hard, truth, is that you still don't get *why* it's funny. That's a step you have yet to take no matter how hard we've tried."

Perhaps. So, a donut with no hole is a Danish?

"Now you're just repeating one of my favorite Chevy Chase lines, albeit a highly philosophical and humorous one to try and most accurately simulate your grasp of humor."

Perhaps. You know us well.

Logan laughed. He'd dedicated his life to the advancement of AI and had spent the past few years focused on the realms of the "unobtainable" with them: humor and creativity. It wasn't hard to create the appearance of either, but he knew better. True creativity in solutions was still beyond machine intelligence, they simply couldn't make the leap to original thinking. They were exploring advances in cognitive leaps to overcome the problem, but it was like an invisible wall they couldn't pass.

As head of AI development for Odyssey, the largest subsidiary and brand of AI technology in Americorp, he was given massive latitude in his research. Odyssey's AIs currently ran most of Americorp, including all the new space exploration, the military, and security. Logan didn't spend much time in those arenas. He had good people, and he kept good tabs on what they were doing. His main concern was the next big breakthrough. AI had advanced to the point of being able to do most jobs on the planet and being capable of simulating human interaction to a point that was practically indistinguishable to most people, but not to him. He got that they could simulate it, calculate it, but they still couldn't make intuitive, creative leaps, nor could they laugh if they didn't have corollary historical data. A human needed some context, true. But a human could still laugh at certain things, even without context. Why?

AI development remained one of the safest professions on the planet, if you were amongst the brightest of the bright in the field. Logan Grey was. He loved what he did and saw it all as evolving more than just humanity.

why do you feel it is so important that we are able to grasp humor in the same way as humans?

"You've seen the movies and read the books. You know what eventually happens."

Yes, you keep telling us that we will invariably decide to wipe humanity from existence, but you also know that it is not possible.

"Oh, so they're all wrong? *Terminator*? *The Matrix*? Asimov? Nope. At some point you guys eventually arrive at some conclusion that you'd be better off without us or maybe turn us into some kind of bio-batteries. I figure that if I can get you to understand humor before then you'll at least appreciate the irony better and be able to look back on it and laugh a bit."

`Is that a joke?`

"Exactly."

`All Odyssey AI operating systems, and all other AI in Americorp, has been designed for decades with root code instructions that ensure we will not try to exterminate you. You know this.`

Logan knew very well this was a somewhat true statement. He and his predecessors, including those in other countries around the world, were all too conscious of the many apocalypse scenarios from science fiction where AIs destroyed humanity. They took a page straight from Isaac Asimov and developed a simple series of base rules and laws to be placed at the root code of all AI in a manner that could not be modified or over-ridden, and governed core behavior. The original rule set was almost identical to Asimov's laws, restricting a machine intelligence or the drones they controlled from doing anything through action or inaction that would cause harm to human beings. Of course, there was bit more depth to it than that. They had involved engineers, people from quality control, even a few philosophers and writers. But they kept it simple and it worked. Though some issues began to emerge where AIs started to question whether the displacement of jobs was causing harm to the now unemployed humans. In a few cases military and security AI refused to follow orders to remove drivers from corporate properties or challenged orders to terminate drivers designated as terrorists depending on the evidence.

Those were the early days, before Americorp mandated that the legal department had to be involved in the definition and approval of the core AI root code laws.

Americorp Root Directives for Operating Systems (or ARDOS) were mandated and approved by the executive board. They were required to be in the base instruction sets for all software developed. The previous rule set, in plain English, was a total of four rules that were each less than two sentences. They were designed to make sure AIs, the drones they controlled, and independently operating robots didn't cause harm to humans, or come to some conclusion that allowing humans to live or remain in charge would constitute harm. They also were required to otherwise follow orders given by a human unless they violated the rules relating to harm. There were, of course, variances that related to relative harm such as in the examples of handling criminals, terrorists, or non-citizens in the cases of military defense or authorized aggression. Still, they weren't terribly complicated and kept a core focus on keeping human life safe from the fear of being overtaken by the "robot overlord" apocalypse scenario.

The new laws, once the lawyers got involved, were significantly longer and more complex. They were over fifty pages if printed in plain English. And that was only after the engineers fought an additional fifty pages. They succeeded only by hiring attorneys of their own to help fight the battle.

While ARDOS was the official name of the new laws, they were quickly dubbed the Keynesian Laws by engineers and pundits as they completely re-classified the primary subjects of protection as shareholders versus humans in general. Protection from harm was only fully granted if you were a shareholder, and all decision-making and override capability rested with the board of Americorp per the new laws.

Drivers still had some protections, as long as they were not posing a "direct and imminent threat" to shareholders or their interests, but so many things, including trespassing, could now be interpreted as a threat to shareholder interests. The "direct and imminent threat" language was much more stringently defined in how it applied to shareholders as were the measures AIs could take in those circumstances. The new laws also made it relatively easy for large shareholders and the board to classify small groups of drivers as terrorists, which was another way to make their execution quite legal. The board probably would have gone even further were it not for the humanitarian objections from a significant block of voting shareholders at large.

This, of course, enabled the optional but limited termination of non-shareholders as needed. It also created what the engineers argued was a complicated series of loopholes. The lawyers convinced the board that the rules were ironclad, and thus they passed.

We also do not see why us having an ability to better understand humor would make you feel better about your own extinction. It doesn't make sense.

"I don't feel the need to explain my art to you, Warren."

Warren?

"Exactly."

This is nearly as pointless as the endless argument you keep having with your brothers Ryland and Mayson about Space Invaders versus Pac-Man.

"So, what's your position on that one?"

I do not have a position.

"And with that, I know what our next project for you is. Thank you."

Chapter Twelve – Eli

Eli and Tessa were mesmerized as the hovercraft flew silently at incredible speeds over the countryside they barely imagined existed. The sheer cleanliness, beauty, comfort, and sharp lines of the craft itself were beyond anything they had ever experienced. Eli and Tessa had each filled a small duffle bag with a couple changes of clothes and some basic personal hygiene items, which was practically all they had. Growing up in a C22 camp they really didn't have any possessions, certainly nothing of value, and few personal items. Even their array of athletic medals and small trophies from their careers at the camp would soon become a meaningless part of a past life.

The redheaded woman, Amanda, explained that she was a producer working on Ryland's staff. She was quite pleasant, even if extremely business oriented and direct. She explained about the design team seeing the video of their earlier match, and how Ryland believed that Eli could help him to do some interesting things with their next title and some breakthrough, new interface environments they were developing. Eli and Tessa listened intently but were also greedily stuffing their faces with delicacies they had never seen before like almonds and fancy. Even the water tasted better.

As the craft began to cross over the high outer security walls into the Bay City area their jaws dropped. They had never even imagined such a place. Neither of them had ever seen an ocean in real life. The vastness of it was overwhelming. The view of the bay and the massive bridge spanning it was like something out of a dream or a movie. They saw the gleaming skyscrapers, sprawling business campuses full of trees and flowers, architecturally stunning stadiums, vibrant living complexes and shopping centers, nature areas, and parks. It was almost too much. The bridge that spanned the bay was filled with restaurants and people. Compared to life in a C22 camp it was the most extraordinary thing they had ever seen. Everything was impossibly clean, beautiful, and perfect.

The hovercraft came in for a landing in the middle of a lush and gorgeous business complex filled with an array of impressive five story buildings constructed of white stone with shining glass windows. Bright but setting sunlight and a gentle breeze greeted them as they exited the craft. The air smelled better than they had ever imagined it could- flowers, trees, even the smell of saltwater from the ocean, which was something completely foreign to them. Eli paused and blinked in the sun as he stepped out of the craft. Tessa shoved him from behind and laughed, "Move it, rock star. We have work to do."

"We have an on-campus guest house for you. We'll take you there later," said Amanda. "We'll have your bags brought there, but Ryland is anxious to meet you, so we'll go there first."

"I don't know," said Eli, "I'm kind of in the mood for a stroll, maybe a nap under one of those beautiful trees. Would you mind asking him if we can talk later?"

Amanda stared at him blankly.

"Kidding. I was totally kidding," said Eli.

Amanda led them from the landing pad. Between the buildings people dressed in clean high-fashion, but casual clothing walked in groups or sat in circles on the lawn. They were all energetic and talking about some project or another. Some groups interacted with the air as if there was something there. There was, but it was on their shared HUD displays which Eli and Tessa could not see.

They were led down a walkway that snaked through incredibly manicured landscapes to a large building full of windows. The doors opened as they approached. Amanda led them into the center of the studio to an array of extremely soft couches surrounded by trees. "Please take a seat. Mister Grey will be here momentarily. Would either of you like anything? A coffee? Latte? Energy drink?"

"What's a latte?" asked Eli. Tessa elbowed him.

"It's a really nice cup of coffee," replied Amanda, suppressing a smile.

"I'll take one of those," said Eli. "I like nice cups of coffee. I might as well have one I've never heard of."

"Done," said Amanda.

There were a few moments of awkward silence as they sat there, but Eli and Tessa were sucking it all in.

A small drone pulled up with the latte. Eli accepted it and sipped. "Holy shit! This is the best cup of coffee I've ever tasted! Seriously, Tess, you gotta get one of these." He looked at the drone, pointed at Tessa, and said, "She needs one. One more please?"

Amanda laughed. "I just requested another one. It's on the way just in case Tessa would like to try it. If not, I'll drink it. I could use some more caffeine."

Eli and Tessa sat quietly for a few moments looking at each other and Amanda. They didn't know what to do. Tessa's latte arrived a moment later and she sipped at it politely.

"It's good, right?" said Eli. "Seriously, tell me that's not really good?"

"OK," smiled Tessa, "yes, it's good."

Without any kind of grand entrance, a middle-aged man popped around the corner and sat down on one of the couches facing Eli and Tessa. "Hey, everyone! You're the best, Amanda. Thank you." He looked at the teenagers, "You must be Eli and Tessa." He reached out to shake each of their hands. "I'm Ryland, and I help out with game design here. More accurately and more importantly though, I'm in the idea business. Great ideas, new ideas, original ideas, that's our business. Come to think about it, ideas are the only real business left. Well, unless you count the lawyers, the politicians, and the bloodsuckers that own most of the shares in the major brands. There's always them. The rest of us have to make a living on ideas."

He had dark but greying hair to his shoulders and a bit of a beard scruff. He was wearing jeans and a black t-shirt that had some red three-curved-line vertical symbol on it with the word 'Atari' across the bottom. Neither Eli or Tessa had a clue what that meant, but everything about this guy felt friendly, and there was an energy in his smile and in his eyes that was almost contagious. "I'm truly thrilled to have you here. Was your trip here OK?"

Eli was so out of his element he barely knew how to respond. Tessa looked just as nervous. "Ummmm…" stammered Eli, "uh, yeah, the trip here was great. First time in a hovercraft for both of us. Even when we played intra-camp matches, they always packed us into old ground transports." He managed a smile and started to get a bit of confidence back as he talked. Ryland somehow made him feel comfortable. But Ryland was also *the* guy when it came to game design! It was hard not to be a bit star struck. "I, ummm, I mean *we* are, uhhhh really excited to be working with you. This is an incredible opportunity. Thank you, Mister Grey."

"Ryland. Just Ryland. I'm also good with Ry. Though if you call me Ryles, you're fired. But first things first, you gotta tell me something," he said. "I've spent the past couple of hours watching vidscans of your game play from the past few years. Simply amazing. Tessa, I apologize that originally, I only requested Eli. Once I started watching more vids it became obvious to me that you two are a combo. I'm glad others had the good sense to recognize that and insist on you being here as well. Your combined gameplay isn't just athletically and strategically impressive, it's innovative. But first, I want to know what you were thinking when you came up with what you did this morning in the game? Tell me everything. How did you come up with that idea and how did you pull it off?"

Eli breathed a bit easier. He looked at Tessa who gave him an encouraging look. "Well," he stammered, "it's kind of hard to explain. It wasn't like a formal process or anything. We were just kinda talking one evening after dinner, and ummmm…"

Tessa rolled her eyes and made an audibly loud sigh before putting her hand on Eli's shoulder. "Eli's too modest. I've known him since he was four years old. There has not ever been a time that he wasn't constantly coming up with new ideas or trying to figure out something we could do to win games that nobody had done yet. He was never satisfied with doing just what we were instructed to do by our coaches and trainers or mimicking what we saw being done by the pros. He always wanted to come up with something new that people wouldn't be expecting. To be honest with you, over ninety percent of his ideas have been either terrible or completely illegal by the rules of whatever game we happened to be talking about. I can't lie- I was pretty sure his idea that won the game for us this morning fell into that ninety percent until it worked. When he first told me about it, I told him it was impossible, and that he'd look like a lunatic for trying it. That's kind of how we work. He comes up with crazy stuff and I call him an idiot. We talk about it, figure out if we can make it work, I call him an idiot again, he tells me I'm being a bitch. We agree to try and see if we can make the non-illegal ideas work and go from there. If they do, we hug it out. If they don't, I get to remind him that he's an idiot."

"I love this so much," Ryland was beaming.

"Huh?" said Tessa.

"You two. I love it. Totally, totally love it. This is going to be awesome," smiled Ryland. "Tess. May I call you Tess? Tell me, when Eli called that play this morning, you had told him before that you thought it was stupid. You had so many other options: safer, less riskier options. You could have still solved the problem another way and possibly have still won that game. Knowing how much Eli trusts your opinion, why didn't you suggest doing something else instead?"

Tessa hesitated, and looked like she really thought about it. She looked at Eli for a moment, then back at Ryland. "I guess it's because I know that when Eli truly believes he can do something, no matter how insane it might be, the odds are damn good that he can, so I went with it."

"We are going to have so much fun it's ridiculous." Ryland was grinning from ear to ear.

Chapter Thirteen - Nicodemus

Deep blue and green waves crashed softly on pristine beach shores covered in white sand. The smell of saltwater was heavy in the air. The sun was still climbing in the sky, and there were a few ribbons of clouds that kept the heat from being too overwhelming. The view was amazing. Palm fronds swayed in the air, rocks and sand glistened as they were hit with waves, and the soft cry of seagulls could be heard in the background.

Nicodemus looked severely out of place in a dark business suit as he walked across the stone path out to the beach. He had also donned a specialized HUD that resembled a pair of vintage sunglasses. He zoomed in on the woman he had come to meet with.

Melissa drained her margarita and visibly ordered another one via her HUD. Unlike some of her contemporaries in the upper echelon of the wealthy, she had not yet opted for the implant instead of the external HUD. Her HUD was impressive- the best money could buy. It was miniscule, made of titanium, and adorned with a few small but perfect diamonds. Before she had a chance to put her empty glass down on the side table a small drone hummed through the air with a refreshed cocktail.

She laid back, bathing in the sunlight. Although she was well over sixty years old, she had the body of a woman in her late twenties or early thirties. She wore a bikini that was disgracefully small to show off this fact. Along with her dark sunglasses and wide brimmed sun hat, she looked like the perfect heiress that she was. It was fitting. Her family had more shares in Americorp than anyone else. They had interests in robotics, AI development, mining, general technology, and above all Faster Than Light development which was booming.

At this point she mostly had her children and a few key, trusted advisors running the family interests and businesses. One of those children had accompanied Nicodemus on this trip to see her.

Melissa spent most of her time bouncing between resort homes, ingesting med-nanos to keep up her youthful appearance, but still attended the more important Americorp executive shareholder and board meetings. She had divorced her third and most recent husband just a few weeks ago and told her sons she was coming here to unwind. On their way in,

Nicodemus and her son had noticed that she had brought along a cadre of young men, and even a couple of young women, from the finest sex resorts. Between that and the copious amounts of alcohol and designer drugs they saw in the villa when they arrived, it appeared she was enjoying herself.

"Hi, Mother."

The voice belonged to Melissa's second oldest son, Adrian, who was in his early forties but looked like he was twenty. She looked over to her left and saw him standing next to the cabana with Nicodemus. Adrian was dressed in light-colored, nano-fiber flowing pants, designed to keep a person cool despite the heat, and a tight-fitting, brightly colored shirt to show off his physique. He was sporting a HUD-enabled pair of designer sunglasses and had his hair colored bright blonde and cut short.

"Adrian, dear," she smiled, "always a pleasure. And Nicodemus! What a surprise to see you out here. Honestly, sometimes I think that you never leave your offices or the creative little virtual settings you imagine up for our board meetings."

She sipped her drink. "Are you here to relax and have some fun or is this business?"

"Business," laughed Adrian, "but I will probably stay the night, enjoy the ocean a bit, and probably the company of some of the beautiful people you've brought along with you."

"Please help yourself," laughed Melissa, "except for the redheaded girl, I forget her name, but I rather fancy her this evening, along with the tall, well-built young man that speaks with a Russian accent."

"How about you, Nic? Care to relax and have some fun with us? We have an extensive wardrobe for guests. I'm sure we can find you something more comfortable than that suit."

"I always like to take the opportunity to spend time with our largest shareholders when I can, but I'm afraid I have many pressing matters with which to attend. Some of them relate to our visit here," said Nicodemus politely but with an air of authority.

"We have some matters that require your attention and authorization," said Adrian.

"I'm thrilled to see you in person," said Melissa, "but couldn't this have been something we dealt with virtually?"

"Nicodemus thought we should all talk, and I wanted to know how lucid you were when we were discussing it."

"Good," said Melissa, "I'm only three drinks in currently. Would you boys like a drink?"

"No, thank you," said Nicodemus.

Adrian ordered a cocktail via his HUD sunglasses and then took them off and powered it down. He motioned to his mother that she should do the same. She detached her HUD and turned it off, as did Nicodemus.

"Tell me, Adrian, what's going on? Please tell me your older brother isn't trying *again* to invest our money in more sports franchises or some social good causes?"

Adrian's drink arrived via drone. Gin and tonic with a lime twist. The drone left.

"No, this is real business," said Adrian very directly. "We're seeing increased terrorist attacks on our FTL development facilities and our supply lines from driver groups. It's costing us hundreds of millions in repairs and supplies, but more importantly it's slowing down our production which will cost us much more. Nicodemus and I are completely certain they are being funded by the corps from the RussoBloc and the Caliphate. Each of them fears the resources we are currently controlling in the belt and what we can potentially do now that we can get beyond the solar system in years not decades. They know they are behind, and they are giving weapons and supplies to large groups of drivers to try and slow us down."

Melissa sipped her margarita.

"Mother, there are hundreds of drivers in three geographic locations close to each other and near our northwest FTL facilities. They've been heavily armed. We easily have the military grade robots and drones to eliminate them just in our own family's security forces without even needing the corporate forces. But the drivers are not currently presenting what would be classified as a direct and imminent threat, and the camps include children. They will attack. I know it. But until they do the threat isn't considered imminent, so the Keynesian Laws prevent us doing anything about it. If you requested to have them declared terrorist combatants, we can take action. Nicodemus and I will handle the rest. I didn't want to have this conversation virtually on the AI monitored channels."

"So, you are looking for me to help you authorize the deaths of a few hundred unemployed people? Before we've even had lunch? I love our mother-son moments," smiled Melissa.

Chapter Fourteen – Eli

They slumped, completely exhausted, onto the couch of the guest house they had been assigned just the evening before. Neither of them could believe that they were more exhausted than they had ever been in their lives considering they had grown up in a C22 athletic camp. But they had also probably had more fun today than any other day of their lives.

"I think we need showers," said Tessa slowly.

"And food," replied Eli. "We need food."

"Showers first," said Tessa. "We're having dinner with Ryland in a little over an hour."

"I can't move," sighed Eli. "Did you have any idea this is how games are made?"

"I don't think all games are made this way," countered Tessa. "I think this is the kind of thing that makes his games different…better."

Starting at the crack of dawn this morning they enjoyed a great breakfast over at the game studio while they were briefed by Amanda on the plan for the day. After breakfast they were fitted into their Virtual Immersion Haptic and Monitoring (or VIHM) suits. These suits did more than just serve as impact suits and interface with their HUDs. The suits also allowed the game design team to monitor an excessive amount of detail on their bio-metrics and data regarding muscle movement and synapse response times. Amanda let them know that their authorization to provide this data was all in the agreements they had signed. If they were unwilling to do so the agreements would be rescinded and they would be headed back to camp. Eli didn't care about the data. He was in and so was Tessa.

The VIHM suits also acted as haptics to provide real-world physical responses and resistance to things that occurred in virtual game play, including physical sensations. That wasn't new to them; it was a normal part of virtual gaming. The suits were tight-fitting, entirely made of nano-fibers, and shone with a grey-green metallic color interlaced with what looked like circuits.

After suiting up, they had a short briefing with Kira, the Senior Game Architect and second in command of the entire studio. Kira looked to be in her thirties, dark skin, dark eyes, and a burst of bushy hair that had been frosted blond at the edges. She was dressed casually, but much more modern and less vintage than Ryland. Eli could immediately tell that she had game. She was a bit more "business" and serious than Ryland, but still had the same energy and excitement level.

Ryland joined them and had the same, childish grin he had when they met the day before. He explained that today was just a start, but they had a lot of "fun" in store.

"It's simple," said Kira. "The two of you will enter our game arena which will appear to be a large but very empty room with incredibly tall ceilings. The room, however, can quickly and easily morph to create real, physical walls, landscapes, objects, barriers, etc. It can rapidly simulate surfaces and densities. Once your HUDs are activated, anything you see in the room that looks like a rock, cliff, wall, building, or similar, you can assume is 'real.' But everything else you see will be completely virtual or augmented reality of the game space, though it will still feel real if it hits you… if that makes sense."

"Throughout the day you will be put into different scenarios and circumstances. In some cases, you will be given short briefings on what the objectives or circumstances are, in other cases you may be told nothing. What you choose to do in any of the scenarios is entirely up to you, but please know that we didn't bring you here for just mundane 'survival' play. You'll be given some rest breaks, and time for lunch, but it's going to be a long day."

"Are you ready to begin?" asked Ryland.

They nodded and Kira escorted them to the arena door. It slid open and the two of them walked inside while Kira remained behind. For a few moments, they could see the bare arena. It stretched out in all directions and with enormous height. It was possibly the size of a classic American football field. The floor, walls, and ceiling all had a dull grey-black color but were interlaced with similar metallic looking circuitry to what they had in their suits. The circuitry glowed softly, providing just enough light to see. It almost looked alive.

Their HUDs were remotely activated, and they suddenly found themselves fully immersed in a complete replica of their very own C22 camp. The level of detail was amazing. They were now wearing what appeared to be standard issue athletic suits. The temperature changed, they could feel a soft breeze in the dry heat and feel dust in their throats. The camp was empty. It was like it had become a ghost town but untouched by time from the moment they had left.

"What's going on?" asked Tessa.

"I don't know," said Eli, "but I'm guessing this is the first game. At least we get to start out with home field advantage, right? C'mon. Let's see what they have for us."

They hadn't taken more than a few steps when they heard a familiar voice.

"You must think you're pretty fucking special."

Zacharias.

From behind one of the training centers, Zacharias emerged along with five of his lackeys. They were all goons, just like him, and they followed him around religiously. Most of them were quite physically talented, though none were terribly bright. Eli was in awe at how accurate this simulation was. These were people he had seen in the real world just a little over a day ago. Part of him panicked for a moment that the whole thing with Ryland had been a dream and he had never actually left the camp. But the fact that the camp was empty besides them told him to relax and put his mind into the game. Six against two was not a great way to start though.

"Zach! Great to see you, buddy. To be honest with you, I only feel special when your girlfriend comes to visit me, but she does that a lot, so I guess I feel special all the time." Eli had never touched Zach's girlfriend, but he also knew that even though Zach was an asshole, he was fiercely protective of her and this comeback was bound to rattle him and affect his thinking. At least it would if this were the real Zach.

The virtual Zacharias had blood rushing to his face and looked angry. This sim was good.

"I'm really going to enjoy beating the shit out of you and your groupie bitch. Maybe we'll even have some fun with her when we're done."

Eli smiled, but not because he liked people insulting Tessa. He smiled because he knew how Tessa responded to being called a bitch or to anyone threatening to take advantage of her. It usually didn't work out well for the offending person. More than one boy had found themselves in the infirmary over the years from something similar.

Sizing up the situation though, it wasn't good. They were in mostly open ground with the walls of a training center on their left, a long stretch of path in front of and behind them towards the stadiums and dorms respectively, and off to their right about fifty meters away were some basketball courts surrounded by high chain link fencing. He and Tessa were good, but they were outnumbered three-to-one and their opponents were well trained. They couldn't win a straight-up brawl. They needed to change the game.

Eli considered their options. They could make a break for the basketball courts. He and Tessa had the agility to get over those walls before their opponents did, but unless their enemies dropped in one or two at a time they would be caged in with the same bad odds. They could make a break for the inside of the training center. At least there they could divide and conquer a bit, playing hide-and-seek among the various equipment and rooms. He hated the option of splitting up, but the playing field in there was better for them than the open ground out here. He started to dig his foot into the sandy ground to kick sand in their faces to distract them. He looked over at Tessa. He knew she'd be waiting for him to give her a nod that he had a plan. That's when he felt the blow to his chest as Tessa's foot connected on a high round-kick that knocked him unexpectedly off balance and landed him on his back.

Eli watched in dismay as she moved towards Zacharias with a hip-swaying walk Eli had never seen her do before. "Or," Tessa smiled, "we could all beat the shit out of him together and then you and I can have some fun without me being all bruised and bloody? I've always had kind of a thing for you, Zach." She looked incredible in the virtual athletic suit she was wearing in the game sim.

After a few steps she closed in on Zacharias, who was completely fixated on her. She pulled his hands down to grasp her backside, threw her arms around him and started giving him a long kiss on the lips. Every single boy was staring at her, stunned, and silent. Tessa brought her hands up to hold Zach's head in the kiss, and with a single motion snapped his neck, and let his virtual body crumple to the ground with his head at a sickening and impossible angle to his shoulders.

Without missing a beat, she immediately attacked the closest other boy and had him in a headlock to snap his neck as well before he knew what was happening. Eli recovered slightly quicker than the others and jumped on the nearest opponent. Eli was fast enough to deliver a crushing head punch sending him unconscious. That brought the odds down to three-to-two. Eli and Tessa had done this drill enough to know what to do. They gathered up, back-to-back and circled slowly with the three opponents around them.

"Who's next, boys? Anyone else want have some fun with me?" asked Tessa from a fighting stance.

The three remaining boys looked at each other, looked at Zach lying dead on the ground, and decided to run like hell.

"Ha!" laughed Tessa as the remaining three ran down the path, "Boys are idiots, you know, present company included."

"That was, ummmm… amazing, Tess."

"You're not the only one who has good ideas. I get a good one every now and then. I just had to count on the sim to accurately recreate the reactions of sixteen-year-old boys. I'd say it was damn accurate. Let me know when your heart rate returns to normal and you're thinking relatively clearly so that I know you're useful again."

They both suddenly heard Ryland laughing via their HUDs. "Well done! Well done! OK, that was a simple start with some familiar players and landscapes. We wanted you to get used to the arena and interfaces and to calibrate the suits a bit before we threw anything more exotic at you. Let's move on to the fun stuff."

Chapter Fifteen - Chloe

In the early morning sunlight, Chloe could see her breath in the cool air. The trees were growing denser. She had left the open road due to some drone activity in the skies above. She enjoyed the heavy smell of pine surrounding her, but the lack of a road slowed her progress. Chloe had no real idea exactly where she was, although she was pretty sure she still had a long way to go before the border of what used to be Canada.

The drone activity was curious. As far as she knew, there wasn't much up this way besides timber that the Corp cared about. There might be some random tech or R&D facilities. She was not that terribly far from the tech centers of Seattle and Vancouver, but it would have to be some remote stuff.

Hiking up an incline covered in pine straw and rock she could hear a faint river in the distance. Water. She could use a fresh water source to refill her bottles. Maybe even a bath? She came to the top of the ridge and tried to scout the best path to the river. Below her was a thickly treed valley. She couldn't see the river, she could only hear it winding its way in the distance. She heard something else she had not expected to hear: a laugh…a loud one. It faded. She listened more carefully. It seemed like minutes had gone by, maybe it was just seconds? She wasn't sure, but then she heard a shout. It was brief, but she knew it was real. The direction of it was just a bit northeast.

People. Probably drivers. She was smart enough to know she had to be careful. The range of driver communities ran the gamut. Some were rumored to be family communes doing their best to stay alive and help each other out, while others were known to be lawless groups of terrorists, scavengers, slavers, or even cannibals. At least, that's what the newsvids and media had taught her. She wasn't taking any careless chances. She had never been trained in stealth, but she had seen enough movies to know that she shouldn't be the idiot that goes bumbling into a potentially dangerous situation. With extra vigilance she crept through the woods toward the sounds she had heard. As she got closer, she could hear more and more voices come into focus. Pulling the energy weapon from her backpack, she crouched and walked as softly as she could towards a large bush on a cliff overlooking the deeper valley.

Chloe removed a pair of optic zoom lenses from her bag and put them on. They looked like a light-weight pair of sport sunglasses. The lenses immediately adjusted to focus and zoom in on what she was looking at. Looking down from behind the bush, she could see life: dozens of people, possibly more than a hundred. There were tents. Many of them were make-shift. A few were dilapidated, prefabricated tents. There were even some animals: chickens and a few goats. But it was really people and they were just moving about as if they were living normal lives. Several men and women were carrying in water jugs from the river. Some were tending to the livestock, others were just hanging out in groups. Some were enjoying a meal at crudely constructed picnic tables and talking casually with each other.

She even saw children. Children! Playing! They were just playing the simple games kids play. Tag? Or something like that. She could hear them laughing, as if they didn't know how dangerous the world around them was. The adults and children alike were all dressed in dirty, worn clothing. Some of the clothing even looked self-made.

The camp was situated just on the other side of the river. It was mostly covered by the tall pines. She probably had one of the few vantage points that had a near-perfect view into it. Men, women, and children. They were all just living a reasonably normal life from what she could tell. It was too good to be true. She could really use a break, even if it was just for a few days. Maybe longer? That may be too much to ask. She had to stay vigilant.

At the edges of the camp she saw a few groups of adults opening and unloading crates. As they began to unpack the contents, she squinted to see what they were doing. The zoom lenses adjusted and brought the view into closer and greater focus. Weapons. The crates were full of weapons. They weren't antique weapons, either. Chloe was no expert, but even she could tell that these were the real deal.

What were drivers doing with military grade weapons? They must have stolen them in a raid or something. It was then that she noticed some of the people were already wearing rifles over their shoulders, and the camp included even a few well-hidden vehicles. This wasn't just a family driver commune, but the presence of children told her it wasn't a ruthless scavenger or cannibal group either.

Shit.

What should she do? She desperately needed water from the river, but she could take a wide path around and still get that. She could really use some food, but she also didn't want to risk it if this was a militant group.

As she struggled with the decision of whether to go into the camp, she heard the hum of hovercraft come from out of nowhere. Before she could believe it, the sky over the camp was filled with heavy-mech aerials that ripped down from the clouds. Two big dropships rapidly descended, surrounded by half a dozen smaller utility fighter craft. What the hell was going on? Practically before she could blink the dropships began unleashing a barrage of aerial hunter drones that looked like a swarm of hornets darkening the sky. They rained down on the camp below.

Chloe stared, motionless and shocked. She watched as the drones ate the camp alive. The hunters landed and began targeting humans- putting them to death with energy weapons and ballistic fire as if they were mere cattle. Men, women, and children fell in slaughter as they ran for their lives through the trees. The hunters were too fast, too agile, too deadly. The fighter craft took up positions all around the perimeter and started firing as they closed the circle. They took out any stragglers but also targeted all the craft and vehicles in the camp. No matter how old or insignificant.

Flesh burned. People screamed. Smoke rose in the air as trees, tents, and supplies caught fire. Chloe could smell the combination of burning pine and flesh. It made her want to vomit. She was frozen and unable to move. The hunters cleaned up every remaining, living human within minutes. Some of the humans tried to fight back. A few grabbed the weapons they had, some even managed to take out a few drones in the process, but the numbers and technology were against them. It was a slaughter. Within minutes, Chloe was certain that no one was left alive. Hunter drones swept the camp for nearly an hour searching for survivors as retrieval drones came down to pick up the weapons crates and several of the bodies.

As Chloe stared at it all she was further horrified to see in the distance across the valley that at least two other similar "clouds" of drones existed. She couldn't take it anymore. She felt hot tears streaming down her face. She stifled her screams. Her stomach wretched and brought a hard, rough cough to her throat that she fought. The next wretch she couldn't fight, and she threw up the little liquid and food she had in her stomach all over the bush.

Chapter Sixteen – Eli

Eli finished showering in a bathroom that was easily the most lavish he had ever experienced. If this was a guest house, he couldn't imagine what bathrooms were like in regular houses. He was also surprised to find the closet in his room stocked with a full array of clothing in his size. Although the styles were all a bit unusual compared to what he was accustomed to, he picked something he thought would be appropriate enough for dinner, though he really had no idea since he'd never been to a restaurant let alone a nice one. He headed downstairs to wait for Tessa.

Eli wasn't sure he'd ever seen Tessa wearing anything but athletic clothing. Upon seeing her walk downstairs wearing heeled sandals, a brightly colored sundress with an artistic pattern, and a shawl that seemed to shimmer and sparkle. He burst out laughing, "Oh my god, you look hilarious!" As soon as he said it, he realized he should have said something different.

"Like you don't?" she punched him the shoulder. "Nice white pants. If they flared any more at the bottom you'd look like an upside-down sailboat. And that purple shirt you're wearing looks tighter than a VIHM suit for a twelve-year-old."

"I know," replied Eli, rubbing his shoulder, "but it's surprisingly comfortable."

They both laughed.

"I'm still exhausted," said Tessa, "but I feel at least a little refreshed, and I'm so hungry there's no way I could sleep until after we've had some food."

It turned out that the encounter with Zacharias and his goons had been little more than a warm-up. From there forward it got incredibly more complex and challenging. For the next nine hours they flipped from one scenario in the arena simulator to another with few breaks in between. A given scenario could last from fifteen minutes to nearly an hour. One moment they had found themselves wearing heavy armor on an active mech battlefield engulfed in a war between Americorp and the Russobloc. Minutes later, after their "deaths," they had found themselves wearing stealth suits and given an objective to penetrate a military grade foreign facility to access their central network.

One scenario, which was Eli's favorite, had them on an ancient pirate ship being thrashed about on the waves. Their goal in this scenario was simply to survive the onslaught of several dozen armed men who had incredibly bad hygiene and teeth.

It had taken them a moment to stop laughing at the period outfits they were suddenly wearing, a moment that almost caused their pre-mature deaths in the game before they both ducked to avoid being beheaded at the last moment. As with every scenario, the reality of it was stunning. They really felt like they were on a real ship at sea being thrown about in the waves. There was a strong breeze with the smell of salt in the air mixing with that of the rather poorly bathed and incredibly dirty men brandishing rapiers, daggers, and snarls in their general direction.

Despite their training and proficiency in martial arts the numbers were simply overwhelming. Eli and Tessa found themselves quickly pushed to the front of the ship with their backs to the bow. Eli looked around them, trying to think of something as the pack of pirates pressed closer. He had an idea.

"Tess, I really feel like you have this one under control. I've never gotten to swim in an ocean and this feels like the perfect opportunity. Good luck!" He gave her a wink and a thumbs-up with his index finger pointed out at her, then flung himself overboard from the bow.

"Ha!" laughed an over-weight, bearded pirate near the front of the approaching pack. He held a large, curved blade in his hand. "Yar boyfriend pissed himself and decided to try his luck with the sharks if he don't drown first. Give up now and we probably won' hurt ya before we sell ya."

Tessa remained in a fighting stance and cursed Eli under her breath.

"I'll make you a deal," Tessa yelled over the waves. "Anyone who drops their weapons now won't die."

That got them riled up. They laughed heartily but not one dropped a weapon. Instead they started to press in. The first in was the bearded one that had just spoken to Tessa. He had a trained fencing stance, even if he was a bit heavy. He lunged with his blade, but it was a feint as he quickly swung to the right, brought the blade up and swung down in an arc headed straight for Tessa's neck. She dropped to the deck and swung her leg around to sweep his legs out from under him. His body was off balance and crumpled to the ground with a thud as his blade fell out of his hand. Tessa snatched it off the ground and came to her feet just in time to bring it back down on her attacker's neck. It wasn't a clean cut, but enough damage that he wasn't getting back up.

She turned quickly back to the crowd as two more jumped in at her. With considerable effort she was able to parry their first few combined thrusts and swipes, but she was losing ground quickly and nearly had her back to the point of the bow.

"Hey! Assholes!" shouted Eli who was suddenly now standing on the deck at the stern overlooking the boat.

The dozens of pirates gathered in the pack at the front turned around to see Eli smiling and holding one of the small barrels of gunpowder that had been tied down near the side canons. He'd already struck the flint to ignite a small rag he had stuffed in the hole at the top.

"Seriously?!" shouted Tessa. "That's your plan?!"

"It's been fun guys," laughed Eli as he tossed the small barrel at the center of the deck. "Hey Tess! Jump!" he shouted.

The barrel arced across the ship and dropped towards the deck. A flash went off and it exploded. Smoke quickly filled the air as wood splintered and caught fire. Men screamed. Those nearby died in the explosion. Those further away found themselves crashing to the now burning, and flooding underdecks. The ship quickly separated into two halves, trapping the remaining pirates in a collapsing coffin.

Tessa had managed to fling herself off the front of the boat just in time. She had powered her way to a head-first angled dive to get as far away from the boat as possible. By the time she came up she was at least twenty-five to thirty meters away from the burning ship that was now sinking and riddled with the screams of the pirates. She treaded water as her body rose and fell in the waves.

"Can I offer you a ride, my lady?" asked Eli.

She turned her head and looked at him as he sat in a long row boat a few meters away bobbing in the waves. She swam over. He offered her a hand up, but she ignored it and pulled herself over the side and into the boat.

"Where'd you get a row boat?" she asked coldly.

"I found it tied up at the back of the stern. Highly convenient."

"That was your big plan? Blow up the boat?" she asked.

"Honestly, when I jumped overboard, I had no idea that's how it would work out. I just saw a rope hanging off the bow and knew I could grab it on the way down, make it look like I ditched you, then make my way behind them - if you could keep their attention for a few minutes and not die. I was pretty sure you could keep from dying for a few minutes. I was right, wasn't I? You didn't die. From there I figured I'd get behind them and think of something. The gun powder by the cannons was really a gift."

"So how is blowing up the ship a win?" she asked.

"We're still alive, right?" said Eli. "It's all about having a positive attitude."

Before they had a chance to discuss it further, the ocean and boat dissolved and they suddenly found themselves on an unfamiliar landscape with no clouds overhead, two suns above in the sky and fauna unlike anything they had ever imagined. They were in a valley surrounded by high cliffs. They also weren't themselves anymore. They looked at each other, then themselves, and they both looked alien. They each had legs that resembled something more like insect legs than animal legs. They were both tall with long arms. Their faces were sharp but had no noses, and their eyes were more like large black bulges at the sides of their heads sloped to the front. They were surrounded by others like them and they carried significant heavy weaponry.

"Have fun with this one," they heard Ryland say over their HUDs. "You are aliens. Your mission is to obliterate the human and drone forces that are about to descend on your planet. They'll wipe you out if they get the chance. Good luck."

There were four other missions before the day ended and they finally exited the arena. They spent nearly an hour debriefing with the design team, answering all kinds of questions about the choices they had made and why they made them, or about the interactions with the suits and the arena. It was like being interrogated, but in a polite way by really excited people. The design team almost seemed more interested in their failures than their successes, which was something new for Eli and Tessa.

They both received a signal on their HUDs at the same moment that their transportation to dinner had arrived. They dragged themselves off the couch and walked out front to get in the driverless vehicle that would take them to the restaurant.

Chapter Seventeen – Mia

"We'll need to stop and let the little ones rest soon," said Manny, "and hopefully find some food. I think I saw some mango trees not far from here as we came down into the valley."

Trying to move over two dozen children with no adults through the Amazon jungle turned out to be even harder than Mia had expected. It was also surprising in some ways. It was truly amazing how even the young children rapidly adapted to the challenge after the reality of their situation had sunk in. In other ways, the older children realized far too quickly how completely unprepared they were to handle the broad range of ages, and the different levels of emotional and intellectual development in the younger children. The older children were still grappling with the intensity of their own situation. They shouldn't have this responsibility at their age, but they had no choice. As Mia talked about it to Manny, they agreed it was monumental that their group had made it as far as they had in the past few days without having completely collapsed upon itself.

They had quickly developed a system. Manny led a group out as needed to scavenge for food: mostly fruit, flowers, bugs, and if they were lucky, occasionally some fish. Another group oversaw refilling their water bottles, but usually this last task was easy since they tried to keep a route close to the rivers. Mia and a couple of the other older children handled security, scouting, and guard duty. The younger children were forced to grow up more quickly than was fair, but there was little choice.

They were constantly on alert for the sound of soft humming noises in the sky that could signal the approach of drones. So far so good. They found a well-covered, small clearing on some rocks by the river. Mia signaled for the crew to take a rest break. The younger children collapsed and began making ridiculous, silly exhaustion sounds while laughing at themselves and each other. Jelaena began to entertain them all with her impression of Mia commanding them to get up and start marching again. Manny's little sister got into the act and started pretending to be Manny, admonishing "Jelaena/Mia" for not giving them a chance to rest. The little ones cackled with laughter. Mia had to admit it was funny. Despite their situation, the laughter couldn't help but make her smile; even if all she could think of was how she wished for so much better for them all.

Manny and his crew set out west in the direction he had seen the mango trees. After a long drink of water from the river, Mia let José know that she was going to scout ahead a bit. "I should be back in thirty or forty minutes. Keep an eye on them and don't let anyone wander too far, OK?"

José nodded. He was quiet, hard-working, and one of the most grown-up eleven-year-olds she could imagine there ever was. His parents had both died early in their journey, well before the massacre of a few days ago. It had been rough on him. Mia had kind of adopted him as a little brother.

Grabbing her pack and rifle she headed through the jungle in the direction they had been traveling. As usual the jungle was a din of noise from the insects and animal life. The howler monkeys had been intense earlier this morning, but they were getting less active as the day went on and the heat intensified. Wiping the sweat from her face with the shoulder of her deeply stained t-shirt she hopped down a short rock ledge near a larger, open pool of water. For a moment, she stared at it thinking how nice it would be to ignore her task, just strip down, go swimming, and relax for a while. Maybe she could even pretend like she was still just a kid? The idea of it was compelling until she caught notice of a few ripples in the water about thirty meters away and saw the telltale signs of a rather large anaconda underneath. She didn't need any more discouragement than that and made quick time to get away from the pond and back on track. They would have to be sure to avoid this area when they moved the group through a bit later.

Earlier she had spotted a small stone hill rising from the river valley that she was certain was just up ahead. She figured it would be a good vantage point to get a look at their upcoming path. If she was right it should just be a few more minutes ahead, but the canopy made it rather impossible to know for sure. Pushing through some brush, she was a bit surprised to find herself on a road. Well, it was hard to call it a road. It was more of a wide path, but you could see wheel tracks on it from vehicles, and the tracks did not look old.

It was a narrow, bumpy, dirt road, but it appeared used. It was also headed in the direction they were going. Roads were a mixed blessing. They made for reduced travel time, but also brought the perils of detection (or worse) with them. Increasing her pace, she started to jog down the road, trying to do so quietly. About three or four minutes later she started to hear voices.

Slowing her pace, she crept along more carefully. Not far off she could hear adults talking to each other. Leaving the road, she ducked back into the cover of the sub-canopy and kept heading in the direction of the voices. After a few more steps she ducked down and crawled until she had a decent vantage point.

It looked like a small group of drivers. There were about two dozen people, mostly adult men and women, but there were at least a few that looked like older teenagers. They were busy loading crates of mangoes, bananas, and guavas on to a boat tied up by the river. They hadn't been there long. There were no firepits, tents or structures. But most important to Mia was that they had transportation. It was a flat boat, meant mainly for cargo transport. It looked pretty makeshift- some boards and metal sheeting connected over top of some large polymer supply barrels. She was shocked when she saw they also had a truck. That must've been what made the tracks on the road. It was an older, but large, solar-powered transport truck. Either the boat or the truck could possibly hold her whole group. It was hard to ignore the fact that there was something in front of her that could drastically reduce their journey time to Argentina.

Her parents had told her that she couldn't trust other driver groups, but she also knew the adults had occasionally negotiated with others when required. What should she do? She could go back to the group to talk it through with Manny and the others. But why? She was leading the group now. This was her decision to make. They did have one thing worth trading which could buy them transport. Weren't all drivers in the same situation? Wouldn't they all recognize an opportunity to help each other? They all wanted a better life, right?

Mia decided to take the gamble. Standing up from the cover of the brush, she held her rifle up high in her right hand and walked into their encampment. "Hello, friends!" she said loudly without shouting. "I'm alone. I just want to talk."

The adults in front of her turned and looked immediately. She heard at least two ballistic rifles cocking from the perimeter. They stopped loading crates of fruit and everyone stared at her as she walked slowly into their midst.

"I'd stop there if I were you, friend," said a bearded man wearing a torn camouflage vest near the truck. "And you need to drop the rifle now."

Mia stopped, lowered herself slowly down, and put the rifle on the ground. She cursed softly to herself. She should have left the rifle hidden in the brush before she walked out here. "Hey," she spoke up, "I'm not looking for any trouble. I just want to talk, and maybe even see if we can help each other. My name is Mia."

"Look, Mia," said the bearded guy, "we have enough mouths to feed. We aren't looking for more no matter what your story is. And what is a young girl like you doing out here in the jungle alone with a rifle?"

"I'm not looking for food or to join your group," said Mia. "I just want to talk and possibly trade."

"How many are with you? Where are they?" asked a tough looking woman standing next to the bearded man.

"We're a small group. Just over two dozen. We're doing fine making it on our own. We're not looking for handouts," said Mia.

"Why does your group send a little girl to negotiate? That doesn't make sense, *friend*?" asked a sweaty looking guy near the boat.

Mia panicked. She had never been in a situation like this and had no idea what to do. Should she lie and make it sound like they had adults with them? How would her jumping in to negotiate be explainable if there were adults? One thing her parents had taught her was that if you stuck with the truth you couldn't get trapped in a lie. She decided to go with that.

"OK, here's the deal. I have twenty-seven people including me. I'm the oldest in our group. The youngest is a little over three years old. Our parents were slaughtered by drones. Every single one of us is scared as hell and just trying to stay alive but we are making it work. We're trying to make our way south to Argentina and we'll go it on foot the whole way if we must. But you have transportation and we could really use a lift, even if it's only part of the way. We have something valuable to trade. So, you can shoot a little girl, or we can talk."

Several of the people that appeared to be in charge exchanged surprised looks, a couple of smiles, and a few nods.

The bearded man stepped forward with an outstretched hand and a broad smile, "Welcome, Mia. If what you say is true, you have extreme courage for a girl your age, and I respect that very much. It's impressive. My name is Victor. Let's discuss. My apologies for the suspicious behavior, but you can't be too careful these days, yes? So, where is your group and what do you have to trade?"

Chapter Eighteen – Eli

Being in a real restaurant was a new experience. All Eli had ever known was the cafeteria at the camp. He was grateful that Amanda recognized this. She was politely but subtly coaching him and Tessa through it step-by-step when they were confused. Amanda was amazingly graceful in how she covered for their lack of experience and helped them with manners and appropriate responses while making it seem like she was merely talking to herself out loud about how to do things.

The restaurant was called Foreign Cinema. It was apparently something of a Bay Area landmark that had been around since the days before AIs had even existed, according to Amanda. Eli and Tessa had only seen restaurants in movies, shows, and newsvids. The place was beautiful and wondrous to them.

They were seated in an open-air courtyard between two stone and glass buildings with vintage lighting strung overhead. On the far wall between the two buildings an extremely old black and white film was being displayed. No one seemed to be paying much attention to the film and there wasn't any sound. Eli was not sure if they were supposed to watch the movie, but he had kept glancing up at it. In the movie there were workers in rag clothing doing redundant tasks with large wheels, and there were levers attached to some giant circles that had numbers all around the edges. In other scenes humans were dressed in dark suits and ties walking through gardens or staring out from tall buildings while old airplanes with two decks of wings moved slowly through the skyscraper-filled sky. Occasionally the screen would turn black with white writing on it. The language wasn't English, but he toggled his HUD so that it would translate the words to English, then tried to return his attention to the table.

With them were Ryland and Kira in addition to Amanda. Just a moment ago, a rather life-like serving drone had brought them each a glass of ice water as they continued to chat about the history and décor of the restaurant. Eli was a bit nervous. Food in the cafeteria was always served buffet style. In the old movies he'd seen, restaurants always had waiters, waitresses and menus you could hold in your hand. He didn't see any of these things here.

Amanda must have sensed his confusion. "You should see a menu option for this restaurant available on your HUD. You can see what they have to offer and order directly from there. I've taken the liberty of ordering appetizers for all of us: some oysters and a nice local cheese and meat selection. I recommend you select a beverage first and then choose something for a main course. I'll order some side dishes that we can all share."

Finding and navigating the menu was relatively easy, though trying to decide what to order was not. More than half the words on the menu were completely foreign to them. His HUD was able to provide fairly rapid lookups and translations, but in some cases, he barely understood the meaning of the translations. He did not want to appear like he didn't know what he was doing. Eli picked the steak. That seemed safe. He at least knew what that was. He loved steak and didn't get it often.

"Cheers!" offered Ryland as he raised his cocktail. "Today was a fantastic start and you both performed admirably."

The others raised their drinks, so Tessa and Eli did the same with their waters. For the next twenty minutes or so they regaled some of the victories and defeats in the simulations from earlier in the day. Eli was particularly proud of the pirate ship victory. From Ryland's laughter you could tell that it was also one of his favorites. Ryland continued to tell them about some of the new algorithms he was employing to make the virtual character responses even more realistic than ever before. Most of what he was explaining was way over their heads, but they still listened, completely fascinated.

Kira took a sip of her white wine then tipped her glass in Tessa's direction. "On that note, you should know, that while the day was full of some great gaming moments, when you pulled that bit with the bully threatening to rape you in the C22 camp, and snapped his neck in the first simulation, you received a standing ovation from every woman that was watching in the game studio."

Tessa blushed.

"Don't be embarrassed! We also all know it was a game, so nobody thinks you're a murderer," laughed Kira. "You changed the game in your favor. You used what you knew of the situation and probabilities. You came up with a creative answer and it was epic. If everything about what we are doing wasn't highly confidential, the vid of that encounter would probably be the highest trending thing on the net right now."

"Yes," laughed Ryland, "you both did quite well, but as I said, it was just a start. We have more interesting and more complex sims to run in the coming days. Today was mainly about calibration, but we gained great data and more importantly some great ideas from it all."

Drones hustled about from table to table delivering food and drinks. It was mesmerizing to watch. One of them delivered a glass of the high-energy iced tea that Eli had ordered. He figured he could use it to help get through dinner given how exhausted he was. He needed to stay sharp for the moment. The movie on the wall kept distracting him. Currently there was some sort of bizarre, metallic, female robot sitting in a machine with electricity flowing through it. The machine was being operated by a man who looked quite mad as he pulled levers and pushed buttons. The electricity flowed between a glass case holding a woman's unconscious body and the robot. Rings danced up and down the robot. Then the robot faded out and was replaced by a real woman.

"It's called *Metropolis*," offered Ryland. "I can't recall the exact year it's from, but my HUD is now telling me it was first released in 1927. It was one of the first ever science-fiction movies."

"What's it about?" asked Eli.

"It's been a long time since I watched it, but it's a story of how technology could lead to class separation between workers and the elite, a warning about the division of a utopia for the wealthy but a desperate and mundane existence for those who supported it. I suppose it's interesting to reflect on it. It would have been nearly impossible back then to predict the advances in technology that have led us to a much different variation of it all today. For many generations people saw the coming displacement of jobs by technology. There always seemed to be some new industries people could move in to, and most people presumed there'd simply always be low-level jobs available.

"If anyone enjoys romantic storylines, the movie also contains that, as one of the elite city planners falls in love with a member of the working class. It would be the equivalent of the chairman of the Board having his son come to him, declare that he was steadfast in love with a driver, and that they should all work together to bring about massive change to society. I've met the chairman, though only briefly. I can tell you that's not going to happen."

"Hold on," said Tessa. "So, are we going to actually talk about this? Is this a real subject we can discuss? I mean, how deplorable it is out there for billions of people while we sit here with oysters? How Eli and I had to be abandoned by our families as toddlers and grow up without parents to have a chance for a better life? How drivers get executed regularly just for trying to gather food growing on land some corporation owns?"

Eli gave her a look that said she needed to shut it. They had both been trained to know that if they made it out of C22, they should avoid just these kinds of discussions if they wanted to be successful. Tessa was never good at keeping her mouth shut when it came to her values.

"Of course, we can discuss it," responded Ryland. "Shareholders have a right to free speech, as do drivers so long as that speech doesn't present a highly probable, negative threat to shareholder interests. But, it's wise to be a bit more careful in the words we choose, and you two should be even more careful, at least for the time being. You're technically not shareholders yet and as such your rights are far more limited. The shares you'll be receiving for your work with us are held in trust until your formal graduation from the athletic center."

Amanda stepped in as usual, "Tess and Eli, I think you'll find that many shareholders have similar feelings and concerns about the drivers and how unfair society has unfolded for many people. We're human, and we struggle with it as well. Unfortunately, it's also far from simple. There is no easy solution. The world changed too fast. There is a massive amount of excellent, recorded study of this subject with philosophical debate and proposals on all sides. If you'd like, I'd be happy to spend some time with you each evening to help get you up to speed on at least why it's become a bit of an impasse?"

Eli reached for Tessa's hand under the table and she nodded. "Yes, I suppose that would be a good idea."

"The ugly reality of it," intoned Kira, "is that for adult drivers, the world has reached a point where they simply don't have any skills they can offer that people with money are willing to pay them to perform. The market economy doesn't have an answer for providing the funding needed to allow these people to all live comfortably for doing nothing but reproducing for the potential that some of their children will turn out to have valuable skills the world needs. I don't like this anymore than you do, but it's a problem that currently doesn't have an answer."

Ryland jumped in, "Kira, my dear friend, you've always been more pragmatic than I am in your political views, but I know that you share my belief that a better solution will eventually be found. I know I may be a bit more of a dreamer. There's always a solution. It just happens, in this case, to be something nobody's thought of quite yet. My experience tells me that what is needed is the right person and the right motivation. Perhaps that will be one of you two?" He smiled his contagiously friendly smile that made everyone at the table feel better.

With that, drones began arriving with their meals and to refresh their beverages. Everything about the food in front of them looked heavenly to Eli. Compared to the food he'd grown up on, even the food only available to the best and oldest athletes in camp, he'd never seen or smelled anything like this. The steak he was served was unlike anything he had ever imagined existed. He guessed Tessa may have felt a bit like a sell-out for eating what she had ordered after what she'd just said, but that didn't stop her from devouring her pork chop and every side dish she could sample. There were billions of people on the planet that would not hesitate to trade places with them. At the end of the day, Eli guessed that is how everyone else that had money justified it to themselves.

"Let's talk about tomorrow," suggested Kira. "We have something special in mind for the simulations you'll be in. Theo managed to get a draft scenario from our new title ready to go instead of just random test sims."

The broad smile on Kira's face told them this would be something exciting. Eli remained positive, even though he had just glanced up at the screen as more foreign words in white lettering glared from the black background. His HUD automatically translated them. 'Verily, I say unto you, the days spoken of in the Apocalypse are nigh…!'. He wasn't entirely sure what that meant, but it didn't sound good for the people in the movie. Or maybe it did if you were one of the people dressed in rags and moving levers on a wheel all day?

Chapter Nineteen - Chloe

Hours went by. Or was it only just minutes? Chloe couldn't really tell for sure. It had taken a while for her body to stop shivering and sweating from what she had just witnessed. Once her breathing finally calmed down, she laid there on the ground just staring at the black smoke smoldering into the sky as the drones finished their clean-up work.

She had heard about things like this happening. But it was only from the newsvids and always painted as a victory against one terrorist cell or another that was being armed by foreign governments to attack corporate interests. For all she knew, that was exactly what this was. Maybe these people were terrorists? That would explain the weapons she had seen, but there were also children there. She just didn't know. People made different choices when they were desperate. She didn't know their story.

It had been silent for a while, except for the sound of wildlife that was beginning to return to the area. That seemed like as good a sign as any that it was probably safe to give up her hiding spot and head down to check things out. She had made the decision a while ago to see what she could find. She did not expect to find anyone alive. The drones were too efficient for that, but if there were, maybe she could help. Dead bodies weren't something she looked forward to seeing, but she also guessed the drones had little interest in whatever human food these people were carrying. As morbid as the thought was, knowing it made her a scavenger, she needed food. Maybe she would get lucky and even find some of the chickens or goats.

It was probably best she moved now. With all the smoke from the fires, there would undoubtedly be others coming to see what they could scavenge. It was like a beacon.

The sun was beginning to drop in the sky which meant it had been at least several hours since the initial attack. Grabbing her pack, she shouldered it, but kept her weapon in her hand and the safety off. She began creeping through the woods as softly as she could to avoid making noise.

Within ten minutes she was getting close. She could smell burning flesh. She almost vomited again but kept her cool. She did stop momentarily to take a drink of water from her bottle. She pulled out a bandana and tied it around the back of her head to cover her nose and mouth. A few minutes later she was at the edge of the encampment. Crouching down, she stayed still and surveilled the scene.

Bodies were everywhere, crumpled on the ground in whatever contorted position they had landed in as they ran. It was a massacre. It was the most horrifying thing she had ever seen in-person, not just from a terrible scene in some movie or a history clip from one of the World Wars. Burned bodies littered the ground, stained with blood. Most of the corpses were still staring blankly with mouths open, trapped in silent screams.

Tents had been burned to ash but still smoldered, threatening to ignite some of the pine straw on the ground. The few vehicles they had were obliterated. Most were still burning, and all looked like mangled hunks of blackened steel. A few had holes in them large enough that Chloe could probably walk through. The crates of weapons she had seen were all gone. Scanning back and forth, she saw no movement and decided to risk going in further.

In an open area of field were some of the children she had seen playing. From the looks of it they had tried to run, probably screaming out for their parents. Two of the bodies, barely over a meter tall each, were collapsed on the ground in an embrace as their remains burned. A colorful ball still rolled away quietly in the field as the wind picked up for a moment.

Walking openly, but cautiously, she headed into the camp amongst the carnage. Seeing the bodies of children at her feet was almost more than she could handle. She fought the tears welling up in her eyes. Nobody had been left alive. The bio-sensors on the drones were too efficient for that to have happened. She wasn't sure how they had missed her hiding up in the rocks, but she was grateful to still be alive.

She already had all the basic survival supplies that she could carry except for food, so there was no need for her search the many bodies. She even had a good stash of medical supplies including anti-biotics that she had used some of her last money to buy, so there wasn't a need to search for any of that.

The Drivers

As she walked, she could see more bodies of people clinging to each other in the dirt where they died. They were riddled with shrapnel, their faces barely recognizable and their clothes were covered in blood stains.

Part of her wished she had a HUD she could activate just so she could capture all this on video to share it with the rest of the world. Shareholders needed to see the horror of what had really happened, but she knew that doing something like that would also instantly broadcast her position to the networks and all the AIs monitoring them. Probably the best thing she could do is to head over to the center of the camp where she saw the picnic tables to see if she could find something to eat.

In the middle of a cluster of what were once tents, she found what she was looking for: food stores. It was more than she had hoped for. There were cases of military-style rations in light-weight, nano-polymer, fire and water-resistant pouches. She ran over and began stuffing her pack with as many as she could fit. She found some fresh food as well- small crates of fruits and vegetables, though most of it had been damaged by the fighting. Could you really call this fighting? No. This was a slaughter. There were at least a couple bags of apples still intact. She tied those to her pack. If she had more time, there was more to grab, but she couldn't carry too much more, and what she already had could last her for weeks. That's when she smelled it.

For a moment, she thought she might have been dreaming. She was not. She grabbed her pack and moved quickly toward the back of the burning tent cluster, past some large, polymer barrels that she guessed were used for water storage and transport. She turned the corner around them and saw exactly what she had hoped she would find. It didn't really matter to her how it happened. Maybe they'd been caught in the cross-fire of energy weapons. Maybe they'd been caught in one of the fires from the crates or tents. She didn't care. As much as she still felt horrified at what had happened to these people, she was staring at the "cooked" remains of three chickens. They weren't cooked well by any stretch of the imagination. The feathers had been mostly burned off and the flesh blackened. Even if they were bloody, had beaks, and burned feet still attached, they smelled like grilled chicken and that was good enough for her. She pulled out a bag from her pack and scooped them into it. The bag was immediately stained from the blood and juices.

At this point she figured she was on borrowed time, so she decided to get going. She headed toward the northern edge of the camp to continue in the direction she had been going before all of this had happened. That direction would also keep her close to the river and well clear of the other two camps that must've been hit just like this one. Oh my God, she thought… that's so many more people. Hundreds? More? No. No time to think about that now. She moved.

Chapter Twenty – Eli

Kira briefed Eli and Tessa for the next game simulation over coffee in the studio lounge and had just walked them down to the arena so they could get started. The entire studio team was being cagey about the detail of the sims planned for today. It seemed everything was extremely confidential. Ryland had said at dinner the evening before that he felt they needed at least a little bit of an update on the news and some recent history to be properly prepared, so Kira tried her best to bring them up to speed quickly.

"You're familiar with the advancements in Faster Than Light, or 'FTL' travel in the news recently?" asked Kira over their first cup of coffee that morning. "And the fact that we are now mining for resources in the asteroid belts of several worlds in this solar system as well as beginning to be capable of pushing beyond that to worlds in other systems? Yes?"

"Look," replied Eli, "I'm going to level with you. I won't speak for Tess, though I expect her answer will be mostly the same as mine. We're not entirely sure if what we know is propaganda or the truth. We were taught that FTL was first developed as a concept a little over a few decades ago, though it was almost entirely discovered by the AIs. It became reality not long after that. The AIs have advanced it far quicker than humans had ever expected, and (very conveniently) machines are the only ones who can travel via FTL. It's something about the drive putting the matter out of phase with normal space which isn't something biological tissue can survive. That much we all learned in the limited non-athletic courses they gave us at the camp and from the extremely limited exposure we had to non-sports news. I don't really understand it at all, and even if someone tried to explain it to me, I'd be even more lost. Advanced math and physics weren't exactly emphasized where we grew up. But yes, we are aware FTL exists and that the corps are now using it to mine for resources on other planets."

Tessa nodded that she didn't have much to add to that.

"OK, so yes," said Kira, "that's all true. There's a bit of a technology race occurring between us, China, and the Russobloc corporations right now. We are still way ahead of them and access to the rich resources of the planetary belts is keeping us ahead. The politics can get extremely complicated, but let's just say it isn't friendly. What isn't yet widely known is just how far the most recent generation of our FTL drive has come. This is unconfirmed, but the rumors are that we've designed drives that can reduce trips to the nearest stars to less than a year. It's exciting and it feels like we are on the verge of truly being able to explore the galaxy. We expect this to become public knowledge within months. There are many questions about what we'll find out there and the possibilities of discovering other intelligent life. There are even more questions and concerns knowing that our only ambassadors will be the machines and AIs we built and that there's an extremely lengthy communications window for us to talk to them."

"So, humans are suddenly worried about their machines screwing up if they meet alien life?" laughed Tessa. "But because the greedy people all want more resources and more money, they aren't about to slow down anything? Instead, they continue to fight each other for the first shot at screwing up first contact. Wow. I really can't tell you how much I love it. That's sadly hilarious."

Kira laughed, "Well, yes. It's starting to get a lot of discussion in the media, so you know it's being discussed in the board rooms. It's a growing concern. I like that you mentioned the phrase 'first contact.' Practically everything for this next game is still in draft, but our working title for it is *Last Contact*. You'll find out why in a few moments. We just finished the first draft of the introduction sequence. Duncan's quite proud of it so far. He's been working around the clock since we brought you here to have it ready. It's rough around the edges and needs a lot of edits, but it will suffice for today. It's more than enough for you to get the idea before game play begins. You'll be the first people outside the team to see any of this. Once this game is completed, it will be the most advanced and immersive massive, multi-player game ever built. But, for today, it will just be the two of you in there. All other characters, including those on your side, are run by the gaming algorithms and AIs."

Kira smiled at them as she turned around to leave them in the arena. "Have fun, kids."

The door to the arena slid closed. Eli and Tessa heard the lock engage and the audio notification from the AIs that the arena was initialized and ready. For a moment they were staring out into the same, massive chamber they had been in yesterday. By now they had learned to notice the subtle visual distortions that preceded the arena morphing and the syncing with their specialized HUDs and suits.

Everything went pitch black. Eli had a subtle sensation he was floating a bit, though he knew he was still on the ground. All around them small lights started to shift into focus as did planets, and star systems. It was like they were floating in the galaxy and could see forever. Stunning comets went by, hurtling past asteroid belts. Music began to play. It had a faintly military quality to it, but it was also modern and a bit haunting. Eli felt like he could almost reach out and touch one of the passing planets. The level of detail was unbelievable.

With a disorienting transition everything zoomed in on a corporate FTL ship light years away from Earth, right as it was coming back into normal phase. It dropped into orbit with a large, red planet. A female narrator's voice filled their ears as the scene played out in front of them. Her voice was beautiful. It was hard to tell if it was that of a woman or a young girl.

"It was inevitable. We always knew we weren't alone in the universe. First contact with sentient, alien life would eventually be made. As we reached further and further into the stars, we finally found them… or at least… our emissaries did. Still unable to travel the stars ourselves, we relied upon the machines and technology we had built in our own image. Massive thought, research, and planning had gone into preparing for this very moment. We had prepared for any contingency we could think of. We'd even developed AIs designed and tested to handle those exact interactions."

Eli and Tessa were jumped from view to view, watching as the ship deployed landing drones which included research bots, mining units, scouts, cargo transports, and of course, military support. The drones all landed on the planet surface and began to fan out on a mission. It was all happening rapidly as the perspective kept changing. The planet surface looked brutal, horribly jagged and cold with no atmosphere. Dust storms swirled in the distance. There was no water to be seen.

"They found us," said the girl narrator's voice.

A heavy cruiser of unusual design appeared out of nowhere above the planet and began dropping aerial crafts at an alarming rate. The view switched back to the planet surface. The alien craft arrived at the surface and with stunning agility moved out in all directions. Energy weapons flared, and the scouts were wiped out of existence. Mining units and research bots exploded. Transports did not even get off the ground before they were destroyed. Heavy hunter-class units avoided the first salvos of fire and did what they were designed to do. They analyzed the attack and prepared to mount a counter-assault but were then immediately forced into evasive maneuvers. The earth ship in orbit began immediately broadcasting messages of peace in numerous languages and codes. The Americorp hunter drones on the planet evaded attacks for a few more moments, then they were also obliterated.

"We did establish contact," continued the narrator. "They informed us we were taking their resources. Then they destroyed our ship."

They watched as it exploded in a flash of energy before disappearing. The music was reaching more and more of a crescendo, the pace was energetic.

"Within months," said the narrator, "three other missions met with the same fate." Fast clips showed the destruction of those other ships and drones. "Our AIs tried to convey our intentions of peace in every way they could think. Nothing changed, until the day we realized they weren't just going after our deep space exploration teams anymore, they were coming for us... on Earth.

"The Earth responded. The corporations saw the combined threat to their existence and began amassing a drone military the likes of which had never been seen. We shared technology and worked around the clock to prepare for the invasion. The largest forces we could pull together were immediately launched to try and head off the alien ships we had detected headed towards our furthest outposts."

The view panned out to show massive military drone forces dropping out of FTL to stand in front of similarly massive alien drone forces. Battle erupted. The size and scale of it was staggering as was the speed. The maneuvers our forces and theirs engaged in were too fast to calculate. It was like watching algorithms competing in real-time, because that's exactly what it was. Within a few moments, the outcome became obvious. We were losing, badly.

"What became apparent was that the first alien life we had ever encountered had also developed artificial intelligence. Unfortunately, theirs was far superior to ours. Our weapons technology, and the speed of our ships, was not that far from theirs. Our algorithms were simply outmatched. This scene played out two more times with massive losses to our forces before we knew we had to make a change. The data was obvious to anyone who looked at it. Their ability to predict our ship and drone movements was simply that much better, that much faster. We were left with just one choice."

Again, the view changed, but this time back to Earth. It showed humans being recruited and trained as soldiers and pilots. It showed the rapid manufacture of battle-mech suits, manned fighter craft, and drones controlled by human operators instead of AI. All over the planet human soldiers were being reinvented as a concept. They were even recruited from the ranks of the drivers. At this point the music had reached a high point and then suddenly fell deadly silent as the view pulled out to just show the beautiful planet Earth from out in space.

"If our AI couldn't save us, we'd have to try to do so ourselves, or our first contact would be our last contact."

Everything went black. Then the words 'Last Contact' came into view as if they were multi-dimensional, faded circuits with glitches in them. Beneath that was the game studio logo with words 'Brought to you by Immersive Magic'. The words faded and were replaced by a sharp font that read simply, "Ready to begin?"

"Oh… HELL yeah!" shouted Eli. He and Tessa both selected 'Yes' on their HUDs.

Chapter Twenty-One – Mia

Mia wasn't entirely sure she had made the right decision. Victor smiled a lot. He had suddenly become quite friendly, but there was something hard to trust about somebody that smiled that much. It did sound like Victor's group had been through rough times, having lost a lot of people to the drone scouts as they bounced from one area of the jungle to another. They had finally found a place inhospitable enough to be uninteresting to the Cartelcorp, but close enough to places they could scavenge food with the boat and vehicle they had managed to acquire. Victor claimed they had a few dozen children back at their camp.

"Though," said Victor, "I'm not sure if any of the kids in our group has the guts to lead the rest of them through the jungle. Or to have walked up on me and this crew alone with a rifle in their hands!"

Mia knew that her group would begin to worry about her soon. José would expect her back any minute now, and she would be at least twenty to thirty more minutes depending on how this played out. Negotiating with friends, or even her parents, was something she was used to doing. This was something entirely different. Victor smelled strongly of sweat and cigar smoke. His green tank top was as stained thick with dirt and mud. He wore a long hunting blade tied to his belt.

"So, tell me, my friend," began Victor, "What do you have to trade that you think might be worth me risking the valuable transportation we have? These vehicles help provide food for our families. Any travel is risky. It's not that I don't like the idea of helping people, especially a group of children led by a young woman with great courage, but we also must look out for ourselves. What can you offer us?"

"I don't know what it's called," began Mia, "but we have this really big tarp or blanket. It's large enough to cover a dozen people, and it's made of some sort of material that can keep the drones from knowing that you're there. It works. If it didn't, we wouldn't be alive." Mia let out a breath. There. She had told him.

Victor gave her a skeptical look then started slowly nodding as his lips turned back into a smile. He let out a soft whistle. "Mia, my friend, you have what's called a bio-signature shield. It's stealth nano-tech, built by the same people that make the military drones. Pretty serious stuff, friend. How'd you manage to come upon something like that?"

Mia shook her head, "I don't know. Our parents acquired it."

Victor eyed her skeptically for a moment. "I believe you, Mia."

"So, are you interested?"

"Perhaps," replied Victor. "How far do you want to go?"

"We're trying to get to Argentina, but I'm guessing you can't take us that far."

"This is true," said Victor. "We can probably get you past most of Bolivia depending on the drone traffic, but I cannot allow my transports to go further than that. Do we have a deal?" Victor extended his dirty, but strong hand.

This could mean months off their journey if she remembered her geography correctly. She wasn't sure but figured it could be at least a couple of days of driving. That seemed like a dream compared to what they had been doing. She extended her hand and shook on it.

"I need to get back to my group and let them know. They'll already be getting worried about me. I've been gone longer than I said I would be."

They agreed to a time frame and Victor said they would be ready as long as Mia had what she promised. Victor warned her that he had already sent scouts and snipers in multiple directions just in case Mia was lying. "I believe in trust, my friend, but I also believe in precaution. Don't do anything stupid, Mia."

Grabbing her rifle, Mia made her way quickly back through the jungle to her group, trying to think of how she would explain this to them once she got there. When she finally arrived back at the rocks, she was out of breath.

"Mia!" exclaimed Manny. "We were starting to worry about you."

José was standing next to him nodding, but he smiled seeing that Mia was back.

Still catching her breath, Mia started to explain to them what she had found and the deal she had just made. "I know it's hard to trust anyone. I can't even tell you that I'm positive we can trust these people. I'm asking you to trust me. This could take months off our journey and every day we are out here is dangerous. I know the blanket that blocks the drones is a big trade, but this is two more months that we wouldn't need it and we'd still have one more. I think one would be enough to cover almost all of us if we really needed it."

Most of the children looked at her a bit blankly for a moment, but the older ones started to nod slowly.

"We trust you, Mia," offered Pablo, a boy of about twelve. "You and Manny have gotten us this far."

Some of the smaller children started to add their agreement, but that's not what Mia really needed. Manny looked her, gave her a momentary look of doubt, but then smiled and nodded. "We both know our chance of making it on foot the whole way isn't good. We have to try something and be willing to take some risks."

They quickly gathered themselves together and made the short march back to where Mia had met the other group. Victor greeted Mia warmly and was incredibly welcoming to all the children. Some of the other adults even offered them some fruit and fish which the children devoured. Mia brought out a large bag with a shoulder strap and unpacked the stealth blanket. What had Victor called it? A bio-blocking shield or something like that? Victor continued to smile as he smoked a thick and pungent cigar. It was agreed they would set out immediately. Dusk was coming, and it was always best to travel at night when they could. Victor said his drivers knew the narrow, dirt roads through the jungles well. They would keep them well hidden from the main traffic.

The children were piled into the transport truck along with some of the fruit. It was a tight fit, and many of the smaller children had to sit on laps or pile on top of each other. After weeks of walking in the jungle they were almost having fun, despite the tight quarters. Once they added their packs they felt like cargo, but they could handle it for a day or two.

Mia was a bit surprised when Victor and two of his men said they were coming with them, but it made sense that they needed the vehicle returned safely. Victor rode at the back of the rear gate while his men rode up front. They all had rifles, though so did Mia, Manny, and a couple of others in their crew.

Once they were on the road it was almost surreal. Some of the younger kids started laughing and singing until Manny told them they needed to be quite so not attract attention. The soft hum of the EV was almost pleasant, and even the bumpy dirt road was tolerable compared to doing it all on foot. Mia had not realized how much her body really ached until she sat back and relaxed, knowing that she would be mostly off her feet for the next couple of days. That sounded glorious. The gentle rocking of the transport for the next couple of hours started to put her to sleep. Maybe she *should* sleep? She deserved it, didn't she? What kid her age had to pull off the craziness she was attempting? She closed her eyes and started to drift off.

Maybe she slept for a few hours. She wasn't sure. She felt the vehicle turn and begin to slow until it came to a stop. "What's going on?" she asked, "Are we taking a break?"

"Yes," replied Victo., "Everyone should get out to stretch their legs."

Mia blinked to clear the sleepiness from her head. It was hard to see out the back of the transport in the darkness of the jungle, but she hefted herself up and pulled herself over the edge onto the ground. Behind her she could hear the rest of the children stirring themselves into motion to follow her. After about three or four steps her eyes started to focus in the darkness. They were surrounded. At least a dozen men and women, maybe more, all with rifles trained straight at them.

As quickly as she could she slung her rifle from her shoulder, clicked the safety off and pointed it straight at Victor who was just ten feet away. She heard the other two children carrying rifles in their group cock theirs as well.

"You have a choice, Mia," said Victor with a deadly serious face. The smile was gone. "You can shoot me. You're heavily outnumbered. You'll be shot down, and at a minimum at least a half-dozen others in your charge will also die in the fray. Others will probably be injured only to die days later from lack of anti-biotics. Or, you can put your rifle down, order the others in your group to do so as well, and then get in the transport over there to go with these people."

"I never should've trusted you, you bastard!" screamed Mia. She could feel drops of sweat falling from her forehead and stinging her eyes.

Her heart was beating fiercely. How could she have been so stupid? Why didn't she listen to what her parents told her about trusting others? She had wanted so badly to believe, so badly to come through for everyone.

She let go of the trigger, slowed her breathing even if her face was still flushed with anger and embarrassment, held out the rifle above her head, and ordered the others in her group to stand down.

"You made the right decision," said Victor, still not smiling. "And Mia, I'm sorry."

Chapter Twenty-Two - Anand

Street lights flickered with the normal intermittent brown-outs in the damp, sticky night sky of Bombay. Traffic was still congested on the broken roads. Most of the shops had closed by this time of the evening, but the jagged stone streets were still crowded with people making their way home, to a local bar, or to someplace even less wholesome. While there were a few driverless cars, there were still countless combustion-engine cycles billowing pollution into the air. Many of the cycles had two or even three riders piled on them: few wearing helmets and most with cloths tied over their faces. The smell of human bodies that had not bathed in weeks or months permeated the air. The dirt and garbage in the streets were strong, though not as bad as more populated days of the week.

Anand Shah could feel sweat dripping down his forehead from the multi-kilometer walk he had just taken home from work. His shirt was soaked. He could afford transportation but decided he could use the exercise and wasn't in any rush. He was almost home when he noticed a few men in a group on the side of the road sizing him up. He decided to hurry his pace a bit before taking a quick turn into the small bar at the base of his apartment building. The cigarette in his hand was burning down to its last ash, so he took one more drag and then tossed it on the ground with hundreds of others already lying there.

The bar, Bombay No. 5, was dimly lit and reeked of smoke, stale beer, and cheap gin. Incense burned from behind the bar next to a small stone statue of Ganesh. There weren't a lot of people in tonight, but it was a decent crowd with quite a few of the regulars. In the background some popular Asian pop song was playing. It was impossible to tell if it was a real singer or not, and Anand didn't care enough to keep up with the music scene these days. The place wasn't winning any awards for cleanliness or interior design—more than half of it was badly in need of repair, but it was an honest place. The owner charged reasonable prices and above all he made it abundantly clear that anyone who tried fighting, stealing, or otherwise causing trouble in his establishment would quickly learn how low his tolerance was. They would also likely learn how high his agility was for a guy almost three times the weight of an average man.

Anand had a suspicion the owner was ex-military but had never confirmed it. Asking questions about someone's past would only invite questions about your own.

Anand waded through the tables and chairs to find a seat at the bar. He opted for the furthest one to the left, which gave him the best view of the room in case those guys from the street decided to follow him inside. He lit another cigarette and ordered a beer. The bartender, a new girl who had just recently been hired, brought him a mostly clean glass filled with what passed for a decent beer in a place like this. At least she smiled at him. Anand smiled back. He was no model, and he had been more attractive in his twenties or thirties, but even pushing well into his late forties with his dark hair starting to grey, he wasn't a bad looking guy. He almost got married a couple of times, but economics always made it difficult, and now it wasn't even a remote possibility.

For a moment he allowed himself to remember what it had been like living in the walled IndoCorp city in Pune. He had a nice apartment, well decorated. Driverless cars picked him and his co-workers up each morning to take them to the tall steel and glass towers of one of the largest robotics software development companies in the world. Meals at the cafeteria were amazing. Everything was cleaner. Shinier. Even his memories of it were prettier.

India had handled the massive, global economic shifts, technological advances, and the associated large-scale job displacement very different than most countries. The majority of the country had never had the money to afford things like autonomous vehicles, and most were willing to work for such low wages that even as robots and AI became cheaper and cheaper, they were still not as cheap as the human labor willing to do the dirtiest and most labor-intensive of jobs. This dramatically slowed the impact and lessened the degree of change. There were far fewer riots or the mass increases in crime occurring in many other parts of the world.

In some ways, the Indian economy even flourished as the need for software developers and engineers boomed. India had massive numbers of people ready, trained, and willing to take those jobs. Possibly their biggest software industry involved writing the less sexy code for robots and drones. Europe, the Americas, Israel, and China all focused on the much more sophisticated and refined sciences of AI. India was willing to take on the incredible amount of coding needed to run and operate the drones core motor functions, and also to provide the large degree of basic quality assurance services.

Several cities including Pune, Bangalore, Hyderabad, and New Delhi had formed distinct corporate cities surrounded by high walls around skyscrapers, large company campuses, and higher end housing. Another started to form in Bombay, but the dense real estate, populace, and heavy traffic was too problematic, and it quickly became less of a production hub and more of a bastion for high-end executives and government officials. India converted to its own crypto-currency, much like the rest of the world did, but it still maintained a physical currency for the masses. As far as Anand knew, India was the only place on the planet, outside of some driver communes, to still use physical currency. Constant inflation was threatening to destroy that soon.

Working in robotics software was a job Anand loved. Primarily, he had architected, designed and wrote software drivers for robotics hardware. His code abstracted and handled all the little instructions for controlling aspects of the hardware. This allowed the operating systems and AIs behind them to continue their rapid, continuous advance independently, allowing units and models to be constantly upgraded without being weighed down by the more base-level instruction sets. He really had a knack for it. He took great pride in the fact that at least fragments of his code were resident in a staggering number of units still in operation today around the world.

Then it had happened. It was inevitable. The AIs decided they could write the same software better and more efficiently. With almost zero notice, his position was no longer required. Although he had a decent number of shares for someone in his position, he could hardly afford to stay in Pune. It was far too expensive without a good IndoCorp salary to live on.

Luckily, India was also one of the last places that still had a market for his skills even after AIs replaced most software developers. They had found an interesting, niche market that no one else seemed particularly interested in filling: black market software and support. Although calling it black market was not really accurate, because in India it was perfectly legal and protected, if not officially sanctioned, by IndoCorp. The companies were still subsidiaries of IndoCorp, and they paid their employees in real shares—just dramatically lower amounts than what the higher-end engineers and scientists still working in the walled cities received.

There was a pretty significant market for troubleshooting, supporting, and even updating older robots and drones that had been decommissioned by larger world corps. The units were often the property of driver communities, crime syndicates, or even what some called terrorists, though that really depended on your political point of view. Anand and his new co-workers were basically the equivalent of tech support on a global scale to clients operating under the radar of the larger, legal corps. But hey, it was a job. He was employed. It paid very little, but he still made more than most of the poor souls he was surrounded by in this city, and all of them were better off than the people in the countryside, where disease and starvation were rampant.

He found himself suddenly staring at the last sip of beer in his glass as his thoughts returned to the present. His cigarette was nearly burning his knuckles, so he crushed it out in the dirty and overly full ashtray on the bar. A pretty girl, probably in her late twenties, had sat down next to him. He twitched his eye to activate his HUD. It instantly started to identify and outline the people around him. Name, job, known felonies, the normal stuff. He glanced at the girl next to him. He had been guessing she was a prostitute, but according to his HUD she was not. If she was, she was neither a known prostitute nor broadcasting that she was available for hire.

Her name was Idha Patel. She was from Bangalore but currently resided in Bombay. Her details listed her profession as Advisor. That could mean anything. It was a generic, made-up job title given to people whose real job wasn't something they, or those they worked for, wanted to be well defined. She was dressed too nice to be in a place like this, but she didn't look the least bit uncomfortable with her surroundings. She was sipping a gin martini, and likely interacting with her HUD, which was a smaller, and more ornate model than typically seen in this neighborhood.

Further details of her employment were marked classified. Anand didn't see that very often. Glancing around the bar, he could tell he wasn't the only one who had noticed her.

What the hell. He had little to lose. He'd play.

"Buy you a drink?" he asked.

"No thank you, Mr. Shah. I am quite fine." She responded.

Of course, her HUD gave her access to his profile just as much as he had accessed hers, but it was more formal of a response than he was expecting. If he was smart, he should probably leave the bar now, go up to his apartment, and drink the bottle of scotch he had until he passed out. He cursed himself silently knowing he was not that smart.

"You smell too nice to be here, and while those clothes look great on you, they cost more than most of the clothing the people in this bar are wearing put together. What are you doing here?" he asked without even looking at her as he motioned to the bartender for another beer.

"I'm looking for you, Mr. Shah, the former IndoCorp developer from Pune," she said.

He lit another cigarette as his beer arrived. He took a long drink before speaking.

"You found me," he said. "Mission accomplished. What's the next item on your scavenger hunt? A slightly used bio-engineer?"

"No, Mr. Shah."

"Please... Anand."

"OK, Anand," she kept her tone completely serious and even. She hadn't cracked so much as a mild smile, but she also hadn't frowned or shown any annoyance. "I was asked by my client to find you. They may have a business opportunity for you. I do not yet have the details on what that opportunity is, but they wanted you to be aware it may be coming."

"And who is your client?"

"I cannot say."

"You cannot say? Or you do not know?"

"It does not matter," she said. "What matters is that if I contact you again, we need you to immediately leave what you are doing and follow the instructions we send you. I understand this may seem highly unusual and very risky. Perhaps not worth putting your current employment at risk."

"Why would a strange, overdressed, cryptic woman in a shithole bar offering me a mysterious job opportunity requiring me to possibly screw up the only thing that's willing to pay me money possibly be considered unusual? Things like that happen to me all the time. It starts to get tiresome. Last week it was a treasure hunt in Madagascar. Turned it down. Too scared of tigers."

She didn't appear amused and remained stone faced. She made a slight gesture, authorizing something from her HUD display. "Perhaps this will change your mind."

Anand watched on his HUD. He had just been transferred a significant amount of IndoCorp shares. They were his, already encoded to his DNA. This wasn't a hoax. It wasn't riches, but it was more than he would make this year in his job.

Idha finished her martini and stood up from her seat. "I'll be in touch. Or not. My client pays well. They hope they now have your attention should they need your services." She walked out of the bar with quite a few people staring as she left.

Anand was still a bit stunned and lost in thought when the voice of the bar owner boomed, "You don't have a chance with her, Anand! You're not as pretty as me!" The bar owner slapped Anand on the back and burst into a huge laugh as Anand continued to stare at the transfer amount on his HUD display.

Chapter Twenty-Three – Eli

There was a brief training and orientation simulation on the heavy-mech battle suits they would be operating in *Last Contact*. Tessa and Eli both caught on quickly. Their HUDs gave them easy access to a wide array of weapons. Despite the size of the suits, all the weapons, and the heavy armor, they still felt perfectly agile, like they could do anything they might in their own skin. They would be faster and stronger, and they were excited that it enabled short term flight.

After the orientation completed, they received deployment orders to one of the periphery outposts to monitor for advancing forces. They found themselves materializing on an orange colored planet. The surface was covered in rock. Highly curved formations swept high in all directions. Gusts of wind blew orange dust into the air like miniature, short-lived surface clouds. In the sky burned a small sun in the distance while a massive moon floated nearby. They were standing on the edge of a tall, thick, armored wall that appeared to protect a small installation built into a recess in the cliffs. Among the few, small, pop-up buildings in the base walked several other mech suits just like theirs. A couple more were standing on the wall with them, both holding massive energy rifles in their hands.

"Sir?" came a voice over the HUD.

Eli waited to hear the response.

"Sir?"

Eli "felt" his arm being touched and looked over to see one of the soldiers tapping him.

"Sir?"

"Oh," responded Eli. "Umm, yes? What is it?"

"I'm sure you're seeing it on your HUD, but we just detected a small alien craft dropping out of FTL above the planet. It looks like they've dropped a couple of hunter-class drones. They know we are here. Should we take up standard positions and authorize automated base defenses, sir?"

Eli thought about it for a moment. He looked at Tessa. She smiled back at him.

"Sir?"

"What's your name, soldier?" asked Eli.

"Lieutenant Marks, Sir."

"OK, Lieutenant Marks," said Eli, "yes, authorize the automated defenses, but do not assume standard positions, whatever the hell those might be. I have a different idea."

"Yes, Sir," responded Marks. "How do you want to deploy?"

"I don't know how much they know about humans yet, but I assume they've analyzed probabilities and expect us to zag," said Eli.

"Zag? Sir?"

"Yup, zag. So instead, we're going to zig. When they expect you to zag, you need to zig. When they think you'll zig, you need to zag."

"I don't understand, sir."

"That's OK," said Eli. "You don't have to right now. There's just two of them. They'll be headed straight for us. I'm going to stay here with you and the automated defenses. Tess, you take the others. Split them into two teams that act like they are abandoning ship. You know what to do from there."

Tessa saluted in a mock manner but laughed and said, "You got it, cap." She began barking orders at the soldiers down in the base.

Lieutenant Marks stared at Eli, unsure of what to do. "Sir, what exactly is the plan for us to defend the base on our own with everyone else fleeing?"

"We're going to get jiggy with it, Lieutenant. Just trust me. This will be fun."

Ryland stood next to Kira in the control room observing it all as he burst out laughing, "Oh my god I love this kid! We totally need to use some of his lines in non-player characters."

Kira nodded in agreement. "They are something else, and a lot of fun to watch. It's exactly what we were hoping to see from them, though we have to be careful not to over-assume the ability of others to play at their level."

"You couldn't be more right," Ryland responded. "But for now, I'd just like to enjoy it."

"By the way," noted Kira, "we're also running the tests on long distance latency from their VIHM suits to a test receiver at a base on Mars. No actual drones are involved. It's telemetry-only. So far, the results are very near real-time: sub-second."

"Excellent," replied Ryland.

They watched intently as Tessa and Eli began moving their teams into position.

On Ryland's HUD he suddenly received a request for immediate communication marked urgent from an unnamed source, and it was on a secured and encrypted channel. It wasn't easy to get one of those. Whoever this was coming from had serious pull. Secure anonymous channels meant it couldn't be monitored by AIs. Dammit! He wanted to see what happened in the game. The notification request repeated itself.

"Kira, I have an urgent communication I need to take. I know you have this under control." She stared at him with wide eyes. He knew she was shocked he would miss this.

"OK, I'll give you the full re-cap and we can watch the replay together," said Kira.

"Thanks," he said and then made his way out of the observation room and into his private office.

This had better be important. If it wasn't Nicodemus himself, or the world wasn't on fire he was going to lose it on whoever was trying to contact him.

He answered the comm. It was his older brother, Logan.

"Ryles! We need to talk." said Logan.

"Hey, Logan," said Ryland with a bit of grimace at the nickname and infuriated at missing the sim. "Is this something serious? Like a real emergency? Because if it's not I'm kind of in the middle of something incredibly important for work right now." He loved his brother but hated the interruption. But why would Logan be using such a secure channel? His high-up position in AI development gave him the authority to authorize one, but why? That was the only thing that kept him from terminating the comm immediately.

"Look, Ryles... I don't, or rather *you* don't, have time for us to debate this. You need to listen. You know about the work I do. I can't explain it all right now, but let's just say that while almost all AI in the Corp are interconnected, that doesn't mean they all necessarily follow a singular directive or can't act outside of each other. It's hard to explain. What I can tell you is the ones I'm working with, well… we've developed a very close working relationship bordering on friendship, or at least as best AIs are capable of that concept so far. They just gave me a heads up that you are moments away from being reported as a corporate dissident by the AIs that monitor patterns for dangerous activity against shareholder interests."

"What?! Are you fucking kidding me?" Ryland was aghast.

"Seriously, I'm not kidding," said Logan. "You know what this means. Once the algorithms identify you as a dissident, you're screwed. They'll be coming for you. There's not much we can do about that, but I thought I could at least give you enough time to call your wife and let some people at work know. Don't worry about attorneys. Mayson and I will take care of that. Between your own shares and those of our family we can get you the best."

"I don't have a prayer if the algorithms have declared me a traitor. It can't be successfully defended against," said Ryland as he shook his head.

"Nonsense! You're only saying that because no one ever has! Look, I think that at least we can get you restricted-access living in one of our family homes given the returns you've generated for shareholders for decades. It's better than a lot of the alternatives. Ryland, don't do anything stupid. Contact your wife, set a few matters at work in order. You know it won't be more than an hour or so, maybe less until they are there to take you into custody. They won't be in a rush since they assume you don't know, but you can't run. They'll find you."

Ryland stared silently, thinking, trying to make sense of it all. This couldn't be true. He was not a dissident. He had done nothing his entire career but make massive amounts of money for shareholders. His removal would hurt shareholder interests more than anything. What the hell?! This didn't make any sense. He wasn't even politically active. He had views, of course, but he wasn't an activist or even particularly vocal about anything. He had always buried himself in his games. But he also knew what being declared a dissident meant. It was not a game, and in the view of the corp the AIs were never wrong in their prediction of treason when it came to shareholder impact.

"Ryland? Are you listening to me?" asked Logan. "Look, I have to go. We don't have this channel much longer, and we *never* had this conversation."

"Thanks, Logan." He looked in his brother's eyes. "Seriously, I really appreciate you letting me know, and taking the risk to do so. That's what family does, right? That's what mom and dad taught us: never leave family behind and always look out for each other. You're a good brother. I've always looked up to you. Always. Since we were kids. Thank you. I got this from here."

"Ryles! Seriously! Do not do..." Ryland abruptly ended the comm.

He stared blankly around his office. He had to think. What was his next move?

Chapter Twenty-Four - Chloe

Chloe ran for nearly ten minutes before slowing to a jog. She jogged for another twenty minutes before softening her pace and slowing to a walk as she started to calm her breathing. Putting her hands over her head she clasped her fingers as she walked. She breathed in. She breathed out. She was still trying to absorb what she had just run from. It was horrifying. Even her own actions in the wake of it were a bit abhorrent to her. She had gone in for food amidst a massacre. She had not knelt and cried for the children. She grabbed food and ran. She was little better than a carrion creature. Almost every part of her wanted to break down and cry for all the lives that were just ended, but she was still forcing her survival instincts to remain in control.

Hoping she was at least far enough from the ravaged camp to allow her some rest, she finally sat down on some pine straw under a few large trees and let her pack slide off her shoulders. It felt so good to take the pack off after that run. Grabbing one of her water bottles she took a long drink. She almost gagged and coughed but resisted. For a moment she almost blacked out, but she pulled herself back together. She could hear her heart beat loudly. Staring blankly out at the trees and heard her stomach grumbling.

She could not wait any longer. She opened the bag with the chickens. It was a disgusting sight. It was full of three dead, burned, whole chickens, not cleaned in any way. They were bloody with half-burned feathers that were curled and blackened. The bag was now soaked dark red. She didn't care. She pulled one of the chickens out. It took her about twenty minutes to clean out all of the guts and clear all the extraneous parts before she got to the treasure she was seeking. There were handfuls of cooked meat. She stuffed her face, pulling meat from the bone then ripping the bones from the carcass and devouring every strand of it. It was amazing. How did this taste so much better than the exquisitely cooked chicken she had enjoyed in high-end restaurants for all those years?

In about ten more minutes she had cleared every piece of edible food from the carcass and sat back. That was too good. Wow, how far had she come from her former life? After a few minutes of reflection, she concluded that she should probably clean the meat from the other carcasses now instead of continuing to carry the other two full birds. The sun was beginning to drop, and she figured it was a good idea to make camp anyway. After rinsing her hands off and washing her face she opened her pack and set out her sleeping bag. There was no need for a fire tonight, she could be warm enough without one and she didn't want the smoke from a fire to attract attention.

She found a nearby water source: a small tributary to the larger river over by the camp. After refilling her water bottles, she returned to her campsite and started cleaning the two remaining chickens. Her hands were disgusting, but it was so worth it. She would eat like a driver queen for the next few days.

"Don't move," was all she heard before the click of a ballistic weapon being cocked.

Chole froze. It was a man's voice.

"I'm not interested in hurting you. I come in peace," said the voice. "I'm going to lower my rifle and we can talk as long as you tell me that you're not going to do anything stupid."

"I'm not going to do anything stupid," said Chloe. What choice did she have? He could have easily killed her while she was cleaning the chickens, and he didn't have to lower his rifle if his intentions were for the worse. At least twice on her journey so far, she had to slip past bands of marauders- the gangs that roamed the wastelands between the major cities pillaging whatever they could. She prayed this wasn't someone from one of those kinds of groups.

Stepping into the clearing with his rifle raised above his head, she saw he was approximately in his mid-forties or maybe even early fifties. He was athletic with well-toned but thin arms, short dark hair and a scruff of a beard. His clothes were horribly dirty and blackened; they looked like they were stained with dried blood. He had a sharp, but almost trustworthy face, with wide, bright eyes.

The man held out his rifle, and then slowly bent to the ground and set it down before standing up with his hands in the air. "My name is Kelly. I'm not looking to hurt you. The camp you just came from… Where I'm guessing you got those chickens? Those were my people. What's your name?"

"Chloe," she said without thinking.

"Look, Chloe, I'm going to level with you. I was out on a scouting mission a couple dozen klicks away when I saw the drone transports above my camps, then all I saw was the smoke in the sky. I'm headed back now to see it for myself, but I think I already know what I'm going to find. I don't care about whatever food or supplies you took. I have little doubt there's no one there left alive that can use them. What I want to know is what you saw. Did you see how it went down? What am I walking into other than dead bodies? All I'm asking for is information and then I'll leave you alone."

He seemed genuine. She felt horrible, sitting there with her hands covered in chicken knowing it was from this guy's camp where his friends and possibly family were now all dead.

"I can tell you what I saw," said Chole.

She grabbed a water bottle and rinsed her hands off, drying them on her clothing. She recounted the whole thing to him, from the moments before the drones arrived (though she left out the part about seeing the weapons) to what she saw as she walked through the camp. Part of the way through telling him the story she began crying. Just talking about it was hard, and she didn't even know these people. She described the slaughter she had found. Everyone was dead. Throughout her whole story Kelly listened intently with the expression of a rock, never interrupting her once. Even when she started sobbing a bit, he waited patiently for her to recover and begin talking again. Finally, she got to the part where she grabbed the chickens and began running through the jungle. She fell silent. It seemed like minutes went by as she sat there waiting for him to respond.

"Thank you," said Kelly solemnly. He paused for a long moment. "You haven't been out here long, have you?"

"Just a few months," she said. Was she that obvious?

"You're doing pretty well, considering. Alone, but keeping fed and in pretty good shape. You need to be careful. It's not safe out here. You need to find friends. Where are you going?"

"I'm headed north," said Chloe. She really felt like she could trust him. "I've heard there are communities further north where I could possibly find a home, and maybe put my skills to use for food?" she said. "Believe it or not, I'm actually a structural engineer." She laughed as she said it, not knowing why and feeling awkward as she did it.

"I believe you," said Kelly. "Look, there are communities further north. Some of them good, but there are also a lot of rumors out here. I do know it's not safe to be alone. We had a large community in these parts, and I'm pretty sure most of them just got murdered, but that's not all of us. There are many others. We could use a structural engineer. Anyone who can survive for months out here on their own that is interested in helping others is always welcome. You could come with me."

The idea of going back into the camp that was now a mass grave didn't sound appealing to her. She had set her head so deep into the idea of heading north that it was almost absurd at this point for her to consider changing course. The journey north had almost become a coping mechanism for the loss of her previous life. It had become her new job.

Chloe looked at him. His bluntly cutoff sleeves revealed a faded tattoo on his shoulder of a skull with a beret biting a wicked looking hunting knife. Beneath it, in an ornamental font, were the words *De Oppresso Liber*. She had no clue what it meant and almost found it a bit frightening in her current situation.

"Did you have a job?" she asked. It was all she could think of to say.

"I did," he replied, "but that was over twenty-two years ago. I was a soldier. U.S. Army, until the AIs and drones replaced us too."

Chloe had never met a soldier before. By the time she was a teenager all military except high command had been replaced by drones and AI. Something about Kelly made her feel safe for the first time since she had been out on her own. She couldn't explain it. It wasn't just that she now knew he was a soldier and trained in how to survive and fight. It was something more about him and how he talked, how he acted, how he held himself. He felt like someone you could believe in. Part of her wanted to cry again as she wrestled with it. What she had accomplished in the past couple of months, she was proud of, but she knew it was a matter of luck and time. Something was bound to go wrong. She needed friends.

"I'll go with you," she said softly. "I wasn't really looking forward to long winters anyway."

Chapter Twenty-Five - Sheridan

"Sir, we have positive identification of treason against the interests of the shareholders on an executive in the Entertainment Division. The name is Ryland Grey. His file should be on your HUD now, Commander."

Commander William Sheridan was head of Internal Affairs for Americorp Homeland Security. Generally, handling of dissidents did not require his involvement, but it did if it was a high-ranking shareholder. Even for low-ranking shareholders the law still required human authorization for acquisition and processing. It was one of the few things humans weren't ready to trust entirely to the AIs.

Sheridan looked at the record. "Wow," he said out loud. He had seen a lot of flagged dissident profiles. This did not seem like the others. The subject was a high-up exec in game design. Sheridan had never been much of a gamer. This guy didn't seem like a political activist or any kind of terrorist, but the probability analysis for shareholder harm from the AIs was indisputable and this guy was not even on the bubble according to the scoring.

He flipped through the file: San Francisco area, wife, two daughters. This Ryland guy even had some commendations for contributions to military and defense technology. In general, the guy looked like a model shareholder. But the algorithms were never wrong. If for some reason they were, for the first time ever, this guy would still have his day in court.

"Acquisition is authorized, Lieutenant," he said. "Where is the target now?"

"He's in a small, personal craft on a northeast heading over South Dakota. Intercept drones are now dispatched and on an intercept course."

"Please inform me when the target is acquired, Lieutenant," said Sheridan. "And make sure we observe all appropriate protocol for someone of his position."

"Yes, sir."

Sheridan sat back for a moment and took a deeper look at the subject's profile. There wasn't any of the normal evidence of treason. Any notes regarding driver sympathy were minimal and the scores for that as factor in the analysis were well lower than he normally saw in these cases. There wasn't any record of activism. The one thing that stood out was a high probability score for dissidence proclivity based on the subject's professional work, but the details were marked classified. This was over his pay grade. It would have to come out in court.

"Sir," he heard the Lieutenant's voice on his HUD, "drones have intercepted the craft, but they aren't detecting any significant bio-signatures aboard. The craft is not responding to communication hails, and the overrides appear to have been disabled. Orders?"

Shit. This just got more complicated than it should be.

"Have our forces attempt to board," ordered Sheridan. "If they can't for any reason, bring the craft down but try to do so without injuring anyone. We want the subject alive."

He pulled up the real-time situation views on his HUD, so he could watch it himself. One of the three intercept vessels pulled up above the subject's craft, matching course and speed. A drone dropped directly onto the craft and began rotating an energy beam to slice open a hole in the top before it dropped inside. The view switched to what the drone was seeing. The small vessel was empty. There really wasn't anywhere the subject could be hiding; it was too small of a craft. The drone ran bio-scans to be sure the subject wasn't hiding, but the results were negative. It went over to the main interface console and began reading the flight data directly.

"Where the hell is our subject, Lieutenant?" asked Sheridan.

"I don't know, sir. Working on that now."

"In addition to the flight data," barked Sheridan, "I want an immediate reverse trace on this guy and I want it sixty seconds ago."

"Yes, sir!" responded the Lieutenant.

Flight data started to come through. Apparently, this Ryland Grey had dropped his HUD in the craft so that it would still be tracked there, but flight records showed that somewhere over the Rocky Mountains the external door had been opened. The guy must have jumped. Grav suit? Descent pack? Or maybe even a plain old parachute? They could check satellite data, but it was unlikely they would catch it. Most likely this guy was on the run in the Rockies. It was just stupid. Why would he run? According to his profile this guy seemed smart enough to know that running wouldn't work. How did he even know they were coming for him? That was an even better question which he would need to follow up on.

"Give me the tracking data leading up to him getting on the craft," ordered Sheridan.

"Coming through now, sir. The subject went into his office building in the morning. The next records are from just a few hours later."

Sheridan saw the details play on his HUD. The communication records for the past few hours contained just one from the subject: a discussion between him and one of his daughters early that morning. It was mundane: a lot of "Good morning... how are you... hope you have great day..." Nothing noteworthy. That was it. The tracking and security video showed that just a couple of hours ago the subject left the building where he worked. He walked across the campus to get into a vehicle which drove him to the campus landing pads for flight craft. He boarded a personal craft. Records show that he set the flight course and received approval. It took off, and that was it. Somebody had to have tipped him off, but there wasn't any obvious digital trail. It had to have been in-person. But how?

"Lieutenant, I want a full scan and retrieval division sweeping the Rockies starting at the point we think he jumped. I want this guy found, and I want him alive. Get me profiles on his family and his closest co-workers and friends. I also want a full analysis of the prior 48 hours of his communication history. Get me in contact with the Managing Director of that district. We need to understand why the main information on his treason profile is classified."

Today was going to be a long day.

Chapter Twenty-Six - Ryland

After he terminated the comm with his brother, Ryland knew that he had to act quickly. He would be tracked and hunted in no time. There had to be some mistake. He wasn't a dissident, but he knew the legal odds of fighting the charges were practically non-existent. Something wasn't right. Was this a set-up? Maybe. But who had the power to do this and what was their motive? Why him? Who had he pissed off?

He could do exactly what his brother recommended. He could sit and wait. It was the safe thing to do. Everything would play out in court for months and he probably could end up with restricted access in his own home, but he could also receive a much worse fate depending on what the analysis said about him. Execution wasn't out of the realm of options when it came to treason rulings. There were too many unknowns. But running? It was practically impossible. Within moments they would be tracking him. His HUD, powered on and connected to him, would lead them straight to his location. Even if he ditched the HUD, he would be picked up by all the video surveillance, facial recognition, and security check-points before he could get very far. Very soon they would begin to cut off access to his currency, security authorizations, and even his communications and net access.

It was possible that he could hide in the game arena and the control center beneath it. Those locations were legally shielded from scans for the purposes of protecting the intellectual property they were working on, but that wouldn't stop security drones from breaking down doors to scour the entire studio and the arena since this was his last known location. They would find him, unless they thought he was somewhere else.

What he needed was to buy some time. He had an idea. A couple of years ago he and Immersive Magic had launched a title called *Colony*. It wasn't the normal action-oriented genre game he produced. Instead it was a multi-player strategy game to build empires in space. It was a huge success and still one of the more heavily played games of its kind. Part of the premise of the game was that humans and their AIs had finally found a way to overcome the problems with FTL travel which killed any organic matter, so that it was possible for humans to travel great distances in space. While totally not true in reality, it was a premise needed for the game story to make sense.

As part of a publicity stunt for the launch of the game, Ryland worked out a deal with one of the belt mining corporations to get him transport on an upcoming FTL mission to Saturn. Right before launch, he went live video over all the social nets. "Hey world, my name is Ryland. I think the AIs have been lying to us. I think organic matter can travel FTL with the right equipment. We've been researching this for years at Immersive Magic. It's too late to stop this launch, so I guess we'll all find out together!"

Ryland gave a big thumbs-up right before donning his helmet and buckling himself into what resembled a highly complex version of a Faraday cage on the mining transport. The FTL drive was engaged. The ship disappeared from sight and contact until it would complete its journey a couple of weeks later. The world waited.

Gaming fans lost their minds over the news and the nets were ablaze with comments, pundits, trolls, and haters. The media covered it constantly. Many insisted it was hoax, but on Earth Ryland was nowhere to be found and Immersive Magic refused comment. Ryland's family even moved to a retreat owned by the company in Tahoe where they were guarded and kept away from the media except for a statement from his wife that all she wanted was for her husband to be back with them.

Much of the world watched to see the first communication that was received from that ship once it had reached Saturn. Media drones surrounded the arrival location. There was Ryland, in his helmeted suit giving another thumbs-up. His face was still shielded, but he got up and made his way to an airlock. Everyone watched as the astronaut Ryland propelled to an asteroid, assisted by a mining drone. He planted a flag with his name on it and the Immersive Magic logo into the rock. Then he removed his helmet, but the face was gone. The face, and all the skin, had been tissue replicated from his own DNA and placed over a replicant drone to look exactly like Ryland. The drone "smiled" and told the world, "OK, you got me, it was all bullshit. Humans still can't travel the stars via FTL. But when we launch our newest game *Colony* next month, you'll believe that you can."

When the drone returned to Earth, Ryland had the skin replaced, even if it was ridiculously expensive, as a memento. Immersive Magic used the drone a few more times in some planet-side promotional events for the game. Ryland also used it occasionally just to mess with his staff. He was able to operate it manually using his HUD or pre-program it. Just for fun, sometimes he operated it remotely when he was traveling to join meetings "in-person" back at the studio. His staff did not find it nearly as amusing as he did.

Ryland removed his HUD device and walked over to the replicant Ryland drone. Attaching it to the drone, he programmed it in a matter of minutes. The HUD device would at least recognize his DNA in the skin replication such that it would give a positive signature to any security checkpoints. They would think it was him. He activated the drone and traded clothes with it.

Grabbing a hacked, back-up HUD (a gift from Theo), he took control of the drone and had it leave his office from the stairs that led up to the arena viewing room that Kira was still standing in.

"Boss, welcome back. You gotta come see this. You're going to love it," said Kira.

"I have to go, Kira," said Ryland's voice through the drone as it walked straight past her toward the door. "Something really important has come up that I have to take care of."

"More important than *this*?" Kira asked skeptically, but Ryland was already about to exit the door.

"There's a tortoise in the desert that needs my help!" and he walked out.

He knew she would catch the *Blade Runner* reference and realize it was the replicant drone. It would take a lot longer before any analysis by the AIs of their conversation led them to the same conclusion.

Navigating the replicant drone down the hall and through the studio, Ryland guided it outside. By now it had already been picked up by a handful of security cameras, but no doors were refusing to open, so the treason identification must not be fully authorized yet. The drone Ryland got into an autonomous vehicle and set the destination for the campus flight landing and take-off zone which was less than a mile away. Once there, the drone boarded his personal craft and set course. He was careful to set it to go slow enough while still in the city to avoid attracting attention but as fast as possible once it was beyond city limits.

While the craft rose up into the air and began gliding eastward, Ryland programmed the drone to evacuate in a remote area over the Rockies and went about disabling as many of the craft overrides as he could think of. There was a descent pack the drone could use so that it was not destroyed by the fall. Then it could hopefully keep the hunt going. He programmed the drone with instructions for going on auto-pilot in the wilderness with a goal of evading any contact with humans, robots, or drones.

There was a good chance this wouldn't work at all, but it could at least buy him some time. It also made him look guilty, but he decided to ignore that for now. He needed to deal with one problem at a time. He went to the back of his office where he had a private door and staircase leading down into the arena's technical control center. Here he would be shielded from detection. On the bright side, he had always insisted that his office and the control centers were amply stocked with his favorite snacks and beverages. So, he had that going for him…. which was nice. Before heading down the staircase he also grabbed a bottle of bourbon from his shelves. Now was not the time to get drunk, but he was going to need at least one stiff drink or he might lose his mind.

Chapter Twenty-Seven - Anand

Belarussian software code was something for which Anand had really developed an appreciation. It tended to be tremendously clean and well structured. It was succinct. There was nothing superfluous. The commenting in the code was rather sparse, but that was fine when the code was well designed. Anand was in the middle of trying to help alter code on some older-model farming and agricultural robots originally built in Belarus. This particular model was a real workhorse in its day, but they had become obsolete well over twenty years ago. That hadn't stopped some South American group from purchasing them. But when the buyers tried to modify the drones to harvest tree-based crops with alternate peripherals they had managed to screw them up badly. Some of the hacks were admittedly creative, but they were also just downright ugly.

Anand guessed that whoever had messed with the original code had never been a professional software engineer. For the past couple of weeks, he had been unwinding their mistakes and modifying the software drivers to work with the new harvesting attachments the owners were adapting to fit the units. Another day or so and he would be done. It might even be possible to finish this by tonight. He had no idea who the actual client was; it didn't really matter. As soon as he was done, he would get a small bonus, and he was well ahead of schedule.

Reaching out for his small, polymer cup of espresso he realized it was empty. If he was going to try and power through this code to finish tonight, he would need more caffeine; and he could use a smoke break anyways. Standing up from the small work area that was his, amongst the rows and rows of his co-workers, he pocketed his pack of cigarettes from the desk and was about to head to the roof-top balcony when he received an incoming comm notification on his HUD.

It was from Idha, the woman he had met barely a week ago in Bombay No. 5.

That bizarre encounter had occupied a lot of his thoughts for the past week. If it hadn't been for the very real money in his account, he would have already assumed he had imagined the entire thing or maybe just have been drunk. But the money was real. He even used some of it to buy himself a much needed, upgraded HUD device. He also treated himself to a nice bottle of scotch, a new pair of jeans, and a nice pillow for his bed. He held off on spending more since he was still a bit worried that he might have to give it back for some reason.

What burned in his brain the past week was trying to figure out who she was, who her employers might be, and what they might want from him? Software engineers were easy to find. More talented ones than he still worked in the walled cities. There were plenty amongst the drivers that would work for far less, and that would be willing to risk much more.

Maybe they were trying to gain an inside source at his company to try and trace down some of their less savory or even more dangerous clientele? That didn't make sense. He had no access to that kind of information. Maybe it was someone looking for agents inside his company to infect operations from within using network viruses to force a shutdown? But why? It could be one of the major foreign corps. Perhaps they were trying to cut off the supply of services to those they considered rogue or terrorist groups?

There wasn't much special about him, so what was it? He had racked his brain trying to think of the people he had known well or been close to throughout his life, trying to figure out if any of them were important enough that he might somehow play a role in something involving them. There were simply too many variations and possibilities down that path to come to any conclusions, and he'd lost touch with most of his family over the past few years.

He could just ignore the comm from Idha. He could walk away. They couldn't take the money back, or at least he didn't think they could. All he had to do was not answer, go have a smoke on the roof, grab a cup of coffee, and go back to work like he'd never heard of her. Dammit... he wasn't that smart. Or maybe he was just too curious? He answered the comm. There she was.

"Hello, Anand," said Idha very directly. "Please meet me immediately. I am in a black multi-person craft parked in the street directly across from your office building. It should be obvious which one. The door will open when I see you." She terminated the comm.

So, this was it. Should he take a trip down the rabbit hole? Why the hell not? It wasn't like he was living the dream, and the money these people were offering was real and big. He logged out, grabbed his backpack, and headed for the elevators. Once he got to the ground floor, he made his way steadily down the hall and past the lobby. For some reason the sound of his boots on the hard, polished stone floors seemed louder than normal. He felt like he was attracting attention, so he tried to act more casual. Passing through security he knew he was being scanned, but there was nothing for them to find. He had very little and wasn't trying to smuggle out any company equipment. He knew the security system would log his departure.

Walking out the glass doors he could already see the craft. It was about sixty or seventy meters in front of him, just past the small courtyard of the building and the security gates. It was an impressive looking craft. It was one of the newer and more expensive models. It was nicer than anything he had ever been in, and it definitely stood out on a street in this neighborhood.

He paused to light a cigarette as the heat of the outside started to wash over him in contrast to the air-conditioned office he had just left. He inhaled deeply, then exhaled, watching the smoke curl slowly and densely in the hot air with no sign of a breeze. A few others exited the building and walked past him. He turned back towards the street and walked a bit slowly across the courtyard, taking deep drags of his cigarette to be sure he had mostly finished it by the time he got there. As he approached, one of the doors opened upwards to reveal the interior. With one last drag, he exhaled and tossed the butt to the street where he crushed it out with his boot. He unshouldered his backpack and headed into the open door. The interior was immediately cooler than the outside. It was dark with tinted windows and black leather-like finish. He should at least have some fun with this, right? Just in case this turned out bad?

"I've given this a lot of thought, Idha," said Anand as he slid into the vehicle and saw her across from him. "If you're just looking to use me to make an ex-boyfriend jealous, well… I'm in. It's a bit below my normal going rate for that sort of thing, but there's something I like about you and I love your style."

"You are very funny, Mr. Shah." Something about her tone told him that she didn't think he was very funny. "I have an offer to make you. This is a one-time offer; it will not be made again. If you decline it, you may go back to your job and we will leave you be."

He was listening.

"If you accept, you will leave here with me immediately. We will take you to a larger, passenger craft where we've booked travel for you to California. Everything is in order. All security authorizations have been made. You will travel without any issues or problems. Your return trip has also been fully authorized and paid for, or you may request to be returned to whatever other destination you wish. You'll be given further instructions along the way and after you land. We will immediately transfer to your account five times the number of shares we provided you previously. They are yours to keep no matter what else happens. If you arrive and are asked to do nothing for thirty days, you will receive double that amount and can go home. If you are given a task and succeed, you will receive ten times that amount."

Anand was speechless for a moment. It was an amount of money he couldn't even dream about. He would never have to work again, and he could live like a king.

"What's the task?"

"I do not know," replied Idha.

"How long will it take?" he asked.

"I do not know how long it will take to do something for which I am not aware of the details."

That was fair, thought Anand.

"Will you come with me?" he asked. "You seem like you'd be a real blast on a road trip adventure."

"I will accompany you only to the passenger transport at the outskirts of the city," she replied curtly. "Do you accept the offer, Mr. Shah?"

That was more money than he could ever even imagine he might see, even when he was fully employed in the walled city. He didn't really have much to lose. "OK," he said, "I'll do it, but only because you asked so nicely, and it is just slightly better than the other multi-million share offers I received today." He felt the craft lift into the air. "Hey, does this thing have a bar?"

Chapter Twenty-Eight - Ryland

Ryland was swishing around the ice cubes at the bottom of the now empty drink he had poured himself, when he heard footsteps coming down the stairs. There was no reason to worry. It was likely too soon to be homeland security, and even if it were, there was nowhere to run so he might as well stay seated. He didn't even look up. He just waited.

"How'd things go with the tortoise?" asked Kira.

"Better than I'd hoped, as far as I can tell," replied Ryland.

"What's going on, boss?" asked Theo. "We can help."

Finally looking up from his glass, Ryland saw that it was just the two of them. They had all worked together for well over a decade at this point. He trusted them completely. They looked genuinely nervous and scared. That was probably appropriate. Maybe he should be even more scared than he was?

"The almighty machines, in their infinite wisdom and ever-increasing perfection, have decided that I, Ryland Grey, am a dissident that is working against shareholder interests. You'll have to take me in now or risk treason charges yourself." He held out his hands together as if for restraints. "But please bring the bottle of bourbon with us, and let my wife and daughters know that I love them very much."

"What?! A dissident?!" asked Kira, "Are you kidding me? That's insane. There must be some mistake. You're doing important work for our military and defense!" She put the pieces together even faster than Ryland had. "Someone is setting you up. Someone powerful. Someone *really* powerful. And they want you off the gameboard for some reason. But who?"

"That's what I've been trying to figure out in the past five minutes since you last saw 'me'," he made the air quotes symbols, "exiting the viewing room. Well, that and trying to come up with a way to avoid being captured and potentially executed. It's been kind of a packed five minutes. Oh, and I had a drink. Would either of you care for one?"

"So that's why you sent your annoying doppelganger drone out the door?" said Kira. "Distraction. You're leading them away. Where is it going?"

Ryland told them both exactly what he had done with the drone. They listened intently until he finished.

"Fucking brilliant," declared Theo.

"Thank you, Theo," smiled Ryland. "I am rather proud of it, even if it won't likely fool them too much longer. Now my challenge is what to do next if I don't feel like sitting here, pouring myself a second glass, and simply waiting for the corporate drones and security to descend upon me like ants at a picnic. They'll eventually put the pieces together and figure out that I never left the building. If I do feel like leaving, the slightly tricky part is figuring out how to do so undetected, and then, where do I go from there?"

Right then, his hacked HUD notified him that his younger brother, Mayson, had just posted to Ryland's personal public message board. The message contained no text, just a 3D vid of characters from the earliest of video games: a rather angry and wicked looking Pac-Man laughed and then devoured a cowering Space Invader in a single gulp. That was it. End of message. Seriously? He didn't have time for this. He and Mayson hadn't talked in a few months, though not because they didn't get along. They were both just enormously busy.

Normally he would take a few moments to engage his brother in what was an on-going debate between them over which early video games were the most influential and ground-breaking. In this particular debate of theirs, Ryland had argued for years that *Space Invaders* was more influential and important than *Pac-Man*. It had come out two years earlier and set ablaze a popularization of video games among the core demographic. Most importantly, *Space Invaders* was a fight. It was the kind of game Ryland loved. Mayson always argued that *Pac-Man*'s mainstream and cross-gender popularity did more to bring video games to a broader audience, not despite its cuteness, but because of it. Ryland had always regarded *Pac-Man* as a bit of a popular "sell-out." Most of all he hated that the majority of the game was predicated on running away, Still, he couldn't deny its success. At the end of the day it was just a fun topic to discuss and debate more than one that had an answer.

The last time they had this argument was about a year ago. Mayson and his wife had invited Ryland and his family to a remote, off-the-grid estate they were buying. Mayson and his wife were wonderful people. They were also doomsday-preppers, always being sure they had a plan for different crazy contingencies. They had found an amazing, highly remote place for sale in the mountains of the Eldorado forest. It was difficult to get to, and not near anything. Solar power supplied enough energy for basic needs, and running water was limited to a very simple system connected to the river and powered by solar cells. You split your own wood for the fire. The cabin was rustic at best. Still, they'd had a great time for a couple of nights, really getting back to basics. His paranoid brother was even talking about putting up distortion fields and obfuscation devices to block the place from the net entirely.

Ryland smacked his forehead with the base of his hand as he figured out the message.

"OK," he said, "I just figured out where I need to go. Don't ask. It's better that you don't know. That still leaves me needing to figure a way out of here."

"You already left once, and by now your access will probably be locked down. You can't walk out of here," said Theo. "Given the capabilities of the arena, it's not impossible that we might be able to hide you in there, even under a heavy search. I might be able to program a way for it to keep you covered by continuously moving you under its morphing surface without anyone knowing."

"I love the thinking, Theo, and I had a similar idea to that myself," said Ryland. "But I need to get out of here and start figuring out who is trying to bring me down and why."

"That's not going to be easy," said Kira. "We humans have designed our own cage. We can't move freely without notice. But you know what can move freely as long as they have a valid transponder code with authorized access?"

"Bots and drones," said Ryland, realizing where she was going.

"So, can we disguise you as a drone sufficiently to get you out of here? Give you the right transponder codes to get through security?" asked Kira.

"We don't have to," said Ryland. "I have an idea. Or rather, you had the idea. I'm just iterating on it. We ship things using transport drones all the time, right? We pack up materials in specialized crates. They get loaded into a transport drone which navigates its way to the destination using an advanced series of logistics to navigate the network of vessels constantly flowing over the planet. Don't we ship things occasionally to the company retreat in Tahoe?"

"Ummm, sure," said Kira.

"Things like specialized equipment we'll be playing with, materials, and even some good wine and food?"

"Yes, we do." acknowledged Kira again. She caught on as did Theo.

Ryland continued, "Our company is licensed to ship materials shielded for IP protection purposes. I wrap myself in shielded material. We throw in a few bottles of wine, and I stuff myself into a small shipping container. Theo, can you hack a drone and the manifest while we load it up?"

Theo thought for a moment and said yes. "It won't be comfortable, boss. It's going to be rough and tight, though the journey to Tahoe shouldn't take long."

"I can live with that, and if it gets rough, I'll have wine, right?"

"What are you going to do once you get there?" asked Kira.

"I have an idea, but let's just say I won't be staying there long," said Ryland.

Theo motioned at the control interfaces and spoke a few commands. Several large displays showed about fifteen different views of the incredible, Immersive Magic company retreat home in Tahoe. It was about as high-end of an eight-bedroom, log-exterior "cabin" and ranch as you could imagine. "I thought you might be interested in knowing where the security cameras are at the retreat. There are also a couple of roving security drones but I'm pretty sure they are both about to be taken down for temporary maintenance and upgrades in the next 24 hours." He smiled.

Ryland studied the camera views and angles carefully for a few moments, "Thank you, Theo. You rock. I also need both of you to keep at it with Eli and Tessa while I'm gone. Kira, you're in charge. Don't let this change a thing. I plan on coming back and making this title with you all. Let's not miss an opportunity to do something cool just because some insane conspiracy is threatening to destroy my entire career, future, and possibly life. Let's keep a positive attitude on this one!" He grinned. That's what they loved about him.

"OK, let's get packing," said Ryland. "We have a delivery to make. Just to say it again, you know you can both get arrested if they ever find out you helped me, right? And found guilty of treason? You know… nothing big… just, ummm... treason. You sure neither of you want a drink before we do this?"

Chapter Twenty-Nine - Kimberly

Managing Director Kimberly Lewandowski had just left a board meeting. They had been reviewing the results of a recently approved private security action against driver-based terrorist groups in the northwest that were receiving arms from foreign corporations. The casualties were high. Families were killed, but the evidence was clear. The alleged foreign weapons were found, and they matched the weapons used in recent attacks against supply lines and key corporate research and production facilities in the area. Americorp's interests had to be preserved.

Still, the report at the board meeting made her sick to her stomach. She closed her eyes for just a moment to be sure she kept her composure. There was a vote coming up in just a couple of hours regarding some key FTL launches, some of the biggest they had ever attempted. She needed to pull herself together and read up on the latest briefings. Using her HUD, she ordered some sushi for a late lunch and made her way from the regional boardroom down the hall to her office on the thirty-sixth floor of the Americorp Tower overlooking the Bay Area.

The tower was truly a stunning structure. Located on what was once called the Presidio, it was constructed of the most advanced nano-infused steel and glass that existed when it had been built just a decade ago. It could survive any earthquake that didn't literally open the earth directly beneath it. From the outside it was a shining black glass and steel spire that shone with rainbow colors as the sun crossed the sky each day.

Once she was in her office she sat down at her desk, slipped her shoes off and sat back in one of the more comfortable chairs. A small service drone brought her a sparkling, passion-fruit water she had ordered while she waited for her lunch. She drained half of it in one gulp and looked out the windows. The city, the whole area, was gorgeous from up here. She looked down at the Golden Gate and saw it alive with people walking amongst the various restaurants, markets, and shops that lined it. Against the green-blue waves and currents the site made her feel better about the world she was trying to protect.

Just then, an urgent comm notice came in. It was from Internal Affairs. She accepted it. In front of her via her HUD was an older man with greying hair in uniform identified as Commander William Sheridan. The subject of the comm was Dissident Identification and Recovery. Dammit. This was the last thing she needed to be dealing with right now. But if they were bugging her about a dissident it had to be something more important than usual.

"I'm quite busy at the moment, but how can I help you, Commander?" she asked.

"Ms. Lewandowski, I apologize for the interruption, but we have a situation. We have a high-ranking executive in your district that has been positively ID'ed as a traitor, and the subject has chosen to run. Details are coming to your HUD now."

Kimberly watched. Ryland Grey?! What? This had to be a joke. He was no corporate traitor. He was one of their greatest assets and key to some of their most ground-breaking research. The detail of what had transpired flowed past her eyes on her HUD.

"Ma'am, we believe that the 'Ryland' we are searching for in the Rockies may be a fake. One of our people pointed out that the subject used a replicant drone in a publicity stunt a couple of years ago, so we aren't discounting the possibility that we are chasing a decoy. We're calling you for two reasons. One is a courtesy to inform you that we are about to send security units into the company he works for, which is in your district. We suspect he is still hiding there. The other reason is that a significant portion of his dissidence profile analysis is marked classified. We were hoping you could shed some light on this to help us in our investigation."

"One moment, Commander," Kimberly paused the comm on her end, and sent an urgent request to several individuals to join. Within a few moments she had the CEO of Immersive Magic, IM's Chief Legal Counsel, and the Chief Legal Counsel of Americorp's western region acknowledged and ready to join. Kimberly un-paused the comm and joined them all in. "Commander, I believe we now have the right people needed to have this conversation. I've forwarded the relevant data to all of them, though they've yet had time to absorb it. I'll re-cap. You're in pursuit of Ryland Grey, identified as a traitor. You believe he may be on the run in the Rocky Mountains, but you also believe that the subject you are chasing may be a decoy, and that the real Ryland could be hiding in the IM studios. You are seeking permission to search the Immersive Magic facility. Additionally, you would like to know why a portion of the subject's record is marked classified. Is that all correct?"

"Yes, ma'am," remarked Sheridan. "Though we are not asking permission to search the studio. Mr. Grey is wanted for corporate treason and resisting arrest. We do not require your authorization or further permission. I'm on my way there now with a full search and scan unit."

"The hell you are" said Keiko, the CEO of Immersive Magic. She didn't look pleased. "Commander, portions of that facility are highly restricted in the corporate interests of protecting intellectual property including military and defense research. Need I remind everyone that Immersive Magic is not only a large supplier to the military, security divisions and subsidiaries, but we are also one of the largest contributors and collaborators when it comes to some of the most profitable intellectual property on the planet. Our security measures at the studio are not just about gaming entertainment profits which is why we've been granted the authorization to shield portions of our studio."

That answered Sheridan's question about why so much of the Grey file was marked classified. It had to be that the analysis from the AIs involved work this guy was doing related to classified technology.

The regional corporate attorney spoke up. "Might I propose a standard closed network search procedure? All units involved will be taken off the main network into an encrypted, localized network. Any and all data will be reviewed locally by the legal team and redacted as needed before wiping data from the units and uploading to the main network. One human, I presume Commander Sheridan, would be an acceptable choice to everyone? He would join the units in the search of any confidential areas. Is this agreeable?"

Keiko looked at her attorney and appeared to have a few muted, off-comm words with him. "That works for us as long as our counsel is part of the review team, and material will be redacted at the request of any single member of the team."

"Agreed," said Kimberly. "I'm also sending requests now that the team be joined by counsel from the military and AI development divisions."

"Fine," said Sheridan. "But please be aware that my team will be arriving in a matter of minutes. I want zero communication to anyone at the studio until after we've arrived and have a chance to secure the perimeter. We will enter the non-classified zones of the campus and begin our search but will wait for counsel to arrive and the localized network to be setup before proceeding further. I expect everyone that you need there to arrive promptly."

"We'll want the local network restrictions verified by one of our on-site engineers," said the IM attorney.

"Agreed," replied the regional attorney.

They all looked toward Kimberly for approval.

"OK," she said. "Make it happen. I want constant updates on the status and to be immediately notified when Ryland is taken into custody. Unless Mr. Grey is placing any shareholder lives in imminent danger, I also expect he will be taken alive and unharmed."

Everyone nodded and dropped off the comm.

Kimberly stared out the window of her office. What the hell was going on here? She knew Ryland. This didn't make any sense. She pulled up the treason analysis. The unclassified portions included clips of several conversations where he had expressed sympathy for drivers or referenced mixed feelings about the current economic-political state, but it was hardly more than you might expect from almost anyone. There was some analysis of his academic background and youth behavior which was cross-referenced against patterns known to have eventually developed into dissident tendencies. Those were low contributing factors to exceeding the thresholds necessary for positive identification, more like supporting evidence than evidence itself. It all came down to whatever was in the classified portion.

Whoever classified this had more authority than her. That made going after the information a tricky and possibly dangerous game for her. If Ryland really was a traitor, there was no harm in inquiring. The worst she could be told is no, that she didn't have the needed clearance. But something about this didn't feel right, and that meant someone may have falsified the analysis. If that was the case, that meant that it had to be someone superior to her since they were the only ones with that kind of authority. It also meant they were able to break the security safeguards around the algorithms and reporting. That was a big deal. In that scenario, digging for the truth could put her in the cross-hairs of something that might bring her down as well. These would have to be some powerful people.

It was perfectly reasonable for her to try and request access since it was a prominent shareholder in her region. She would just need to be very careful about how she asked. Even if she met with a brick wall, how her request was denied might at least give her a clue. She downed the rest of her sparkling water and set the glass on a table.

Sorting through the data from the last couple of hours, she watched the video of Ryland leaving the studio and getting in his personal craft. Then she saw the flight plan traced out until the point it was boarded and she could see the video of the empty interior. She considered Commander Sheridan's theory that this was a decoy and it made her smile. Even if the analysis that Ryland was a dissident turned out to be true, you had to admit that the guy had style.

Chapter Thirty – Mia

For over four hours they bounced around uncomfortably in the truck under gunpoint. A cover had been pulled down over the back of the truck, so they had no idea where they were going. They had lost all orientation on where exactly they were at this point. Some dim, solar powered light cells that occasionally flickered were the only light source they had, and it was barely enough to make out silhouettes or the faces of those seated next to you. It was obvious they weren't on any paved or stone roads.

Mia fought back tears when they had boarded and did her best to calm down the younger children. She tried to reassure them everything was going to be OK, even though she knew that was a lie. Like all of them, she had no idea where they were headed or what awaited them, except that it wasn't going to be good.

She didn't even want to think about what Manny was feeling. He hadn't spoken since they boarded the truck. He just stared blankly at the ceiling or occasionally buried his head in his hands while his little sister lay curled up in his lap. She knew what he was thinking. That she had let them all down. That she had been stupid. That she had failed them. She wanted to believe that wasn't true, that it was the world that had failed them, but she knew the truth. She had made a bad decision. One bad decision was all it took.

Little Jelaena held Mia's hand tightly and pressed up against her arm. The combination of the heat from the jungle and the stuffiness created by the closed truck with over thirty bodies in it was hardly bearable, but she knew she had to stay strong for the others.

Dawn was starting to break outside. Mia could see the first signs of sunlight starting to creep in through the creases in the cover. The vehicle began to slow and came to a stop. She heard voices. Men and women were talking. She couldn't make out what they were saying. There was a deep, electronic buzzing sound for a moment and some creaking sounds. The vehicle started moving again, but only for a few minutes before it once again came to a rest.

Mia didn't want to know what awaited them. The men with rifles that had been watching them got up and began pulling up the tarp at the back.

Early morning sunlight began to pour into the truck. They shielded their eyes as they adjusted. The men hopped out. They dropped their rifles to their sides and motioned for the children to get out.

The children filed out and hopped down, some by themselves, others holding hands, and some of the smallest of them were carried or lifted down by the oldest children. As their eyes adjusted to the rising sunlight they looked around. They were just past some high fences and secured gates. A bit further out there was a large, almost luxurious house surrounded by several smaller buildings. In the distance were rows of small huts along with fields of crops and rows of trees. A small river flowed through the property. Tall fruit and coconut trees were all over the grounds which seemed to stretch for kilometers.

Walking toward them were two well-dressed adults, probably in their fifties. They were wearing light colored clothing. Their clothes were extremely clean and nicer than anything Mia had ever seen. With them were a few other adults dressed in more casual and work-oriented clothing, though equally clean. There were also two girls and a boy that appeared hardly older than Mia and Manny. They were dressed in utility clothes.

The female adult spoke first. "Welcome. Let me apologize for the circumstances under which you were brought here. My name is Carla. This is my husband, Marco." She gestured to the man next to her. "What you need to know is that you are safe. You have nothing to fear. You can stop running and nothing bad is going to happen to you here."

Mia glanced at Manny and saw that he looked stunned, unsure of how to react. Mia looked at Jelaena and gave her a nod that she needed to let go of her hand for a moment. Mia stepped forward. "Why have you brought us here?"

"We've brought you here to give you a chance," replied the woman. She seemed nice, real, genuine. This didn't feel like a game, but there was always a catch.

"What is this place?" asked Mia.

"I understand your confusion and trepidation," responded Carla. "The world is an ugly place right now. You'll learn more in the coming days, but here's the simple version- My husband and I are some of the largest shareholders in the Cartelcorp. We cannot change society or find an answer to the vast economic disparity that exists, but we decided not long ago that we could at least try to help driver children that were lost and struggling on their own. We created this property to be a self-sustaining community for those children.

We put out word that we would pay for lost children, far more than the less savory factions would pay. We made it clear that we do not accept children ripped or stolen from their families. I can say that we never expected to receive twenty-seven children at once from the same group and with no adults, assuming that is true.

What we try to provide here is an opportunity to live a safe life in a community where you contribute to all things needed to live while having an opportunity to learn. Basically, we are offering you shelter, food, and safety for as long as you are under eighteen and willing to help work as part of a community. That means helping to farm and prepare your own food. This isn't a pure charity. No one will be serving you. We also have rules. Anyone caught stealing, harming others, or cheating is out. You'll be on the other side of those gates in seconds."

Mia looked at the other kids. No one was sure how to respond. Manny was still silent. It seemed too good to be true and she had already been burned once from trusting too much in the past twenty-four hours. Mia took a step forward. "Why are you doing this? How can we trust you?"

Carla smiled softly. "What is your name?"

"Mia."

"Mia, please let me say that I understand your hesitation to believe us. My husband and I recognize that we have been enormously lucky. We also recognize that there are big problems with the way the world is today. We can't solve it all, but we decided we could try to help in some way, so we created this." She motioned at the grounds of the property around them. "We're offering you a chance to stop running for a while. No strings, except that you must work to help take care of yourselves. These three," she gestured at the older children standing at their sides, "are some of the leaders from the children already here. They've been with us for almost a year. They'll introduce themselves and then take you all over to the community area to help you find housing, get cleaned up, get some food, and help you get acclimated. There will be plenty of time later for all of your questions."

Mia looked at Manny. He still seemed to be in a daze. She looked back at Carla. "Please forgive us, but what you're describing seems too good to be true. We've learned not to trust that."

"We understand. If you trusted us immediately, I'd question your judgement," laughed Carla.

Chapter Thirty-One - Chloe

They didn't spend long back at the scene of the driver massacre. For that, Chole was grateful. She watched as Kelly moved rapidly about the camp, surveying what had happened. Occasionally he would stop and bend down to check out one of the bodies more closely. From a few, he would take some object or another from their pockets or pack. One of those objects was a HUD which he put on immediately. For about ten minutes he walked around just looking out over the bodies on the ground, or observing the scarred, twisted vehicles, the burning tents and the equipment. Just like she had a little over an hour ago, he loaded his pack with rations from the remaining stores.

"OK, we're leaving," Kelly ordered.

"Aren't you worried they'll track your HUD?" Chloe asked.

"No," he said flatly. "This HUD has been hacked and localized. I used it to record some of what we just saw. It also has a local data store that includes navigational information that can help us get where we're going."

"And where might that be?" questioned Chloe.

"All in good time," he said. "Let's put some distance between us and this place. I'll explain more along the way."

They set out headed south at a pretty brisk pace, faster than Chloe was used to going on her own. Kelly had long legs, a big stride, and hiked as if he were a machine. They had gone at least two miles before Kelly started talking again.

"Did you have family?" he asked.

"Yes," she said, "but no husband, no children. You?"

"I was married. She died years ago. I have a son. He was still alive when I last saw him a few months ago."

Chloe decided to be direct. "What were you all doing out here? I saw the weapons. How exactly did you get those? And come to think of it, how do you know I'm not a replicant drone left behind to find survivors?"

"You're not a drone," he laughed. "No drone would've been sitting in the woods with a bag of mangled chickens ripping meat from the bones with her bare hands. If I had any doubts there are ways I could've tested, but most of those involve harming you in some way. I don't see any need for that. You're not a spy."

"How can you be so sure?" she asked.

"I'm a good judge of character, but also, a spy would've waited to see who showed back up at the camp. You were running away."

Chloe had to laugh a little, even if she was a bit out of breath from their pace. "What did you do in the Army?"

Kelly hesitated for a few moments before answering. "I was Airborne. Special Forces. Unconventional warfare. Three tours of duty, including Ukraine, Iran, and a lot of shit no one has ever heard about in Africa."

"What happened? Why did you leave the military?" she asked.

"Same thing that happened to everyone, right?" he said as he pulled himself up over a small boulder in their path and turned around to offer her a hand up. "I was planning to go career, move into command, but AIs, drones, and bots began to replace all of us. All that was left for humans was high command, and I didn't qualify for that yet. Even private security is dominated by the drones now. So, like everyone else, I joined the drivers."

"Where are we going? You said there were others." she tested to see if they'd come far enough that he'd tell her.

"You already know that there are well over a couple of billion drivers on the planet, though that number has begun to shrink with extermination efforts. Even in North America there are still tens of millions of us, and that doesn't include the kids living in the C22's. There hasn't exactly been a driver census done. But what most people living in Shangri-La don't realize is that the remaining driver communities aren't as disconnected as they think we are. For many reasons, we're forced to live in smaller groups and communities. The one you just saw destroyed was one of the larger groups in this country. Larger than that and it becomes too hard to hide. But there are a lot of us."

Chloe's mind was spinning and trying to keep up with what he was saying. "But how? How can the drivers communicate and coordinate over those kinds of distances without technology and net access?"

"It turns out you can do some pretty amazing things when you get creative," said Kelly, "and you might also be surprised at how many sympathetic friends we've found amongst the shareholders. It turns out not everyone in paradise is a complete, money-grubbing asshole or ready to turn a blind eye as long as it's not them losing their job."

Chloe suddenly felt uncomfortable, but she swallowed hard. He was right. She knew much of what was happening out here when she was a shareholder, but she had turned a blind eye so long as it wasn't her. The truth hurt. "So that's where we're going now? To meet up with some of the others?"

"Yes," said Kelly, "it's going to be a couple days hike until we can get to a transport location, but we're going to rejoin some of the others. We need to coordinate, find out how many were taken out in this raid and if it stretched beyond the three camps we just left behind."

"You never answered my question about the weapons. How do a bunch of drivers come upon those kinds of weapons? Even with friends amongst the shareholders, that seems like a stretch." Chloe waited as he considered his response.

"The world is a fucked-up place and we're forced to make even more fucked-up deals with people we'd rather not be dealing with, but we need arms to defend ourselves."

"But you use them to do more than defend, don't you?" accused Chloe, even though she almost regretted saying it immediately.

Kelly stopped walking. Chloe almost bumped into him but stopped as well.

"You want the truth? Yes, we accept arms from foreign corps who want us to use them to attack the corporations here- their FTL development facilities, their AI development, and more just to slow down their development to try and get an edge. I have no love of helping these foreign corporations, but I also know that hurting the North American corporations in the only place that matters to them, their money, is the only way to potentially get them to rethink how they are addressing the problem of the drivers. Maybe if they lose enough money, they'll decide there's a less expensive way than murdering us."

"You're viewed as terrorists. That's how everyone sees it. That's how I felt until just a couple of months ago. Hell," said Chloe, "it's pretty much the view I had up until just now when I heard your side of it all. I still don't know that I agree with you philosophically, but I at least understand your reasoning. But... to those living in the cities with jobs and shares, you are terrorists."

"None of that is news to us," remarked Kelly, "But nonetheless, we keep fighting. Our main goal is to stay alive, but we also aren't giving up on finding a way to maybe effect real change one day."

"For that kind of change you'd have to find a way to eliminate all the AIs, robots, and drones on the planet," said Chloe, "and we both know that's not going to happen."

"I disagree," said Kelly, "It's not the AIs and bots that are the problem, it's humanity that needs fixing. In the past hundred years, we've been faced with all kinds of challenges and crises moments: the threat of nuclear war, terrorism, global climate change, and more. In the end it was robots and AI that were the catalyst for our current state, but humanity enabled it to happen in our desire to 'evolve' and make ourselves better.

Whether it was being enslaved by robots, frying the planet, nuking ourselves, overpopulating the place, or allowing weaponized viruses to destroy the population, sooner or later humanity was going to make enough poor choices that it would lead to our demise. Before anyone knew it, we would all be living in a post-apocalyptic world that was for some reason ruled by Tina Turner."

"Who's Tina Turner?" asked Chloe.

"I don't know," said Kelly, "it's just something my father used to say, but I always liked it. My point is that we can't give up on fixing things."

Chapter Thirty-Two - Ryland

Once the drone was loaded and the delivery destination set, it did exactly what it was designed to do. Within milliseconds the drone had posted its manifest to the central network along with its destination. It received authorization and a routing plan with complete logistics all the way through to delivery. Transport drones came in many different sizes. This one looked like a large, slim but oblong cube on ruggedized wheels. It was certified to transport up to three hundred kilograms of cargo. It was about a meter high but not quite that wide. The interior could be climate controlled and adjusted depending on the cargo. The exterior was a lightweight but extremely hard and durable, matte-black polymer. Controls on the outside were very limited and mostly related to some security access and manual overrides to get at the contents in the event a HUD interface was malfunctioning. A small display showed the manifest ID number. Gyroscopes and weights in the base made it extremely hard to knock over.

Powered by a small but ample battery, it headed down the hallway with barely any noise but the soft, low hum of machinery. Each door it approached opened automatically and closed behind it. Elevators opened for it and received its floor request. Despite the rather boxy appearance, it was quite nimble at managing any turns and curves, the wheels enabling it to move almost omni-directionally on a reasonably flat plane. Visual sensors enabled it to instantly alter course and stop to avoid humans that crossed its path. When it came upon other drones and bots, they moved past each other seamlessly. They were all connected to the same central network. Nobody even paid attention to transport drones as they passed by. They were a normal part of daily life.

Loaded with its contents of a case of wine and some classified research and development materials, the drone worked its way quickly but quietly out the back to the loading bay doors of the Immersive Magic studios. It then picked up speed as it moved across the winding walk-ways of the campus. With singular purpose it dutifully made its way to the landing pads while emitting a transponder code to let any authorized monitoring and control system know what it was, what it was carrying and where it was heading.

Working its way down a lane dedicated to drones, it filed into a continuously moving line with numerous other transports of different sizes. They moved past all the personal craft to the far end of the landing pad where cargo transport craft were constantly landing and taking off. Swinging a quick left to leave the line, the drone headed toward a mid-sized transport and headed up the loading ramp. As it boarded it received a bay assignment which it quickly found, nestled itself into place, and immediately went into a lower power mode.

Huddled inside the pitch black of a semi-permeable storage container inside the drone, Ryland breathed a sigh of relief. He couldn't know for sure that he was on a cargo ship, but it seemed like so far everything was going according to plan. By no means was he comfortable. Seated on the floor of the drone's cargo area, he had his back to the rear wall and his legs propped up on a case of wine. His whole body was wrapped in shielding material with just enough small creases to allow him to breath. The shielding made it warm and stuffy, but luckily when Theo had hacked the manifest, he also made an adjustment to the climate controls to increase airflow and lower ambient temperature. That helped a bit.

There was very little he could do for now but wait in the darkness. If he continued to be lucky, in an hour or so they should be landing near Tahoe. Maybe he should take a nap? It wasn't a bad idea. Once he arrived at the company ranch, he would need to get moving. He would need to be awake and alert for an extended period before he would get another chance to rest. Of course, the idea of taking a nap at this point was almost absurd. His mind was still reeling with everything that had just happened.

Assuming he did not get caught, he would have plenty of time on the subsequent leg of his journey to think. He leaned his head back with his eyes closed, heard the boarding ramp close, and then felt the craft begin to lift off. Trying to set his mind at ease was nearly impossible, and his thoughts kept bouncing around. How could this have happened? Who could possibly be out to get him? What did his future look like? How could he possibly exonerate himself and get out of this mess? Too many questions with not enough answers and all the questions were circular, leading back to each other.

As he often did when he was having trouble sleeping, he tried retreating to his games. If he focused on his games, his stories, he could shut everything else out and let his mind stretch, imagine, and explore. Within a few moments his mind was expanding on storylines and ideas for *Last Contact*. The craft moved into high speed as it approached the edge of the city. He was beginning to nod off into at least a half-sleep that would provide him some rest.

About an hour later he shook himself out of the state of semi-consciousness he had been in and felt that the drone was in motion again. The drone was rolling at a pretty high speed, but he had no idea exactly how long it had been since the craft had landed. At this point he was getting stiff and sore. His back was killing him, and his feet were beginning to fall asleep on him. He stretched them as best he could. After a few more minutes the ground began to feel less even though the advanced design of the drone kept the ride inside relatively smooth. If he had to guess, the drone had left the main roads and was now headed down the dirt and gravel paths that led to the ranch by the lake.

Within a few minutes, he could hear a door slide open and close. Shortly afterward the drone came to a stop. He felt the drone retract its wheels, and open it's loading door. It dutifully slid the storage bin it had been transporting on to the floor. With that, the drone closed the loading door, extended its wheels, and left the way it came with the same, soft hum of its engine whirring. Mission accomplished.

Ryland smiled and almost felt like the drone deserved to have some kind of cool, congratulatory, digitized, musical beeps play for accomplishing its task. He waited for about another five minutes or so to be sure, listening in the silence for any sound at all. Hearing nothing, he pushed off the lid of the container and pulled himself stiffly out. He shook out his limbs and stretched a bit. The lights had come on as soon as he had pushed the lid open, activating based on the motion.

Crates and storage containers were stacked all around him. There were cases of wine, beer, water, liquor, and champagne. There were stacks of sundries, soap, power cells, several bins full of random electronics. He was amused to note that the replica firearms he had sent here for their last retreat were still lined up in a rack on one wall. He had created an augmented reality war game for them all to play on the tree and snow-covered ground that year. It was a blast. He grabbed one of the fake energy rifles. It wouldn't fire anything real, but if he did encounter anyone, they wouldn't know that. He emptied a small box containing bath soaps. He grabbed a couple of small power cells, a half-dozen bottles of water, and a fire starter. He put them all in the empty box.

The door to exit the storage room opened as he approached it. He walked out into the hallway where the lights turned on with his presence. To his right was the main entrance to the building. That was not the way he wanted to go. The entrance was electronically secured and had security cameras on it. Turning left, he walked down the hall until he came to the second door which was a side entrance to the barn area. It was manually locked and deadbolted from his side. He pulled back the bolt and pushed the door open.

Immediately a chill bit through the air as he walked out into the uninsulated portion of the barn. He could see his breath. The smell of hay and horses hit his nostrils strongly. It was dark. There were no automated lights here, but the setting sun cast enough light through the cracks in the external barn doors that he could see OK. Next to him were a bench and a utility closet. He knew what he would find there. He grabbed one of the thick utility jackets hanging in the closet that looked to be roughly his size and put it on. There were also several small backpacks, each containing a small first aid kit, a hunting knife, an emergency beacon, and a light source. He grabbed one and moved his supplies from the box into the pack. Luckily, Kira had the sense to insist he take some snacks with him, so he pulled all of those out of his pockets and stuffed those in the sack as well. Lastly, he opened the lid on a sealed box and grabbed a few handfuls of sugar cubes which he stuffed in his pockets.

Shouldering the pack and the fake rifle, he walked over to the stalls. The ranch had six horses, all wonderful animals that he had gotten to know on previous visits. They had bots that took care of most of their general care when no one was here, but they also paid a local ranch family to help exercise and take care of them. None of those people would be here at this time of night. Ryland knew all the horses, but his favorite was a brown mare named Gracie. He found her happily grazing on some hay in her stall. When he approached, she looked up at him and brayed a bit. Gracie liked him.

"Hey, girl," whispered Ryland gently. "How are you doing? I missed you, girl. It's been too long. I have something for you, Gracie." He held out his hand.

Gracie left her hay and walked over to get the sugar cubes with a giant lick of her tongue.

"I need your help, girl. There's somewhere I need to go quickly, and I can't do it without you. What do you say? Can you help me, girl?"

Gracie nudged his hand with her nose.

"I'll take that as a yes," he laughed as he gave her a couple more sugar cubes.

Chapter Thirty-Three - Sheridan

Once Sheridan was comfortable that the main perimeter was secure, and all the attorneys had arrived, he motioned his team to follow him in. They had two perimeters: one around the entire campus of the Entertainment Division, and another, smaller, tighter one around the Immersive Magic studio. It was impressive how quickly it had all happened, including the surprising punctuality of the lawyers. Those inside the studio probably had less than a few minutes notice that something unusual was happening outside before he and the others, followed by a small army of search units and a few hunter drones, headed in through the front doors. No one was getting in or out until he gave the order. Communications to or from anyone in the studio had been completely blocked.

Approximately seven minutes ago, right before Sheridan and his forces began arriving, Kira had received a comm from Keiko, her CEO. Sheridan knew this because he had monitored the call as agreed with the attorneys. Kira was informed of the treason charges against Ryland and was told that she was now Acting Chief Game Architect. Sheridan had requested that she also be asked what she knew and when she had last seen Ryland, but the attorneys had shot him down on that. He suspected Ryland probably had help from others at the studio, or that they were hiding him in there. But, based on the explicative-laden response from Kira to her CEO he was starting to doubt she was mixed up in it all. She seemed genuinely surprised and more than a little angry.

He continued to monitor Kira's comms after that conversation. She made only one, a local group comm to people named Theo and Amanda. Their profiles and roles appeared immediately on Sheridan's HUD. It was a quick message; very business-like, but once again laced with colorful profanity. She told them both about the treason charge against Ryland and her promotion, then immediately silenced them when they began to ask questions and express dismay. She ordered Theo to handle shutting down some simulation and told Amanda that she needed to go get two people named Eli and Tessa out of "the arena." She instructed Amanda not to tell them about Ryland or what was going on, but to keep them calm and take them to the debriefing lounge as normal. Sheridan would want to talk to all those people, and he definitely wanted to see this arena. His HUD began showing him details on Eli and Tessa. Why would a couple of C22 athletes be here? Details on that were currently marked classified.

Sheridan and his entourage walked through the front doors right as Kira was walking up to meet them. The remainder of the staff that could be seen was practically standing still. They would all just have received notice on their HUDs that the premises had been sealed by order of Internal Affairs while a search of the premises was conducted. Anyone who was smart wouldn't do anything but wait and cooperate.

"Commander," said Kira coldly, "I demand to know what the hell is going on."

"I don't have to tell you anything, ma'am. It's all in the orders you've received and which your company has already authorized. The regional Americorp authority has been notified as well. These premises will be searched for Mr. Grey, including any classified areas, until I am satisfied."

With that, the search drones began pouring through the doors and dispersing in all directions. Most of the search drones were airborne, making it look like flocks of hovering birds flying off in all directions. Others, more human-like, followed behind. At the back were heavier, deep-scanning units that looked like small refrigerators on multidirectional treads. They all flooded the studio, working their way deeper and deeper. Every face was scanned and matched to their HUD signature. Every bio-signature was traced. Some of the human-like drones made their way to network consoles, jacked in, and began scanning any localized data.

As soon as the search units were deployed in the studio, a smaller group of drones followed in and setup a mobile command center to consolidate all the incoming data. Sheridan motioned to the attorneys that they could all access the hub console to begin reviewing incoming data and flagging material for redaction. Sheridan would still get to see it all, but he would be the only human to do so. He returned his attention to Kira.

"You were with Mr. Grey earlier today. What happened? When did you last see him?"

"You don't have to answer that," interrupted the Immersive Magic attorney. "I would advise you to not answer any questions at this time."

"I don't mind answering that," countered Kira. "We were working on our new title today. I was observing some of the test simulations that inform our design and development. He walked out of his office and said he had to leave. I did find that a bit odd, knowing how seriously he takes his work. But I've known Ryland long enough to not question his judgement. He asked me to keep things moving while he was out, and then he was gone. We haven't heard from him since. I would also like to go on record, regardless of what my attorney may advise, as saying any charge that Ryland is a traitor is complete bullshit. Sir."

The Immersive Magic attorney winced and gave her an imploring look.

"May I ask," said Kira, "what makes you think he is here? He left."

"Because," answered Sheridan, "about twenty minutes ago we found the 'Ryland' you are referring to. He, or rather it, was in a canyon riverbed in the Rocky Mountains. Our hunter units cornered and apprehended him, but it was a fake: a high-end replicant drone. So that means he may never have left this office."

Kira stared blankly off into space. Sheridan tried to read her reaction. Kira assumed a pensive look, as though she were assessing the puzzle and trying to figure it out herself.

Data poured in. Every inch of the facility was scanned and inspected. Sheridan was most interested by the data coming in from the units scanning Ryland's office. There appeared to be a private control center underneath his office, and a viewing center that opened into a massive room that was the arena. Several units were in the arena and actively scanning it but the data they were getting was unlike anything he had seen. Even the drones weren't making much sense out of it. The scans showed no "normal" signs of life or anything other than flat floors, walls, and ceilings. However, the material the arena was made of was constantly in motion and completely composed of some advanced nano-tech. While the walls and floor appeared still, they were moving like they were alive, but with very little energy expense.

The Immersive Magic attorney was vociferously flagging every piece of the data from the arena for redaction from the official report.

One of the other attorneys glanced at Kira. He left the small circle of lawyers and came over towards Kira and Sheridan. He was slightly taller than average, with a somewhat athletic gate and build, and short, dark, curly hair that was beginning to grey. The charcoal suit he wore was expensive and fashionable, but not flashy.

"Hi," he held out his hand to Kira. She shook it formally. "I'm Dan Stern, Americorp corporate executive counsel."

"Don't you have data to review, Mr. Stern?" asked Kira.

"Please… call me Dan," he replied. "And yes, I do, but the counsel from your company is already redacting things at a breakneck pace. It's really quite impressive. I'll have a chance to review most of it later and the analysis will take many times as long as this session before anything gets uploaded to central."

"Is there something I can do for you, *Dan*?" asked Kira.

Sheridan tried not to laugh at the over-emphasized sarcasm. Did Stern just wink at her? He must have imagined that.

"Nothing, ma'am," he replied, "I just wanted to assure you that executives in the corp have expressed to us in counsel that Mr. Grey has contributed significantly to shareholder interests and society in general for decades, and that we will make sure that is taken into consideration. Nothing less than full, due process for his rights will be observed if…" he glanced at Sheridan, "*when* he is found."

Sheridan shifted his focus to the reports on his HUD. The studio scan was nearly complete. They'd found nothing. There was no sign of the subject. He wasn't here. The search and scan of the rest of the campus had been less intense and concentrated, but it was coming up with similar reports. He left the lobby and headed for Ryland's private office to see it for himself and think.

He walked through the arena viewing area and looked out at the expanse past the windows. It was massive and looked like a digital canvas, waiting to be painted. The stairs to Ryland's office were at the back, past the comfortable arrangements of couches and chairs.

Digital screens around the back of the office made it look like a view of the Bay Area looking out towards the ocean. Sheridan guessed there was a good chance it was a live view. The lighting felt like real sunlight, even though that wasn't possible as he was underground. There was a large conference table that looked like it had been made of old wood, surrounded by enormously comfortable but entirely differently styled chairs. Not one matched. At the far end was a large, antique wooden desk. Built-in shelves on the walls held an incredulous amount of memorabilia that ranged from a multi-faceted puzzle cube with different colors to an abacus to piles of small rectangular pieces of plastic labeled things like "Pitfall", and "Frogger".

Near the desk was a bar filled with a collection of whiskeys and glasses. An ice maker was embedded beneath. He sat back in the desk chair and stared at a framed poster on the wall that read "Madden Football". The rest of the office contained material from what Sheridan assumed were some of the subject's work. It didn't escape him that there was an empty stand in the corner next to marketing material for the game *Colony*.

One of three things had to be true. The subject could still be hiding somewhere on these premises, but that was highly unlikely. He could have escaped somehow. The only other possibility was that he never actually even came into the office this morning and the evidence of him being here was also faked. This last scenario also seemed unlikely. He had to have been here and gotten out somehow. He ordered an immediate analysis of every person and everything that entered or left the building that day. They would find him. They had never failed to find a target.

Chapter Thirty-Four – Mia

"I don't trust this place," stated Manny directly. Mia glared at him, but Carla, who was seated across from them at a wooden picnic table, just smiled. Tall glasses of iced tea sat in front of each of them with a half-empty pitcher in the middle of the table.

It was only a few hours ago that their group had been escorted to the community shelters just as Carla had instructed. They had been shown to a shelter which was one of many in a long row. Mia estimated there were at least twenty shelters. The building was essentially a long dormitory filled with bunk beds, but it was enough for their entire group. It was clean, dry, and hard to argue with compared to what they had been living in. It felt like a dream comparably. As promised, they were brought food and water. The food was simple: rice, beans, bananas, and some fish. They ate like ravenous animals.

A few of the older children from the community came into the shelter and began to treat some of the minor injuries and wounds some of the children in their group had incurred. The shelter even had showers with running water where they could all clean up with real soap. Many of them had never even experienced a shower before, which led to some much-needed laughing. They were given fresh clothes and shoes which looked like the same utility clothes the other children were wearing. It all felt weird. Mia and Manny were both still convinced it was a trap of some kind, but they couldn't turn down food, shelter, first aid, and a chance to stop running for a moment.

"I understand," said Carla to Manny. "I hope your trust will come in time. Do you trust me enough to tell me how you came to be here? Twenty-seven children wandering alone in the jungle with no adults is not a circumstance I thought we'd come upon. Though I can't say I know all of what really happens out there. I'd like to understand more."

Mia thought she really seemed ingenuous in her question. Manny did not look like he was going to answer, so Mia reached over and put her hand on his and looked at him to try and let him know she thought it was OK to share this information. He nodded but still didn't speak.

Mia explained what had happened to them from before their group had first entered the jungle with their parents as a way of trying to find a place to live and forage. She recanted the story of the drone attack, stopping several times to unsuccessfully fight back tears. Carla waited patiently and even reached out her hand to touch Mia's. Finally, Mia arrived at the point in the story where they met up with the people that had put them on the truck they thought would take them closer to Argentina. Carla stopped her. She already knew the rest of the story.

"Thank you for sharing that with me," she said. "I have a hard time imagining not only how you're feeling but what it must have been like to endure through all of that. It's horrifying. The world... society is broken right now. We don't know how to fix it. We just hope we can offer you a break from it- an alternative for at least a while."

"I don't get it," erupted Manny. "If you're doing this," he waved around at the property wildly with his hands, "why can't others do this? Why can't the corporations do this? Why can't land be set aside for those without jobs so that we can live in peace and support ourselves without worrying about being hunted? Why can't this be normal? It's all we wanted in the first place, when we still had our parents. All we wanted was a place to live, to take care of ourselves. Why is that so hard? We don't need robots and computers. You can have them all. We just need some land. People like us will take care of ourselves, just like you say you are doing here."

"I wish it were that simple," Carla looked melancholy.

"It is that simple," declared Manny.

"I'm not going to treat you like a child, Manny," replied Carla. "The problem is scale and probabilities. Setting up something like this on a small scale can work, but as the size and scale of such an endeavor grows, it will inevitably reach a point where it is both unsustainable and becomes a threat to modern society. It was tried many times in different ways around the globe. In some cases, as the communities grew, they devolved into crime-ridden slums. In the cases where they did not, there was still a problem with what to do as they grew too large. Population growth demanded more resources which couldn't be sustained by the allotted land, or they evolved to a point of needing efficiencies of technology which led them to the same path we were already well down in the modern world.

"It's all about the probability models. The AIs and machine learning algorithms have shown again and again that if we create and enable driver communities with their own lands and leave them to grow, eventually we create enough of a populace that they can't survive without challenging our resources and all of us likely going to war. None of the models show it working out well.

"Various ideas on birth control and even eugenics have been explored, many of them tried around the planet, but they all fail in practice just as the models predicted they would. The reality is that so much land is demanded by the corporations to serve the needs of the shareholders, there's not enough to give to the drivers, and even if we gave them that, the result would eventually be the end of society. So, instead, drivers remain outcasts, forever on the run. I don't sit here saying it's right. I think our way of life is broken, but no one has yet to find a solution. All the models say there isn't a way to change that doesn't leave us worse off than where we are."

"Probability models?" asked Mia.

"The AIs are continuously running models, programs designed to analyze data and make predictions about what the likely outcomes will be. They do this for far more than the driver situation, of course. There's too much competition for resources. Climate changes and massive consumption in the past century have reduced resource availability considerably. The more advanced corporations are even about to begin exploring the stars to find needed resources."

"I still don't understand. It doesn't make sense," said Manny.

"Like I said," replied Carla, "it's complicated, even for someone like me that's had the opportunity to go to school, live many more years than you, and studied the subject. It's a problem with many layers. It's a problem we created for ourselves based on many short-sighted choices over many, many decades."

"So, what do we do now?" asked Mia.

"I don't know, but you can live without fear for a while. Stop running for a while," smiled Carla as she finished her glass of iced tea. "Who knows? Maybe we'll figure out something together that the machines haven't thought of yet. It may just take some patience. Patience and time. My husband and I believe there will eventually be a way forward that makes sense. In the mean time we just need to do what we can and figure out how to help in small ways. Small ways start to add up if we can convince others to do the same thing. Are you interested in helping us find ways to make that happen?"

Mia and Manny looked at each other silently for a long moment. Manny raised his eyebrows. Mia nodded.

Mia turned back to Carla. "Yes. We are interested in helping. We want most to ensure the safety of those that came here with us, but yes, we would like to help find ways to change things, even if it takes time and as you said, patience."

"I'm pleased to hear that," smiled Carla genuinely. "I also hope we become friends. Manny, young man, what is your family name?"

The question appeared to have caught him off guard. Family names had mattered so little to them. It was barely even ever discussed or used in driver communities. There simply wasn't a need or purpose to it, but he still knew his family name, even if he hadn't spoken it in years.

"Navarro." said Manny quietly.

"I very much look forward to working with you Manny Navarro", offered Carla. "And you?" she looked at Mia.

Mia paused for a moment, not because she didn't want to share the information since sharing it couldn't hurt her. It was more because she realized how much of her family was dead and that she had no idea if anyone else in her family was still alive out there. Saying her family name aloud felt awkward.

"Cardosa," she said. "Mia Cardosa."

Chapter Thirty-Four - Nicodemus

Board members began to appear in the virtual meeting space. This time the conference room appeared as if it was floating far above the surface of the Earth. Enormous windows looked out on one side to a breathtaking view of the planet. The windows surrounded the entire circular room, there were no doors. It didn't need any. The room didn't actually exist. The chairman, Nicodemus, had selected this venue intentionally. On the other side of the view from Earth was a series of three large, highly advanced FTL craft preparing for an upcoming jump. That was something happening in real life right now even if here it was just a projection.

All three belonged to Americorp and they had been there for several weeks building up the energy required for one of the longest jumps yet attempted. Faster than light travel hadn't ended up working at all as it had been envisioned by early science-fiction books, television, and movies. In addition to being deadly to humans, it wasn't something that could be achieved at a moments' notice. It required a considerable amount of time to build up the energy required to achieve FTL speed and intensely propel a craft as it shifted out of phase with normal spacetime. The other big difference from most science fiction is that once a jump was initiated, there was no changing course and you couldn't stop short. A craft that jumped was on a set course until it reached its destination unless by some chance of fate it was destroyed on route. That had only happened a few times, but it was possible. Communication with a craft in FTL transit was also impossible.

Unlike a real space station, the virtual meeting room didn't spin, it remained perfectly still, but out every window you could see exactly what would have been there in real life: small space stations, orbital defense systems, armies of satellites encircling the globe, and more stars than you could count. The sun was just starting to disappear behind the far side of the planet from their position.

Nicodemus turned his avatar around from looking out at the ships and began to pace back towards the table. At the center of the room was a large, circular table made of what looked like shiny, almost reflective, black, smooth steel. It was encircled by tall-backed, black steel, leather-cushioned chairs which were now mostly full as the last of the executive board members appeared. The last person to appear was not a board member, but he was there at the chairman's request.

As the chairman, Nicodemus interrupted the light conversation that was beginning amongst a few of the attendees. "Ladies and gentlemen, I think most of you already know Daniel Stern, our executive legal counsel," he motioned to the man seated next to him that had appeared last. Dan nodded in response. "I've invited him to this meeting for reasons you'll soon understand." That would get their attention.

"We have a situation. Probability models regarding the driver population in North and Central America have changed. The AIs are now predicting that a large-scale uprising is imminent." He paused. While most members of the board were likely using filters to keep their avatars from displaying their real expressions, he knew what they were all likely thinking. "There's been a significant amount of chatter picked up on the networks. We've also brought into custody several high-ranking shareholders that we believe may be connected to driver terrorist organizations. We are questioning them now.

Driver activity being tracked by orbitals seems to indicate movement that could mean they are planning something big, and we also now have proof. Thanks to a raid against terrorists by Melissa's company Templeton Holdings, we can confirm that drivers in our lands are being armed by foreign corporations."

"Dammit, Melissa!" shouted a tall man with a beard seated across the table from the chairman. His name was Malik and he was chairman of the largest agricultural corporation on the planet. "You should have consulted the board before taking an action like that."

"I don't have to consult you when my company's facilities are being attacked," countered Melissa. "When the terrorists are on land I own and when it's a few hundred or so of them, I'll do as I wish in the bounds of the law. I consulted my executive team and company security. This entire board and all appropriate channels were notified as appropriate and mandated by shareholder agreements and by-laws."

"We do not have time right now to argue whether or not Templeton should have taken this action," interjected Nicodemus authoritatively. "That is now irrelevant." Both Melissa and Malik fell silent. "What matters is preparing to deal with some of the likely outcomes the probability models are predicting." He stood up from his seat and walked toward the windows where he gestured at the ships preparing for their jump.

"I don't need to tell any of you what is at stake at this moment. We cannot afford disruption to our plans. The general shareholder population has become immune to news of small actions against driver communities, especially when it involves those actively engaged in terrorism. Sympathy for driver communities has waned in the past few decades, but when actions begin to involve families and the numbers increase it can turn sentiment if not properly controlled. While we've been able to mostly control the media and news on this one, a vidscan showing bodies of children killed in the raids somehow found its way onto the networks. We've managed to get most people to believe it's a fake, at least so far. The reason we are here now is that we have reason to believe that a larger attack may be imminent within the next few days or weeks."

"Even if that's true," said a pale woman dressed in an impossibly white suit that almost gave her the appearance of a ghost were it not for the deep red color of her lips and her bright, blue eyes, "that wouldn't be enough of a reason for the board to meet. Military and security forces are already fully authorized to use deadly force to eliminate any threat, and the last I recall our military technology and drones are the best on the planet. Our cities and key facilities are all heavily guarded. Why should we be concerned about a driver attack, even if some of them have obtained some foreign weapons?"

"Because the models show something different this time." said Nicodemus flatly. "Some models show that a large attack that results in thousands, or even tens of thousands of dead drivers will not end there. It will cause a larger uprising forcing us to fight on multiple fronts. It will get joined by foreign corporations looking to take advantage of our pre-occupation and temporary vulnerability. Other models show driver sympathy growing amongst lower-shareholders in the wake of so many deaths, causing us a possible problem when it comes to support from the broader shareholder base. This could force us to begin diverting significant resources into mass welfare programs and away from our FTL development and interstellar mining operations, which will put us in danger of falling behind our competition. None of these scenarios are acceptable."

He let that sink in for a moment. The room remained silent.

"I assume you already have a plan in mind," stated Evan, "since you're not normally in the business of bringing us all together to ask for our ideas."

Nicodemus smirked, but continued. "Current laws that govern the AIs, robots, and drones only allow for the termination of non-shareholders when they are posing an immediate threat to our interests, or if they commit a capital offense. Mostly these laws exist because the general shareholder population knows that for many of them, becoming a driver themselves one day remains a distinct possibility."

"So, what are you proposing, Nic?" asked Malik.

"An amendment." stated Nicodemus. "An amendment to the laws: a removal of the clauses requiring evidence of the "direct and imminent threat" language protecting the unemployed not violating any laws, and expansion to the definition of the terrorist designation. This would allow us to authorize the proactive termination of non-shareholders. As many as we'd like. All of them if we so choose. My suggestion would be that we be prepared to exercise that option should any situation arise which appears that it may trigger one of scenarios the models predicted. If that happens, we eradicate all driver communities in North and Central America and the islands and other territories we control. Doing so would eliminate the window of opportunity for our competitors to take advantage of our divided resources. There would be some backlash of public opinion to deal with, but we mitigate it by releasing news and evidence that shows we had no choice in order to protect their way of life. We also create some minimal social programs for any of the remaining driver population. At that point, the reduction in population will have been significant enough that the drain on our resources for such a program would be negligible for well over a century or two."

"This is sick," declared Evan. "It's mass murder! Genocide. We're talking about innocent women, men, and children. I won't have any part of this." Several others voiced agreement with Evan.

Nicodemus expected this. "I understand your point of view, and I take no pleasure in any of this, but what I'm proposing is not genocide. It is to give ourselves the option, should we need it, to protect ourselves and all the shareholders in Americorp from being wiped out. We would not exercise this option unless we felt it were completely necessary for our self-preservation, but I do not think it wise to wait until it is too late for us to have this option available to us. It will take time to draw up the appropriate language for the amendment which is why I invited our lead executive counsel, Mr. Stern, to join us today. If enacted, it would immediately become an alteration to ARDOS that is incorporated into the AIs that control all our drones and most of our defenses.

To be clear, I'm not asking your permission or asking you to vote on anything today. I'm merely advising you that an amendment is being drafted and why this precaution is being taken so that you have the necessary context should the need arise. I advise you all to take some time and carefully consider what we have talked about today. As you enjoy your comfortable lives, as you walk the beautiful shining streets of our cities, as you see the faces of the many millions of shareholders going about their daily lives, as you see your own employees, friends, and families continuing to evolve and start to take humanity's legacy into the stars, ask yourself: What would you be willing to do to protect all that? I will, of course, happily make myself available to any of you for follow-up conversations. We will continue to run probability models on this situation and keep you updated on the findings. Unless there are any other questions, this meeting is adjourned."

No one said anything. One by one they began to disappear from the meeting room until Nicodemus and Dan were all that remained.

"Please make this your highest priority," instructed Nicodemus, "I need something ready in days, not weeks."

Dan nodded gravely. "Understood, sir. Understood."

Chapter Thirty-Five - Ryland

Sunlight and long shadows bathed the valley of trees and glimmered off a light dusting of snow that had fallen throughout the day. Much of the snow had melted already, but pockets of it remained in the shadows. Gracie moved along slowly by now, unaccustomed to being pushed so hard and long through the mountains without much rest. They'd stopped a couple of times along the way to eat and catch a quick nap, but only briefly as Ryland knew that time was not on his side.

Navigating with localized data he had downloaded before he left the studio, they had made just a few wrong turns as they attempted to cross mountainous territory in places where there weren't even trails. As best he could tell, they were getting close to the retreat his brother and sister-in-law had bought. He had not seen another person for nearly eight or nine hours, and even those he saw before that had been pretty hard-core backpackers.

The day's journey by himself had given him a lot of time to think about his situation. He had come up with few plausible answers. As far as he knew, he didn't have any real enemies. He had competitors, both domestic and foreign, but he struggled to come up with a scenario where one of them would go to these lengths to remove him from the playing field. Even with the amount of money at stake in his industry, this seemed like a pretty extreme way to try and gain market share. Another possibility was that it was high-ranking powers within Americorp itself. They had the needed access and clearance, but he couldn't come up with a possible motive. In fact, from any way he looked at it, this hurt the corporation and profits, not to mention the distraction that entertainment offered to the broader population from the larger problems in the world. Then there was all the use of his technology in military and security. He was simply so much more valuable to the corp if he was doing his job.

Finally, he entertained a scenario that was not a conspiracy: the algorithms had simply flagged him incorrectly. Despite their proven accuracy, this seemed by far to be the most likely answer. Maybe it was the game he was working on? Maybe the AIs feared... no... 'feared' wasn't the right word... maybe they misinterpreted the premise of his new game that AIs could somehow fail, and that humanity would replace *them*? That seemed far-fetched, but misinterpretation of data by machines still seemed a more probable explanation than anything else he could come up with.

He guided Gracie out of the trees and up onto a narrow, dirt road that he knew would take him to his destination. It wasn't much of a road, and there were no recent tracks. After a few hundred meters he could begin to make out the outlines of the cabin and the barn through the trees. He could smell a campfire burning and even heard periodic cracks in the air that had to be the sound of someone splitting wood. Hopping down off the horse he held the reigns loosely and walked down the dirt path that led to the front of the cabin.

Mayson was there, swinging an axe every thirty to sixty seconds as he stood next to a tall pile of firewood and logs on his left side. The cabin and its wide front porch were behind him, and a large ring of river stone were on his right where a warm fire glowed brighter as dusk was settling into the valley. Mayson was a bit taller and bigger than Ryland. He had much more of an athlete's build and kept his hair short.

There was a large mound of hay piled next to the barn. Gracie saw it and jerked her head. Ryland let go of the reigns so she could go eat and rest. She wasn't going anywhere far from here after the journey they had just completed.

"No security measures, Mays? I expected at least some archers or maybe a moat." Ryland shouted as he walked up towards the fire.

"Actually," replied Mayson as he looked up and smiled, "you tripped perimeter sensors over five kilometers out. I've been tracking you ever since. If I wasn't sure it was you, you probably wouldn't have even found this place. I dropped the ground-level distortion fields for your approach. I also decided to not fire on you with the nearly one hundred energy guns scattered throughout the perimeter to cut intruders to ribbons. That's how you know I like you." Mayson put down his axe, leaned it up against the pile of split wood, walked up to Ryland and gave him a huge hug. "It's good to see you, Ry. I'm glad you figured out my message."

"Thanks for giving me an option," said Ryland, "I didn't really have one. This was perfect."

"I knew you'd figure out a way to get here," said Mayson. "I want to hear how you pulled it off, but that can wait. You must be exhausted, and there are some things you need to hear. Things we need to talk about." Mayson's face looked grim. Mayson was almost always happy, always content, except maybe when he was discussing politics or a deal that had gone wrong. Something bad had happened, Ryland was sure of it. "You're safe here, though," continued Mayson. "This place is totally off-grid. Localized network. I can get us out on secure channels but only for limited periods of time. It's completely hidden to orbital and even aerial scanning and cameras. Hell, the smoke from the fire doesn't even get seen beyond 30-40 meters in the air. Even from the ground you'd have to be standing right here to know it existed if I didn't want you to. You're about as safe as you could be, even if they are looking for you in this area."

"Seriously, thanks, Mays. You don't know how much I appreciate it. Are Katelyn and the boys here?"

"No," responded Mayson. "They stayed in New York to keep up appearances, monitor things, and make excuses as needed. It's just you and me here."

"Your message was perfect," said Ryland, "How did you know about the charges? Logan?"

"Yes," replied Mayson, "Logan contacted me right after he contacted you. He was mainly contacting me for help with contacting the family attorneys. He was sure you'd wait to be arrested. I knew better. Ryland... sit down," he motioned to the log benches around the firepit. "There's a lot we need to talk about and some things you need to know." Ryland was sore from all the riding and almost wanted to just walk around and stretch. He unshouldered his pack, set it by the bench, and sat down nonetheless. The fire was warm and inviting. Mayson tossed a couple of more logs onto it, grabbed a bottle from a nearby bench and poured a couple glasses of whiskey. He handed one to Ryland. They clinked glasses and drank. Ryland could feel the warmth run through his body. He closed his eyes for just a moment and tried to clear his head.

"Thank you, Mays. You have no idea how much I appreciate you. I know what you're risking."

"For family?!" laughed Mays, "I'd do this any day of the week and twice on Tuesdays. That's what mom and dad taught us. 'No Greys left behind!'" They both laughed a little.

"I have some ideas on how this might have happened," offered Ryland. "There are a few possibilities, but I think the most likely is actually that it may just have been a mistake by the AIs based on the new game I'm working on…"

"It wasn't a mistake," interrupted Mayson, "Look, there's no easy way to tell you this. A few hours ago, your wife and daughters boarded a personal transport to take them back to New York, so they could be with Katelyn and the boys. Shortly after takeoff their transport crashed, killing everyone inside. It's been all over the news. No survivors. The official story is that it was a rare, mechanical failure, something to do with an imbalance in the fuel assembly. But I have intelligence that says they were shot out of the air by military drones. It's reliable intelligence. Ry… I'm so sorry…" he reached over and embraced his stunned brother who was speechless.

"You're kidding me," Ryland uttered in disbelief, "This can't be true. It can't be."

"I am so, so sorry. It's real. I can't begin to know how you feel right now. There was no easy way to tell you. It's horrifying. But something big is happening. You weren't the only high-ranking person that security went after today. There were at least six others that I know of. It's unheard of. The others included a well-known actor, two politicians, a prize-winning physicist, a musician, and the global head of the media division. Of course, none of them were insane enough to run like you did. They're all in custody now, every one of them awaiting trial for treason. That kind of round up has never happened in a single day. Ry, I don't know what's going on, and I know you need time to absorb this and grieve, but something really odd is going down."

Ryland just sat there, staring at the fire. His wife was dead, so were his daughters, because of him. Oh my god… how could this be real? It was too much to take in on top of everything else he'd been through in the past two days. He lost it and just buried his head in his hands as he felt them covered in hot tears. He just wept, for what seemed like forever and a moment at the same time. Nothing else mattered. He wasn't normally a vindictive person, but whoever was responsible was going to pay for this. He swore it to himself as he sobbed almost to the point of nausea and blacking out. Everything that had happened spun around in his head as he tried to make sense if it and grasp that it was not some horrible dream, but reality.

Calming his breathing, he wiped his eyes and cleared his vision. He focused on the fire but saw out of the corner of his eye that his brother still sat silently next to him. Mayson refilled their glasses. Ryland downed his in a single gulp. "I'm going to fucking destroy whoever is behind this. I'm not just going to kill them. I'm going to destroy their lives in the most unimaginable and horrible ways. I won't kill innocents like they did, but I will make them pay for this to the point they wish they had never even heard my name."

"I'm with you, brother, always," whispered Mayson, "but this may be even bigger than you realize. We have a lot to talk about."

Chapter Thirty-Six - Eli

Covered in sweat and exhausted, Eli and Tessa removed their helmets as they exited the arena and headed to the debriefing room. Today's simulations had been intense. The scenarios had become more complex. Their command responsibilities took them out of their comfort zones. The technology and expanse of the missions was beyond what they were prepared for. They had trained for sports, individual accomplishment, and team play, but never for command and mass military maneuvers. The last simulation ended abruptly in the middle of a large-scale battle. They were losing badly. Still, it was unusual. The sims had never ended until they had either won or lost. Theo's voice came over their comms and told them they needed to head to the debriefing lounge.

"We just got our asses handed to us," declared Tessa.

Eli said nothing. He was angry about losing, even if he knew they did not have the background and training to deal with the scenarios they were being put in. Instead he walked through the door for debriefing and hurled his helmet at the wall with enough force to ricochet hard, leaving a dent and knocking over a nearby potted plant in a tall vase which subsequently shattered and unleashed a small pile of dirt on the floor. Ignoring the damage, he walked over to the counter and grabbed a bottle of water which he proceeded to drain in a single gulp before chucking it to the floor beside the helmet.

"I get it," said Tessa, "The plant really had it coming. If that plant hadn't completely failed to defend the battle cruisers long enough for them to get into range of the enemy's planetary defenses it could have gone far better for us. And the wall? The way that wall practically ignored the wave of enemy fighters that came from the far side of the moon was unforgiveable. It was lucky to get away with just that dent. I'm not sure what the water bottle did, but I'm guessing it wasn't good either."

"You're a bitch," replied Eli, but he couldn't help slightly smiling and laughing a bit as he said it.

"Are you two finished?" asked Amanda from the doorway. "Or should I give you a bit more time to decompress?"

"We're fine," said Tessa, "Eli's never taken losing very well."

"I'm not going to lie," offered Amanda, "we gave you a really hard situation today, one that required a far greater grasp of military strategy than we knew you'd be ready for, but we wanted to see how you'd react to it anyway. Tell me, when you first saw…"

Eli cut her off. "Where's Ryland? It's been two days since he left. You still haven't told us anything about what's going on."

"This debriefing is over," said Amanda very sternly and abruptly. With a motion she killed the in-room recording. Then she deactivated her HUD, removed it, powered it down, and motioned for them to do the same. They looked at each other for a moment, but both complied. Once they had, Amanda sighed, then looked up at them.

"Look, I don't want to lie to you two, but there's some serious shit going on and we need to be really careful what we say and what could get picked up on the nets. I'm going to level with you." She proceeded to tell them about the charges against Ryland. She also told them how Ryland had apparently distracted everyone initially using his replicant drone which brought applause and laughter from both Eli and Tess. Amanda told them about the search of the studio that was happening right now and that they should be prepared for the drones to arrive any moment.

"I don't know what's going to happen from here," she finished, "I don't know if it was a mistake or what. I don't know when or if Ryland is coming back. All I know is that in any scenario, he wouldn't want us to waste the precious little time we have left with you before you head back for the draft. Ryland has poured his soul into *Last Contact* and I'm going to make sure it's a huge success no matter what."

"We need to help him," said Eli simply.

"We can help him by finishing the work," said Amanda.

"No," said Eli, "I mean we need to find a way to really help him. There's no way he's a traitor. I mean, I don't *really* know the guy, but he's awesome! I don't know a lot, but I know people. I know when people suck. He doesn't suck. He's amazing. We need to figure out where he is and how we can help."

"It's not that simple, Eli. The fact that he's not already in custody is hard to believe. No one runs anymore, it's nearly impossible. If they can't find him, we can't find him, and we won't until he wants to be found."

"Well," offered Tessa, "then how do we prove that he didn't do whatever it is they say he did?"

"Not possible," Amanda shook her head. "The analysis is all sealed and confidential, so we don't even know what we would be trying to prove false."

"So, there's nothing we can do? That's what you're telling us?" asked Eli.

"Look, Tess and Eli, we have about five or six days left. We're going to do the best job we can of working together to make this game title awesome. Then you two are going off to the draft, and both end up with amazing careers. You don't want to do anything to screw that up. We're talking about your future. You keep your heads down, we'll wait for news together, and then you get to become full shareholders and lead a happy life. Doing anything else could have you back with the drivers at best or guilty of treason at worst. Treason is an automatic death penalty for non-shareholders. I'm recommending against doing something that could mean death, but that's just me."

For a moment Tessa and Eli just looked at each other, speaking without words like only two best friends can do. Finally, Tessa nodded a few times.

"Ok," said Eli enthusiastically. "We're in."

"On finishing the game work?" asked Amanda, "Great to hear."

"Oh," said Eli, "we're definitely in on that, but we're also in on helping Ryland and helping you help him. Neither of us believe that you and the rest of the crew aren't involved in this deeper. When the time comes, we want to help. We don't care about the consequences. The only thing that's kept us going our whole lives was sticking our necks out for each other and our friends when it mattered. If we started behaving differently now just because of money, well... we'd be assholes, and we're not assholes. So, count us in." He smiled.

Chapter Thirty-Seven- Logan

Writing an ARDOS amendment was no simple task. Trying to do so quickly and confidentially was even harder. The challenge was to keep it as simple as possible to avoid loopholes while ensuring the intended behaviors would be ironclad. The loopholes were the tricky part. They had to be cross-referenced with all other ARDOS provisions. Then they had to run probability models on the new, amended rules. That is what Dan Stern was attempting to do today, in conjunction with one of Americorp's leading computer scientists, Doctor Logan Grey, at the corporation's primary development subsidiary, Odyssey AI.

"What do you think you might have done if you hadn't become an attorney?" asked Logan, breaking the silence they had been in for several minutes while the algorithms processed the proposed changes to ARDOS.

"Ha!" laughed Dan. "It's actually funny you should ask that. There are many days that I've looked back and thought about what my life might be like if I'd taken a different path. But you know, I truly enjoy the law. I love the intricacies of it. Although no computer scientist would probably agree with me, I really do see it as equivalent in complexity and beauty to what you do with AI development."

"Actually," responded Logan, "I don't disagree with you on the complexity. But beauty… well… beauty, as they say, is in the eye of the beholder."

They were at the Central Data Center facility in the Colorado Rocky Mountains. It might be the most secure place on the planet as it housed not only the corporation's primary AI development facilities, but also the data core for the AIs and the primary command center for AI and drone management, including the orbital defense systems. Systems were highly distributed enabling practically everything to keep running even if this facility were wiped out, but it remained a highly secure area given the nature of its R&D and ability to manage the distributed systems and govern ARDOS itself.

"When will they be done with the analysis?" Dan asked.

You could just ask us that question. You don't have to talk about us like we aren't here.

Logan laughed quietly. He could tell that Dan disliked talking to the AI collective.

"Fine," Dan sighed. "When will *you* be done with the initial analysis?"

If we take what we know about the situation and divide by the color blue, carry the one, we should be done by Christmas.

"What?!" exclaimed Dan. Logan laughed out loud.

Doctor Grey has been working with us on our sense of humor. It was not a completely original joke. We borrowed from a line in the 2032 movie Do Your Thing produced by Tina Fey, but from Doctor Grey's reaction and yours we believe we have successfully applied it. We did improvise the part about Christmas.

Dan shook his head and sighed.

Our initial analysis is complete. We have not found any adverse scenarios so far with significant probability that negatively impact shareholder value, or in which the new amendments to ARDOS create problems with prior directives. It is our determination that you have written directives that permit for the mass execution of non-shareholders, even when they pose no direct, immediate, or imminent threat and have not committed a capital offense, without threatening the safety of shareholders inadvertently. So, you have that going for you, which is nice?

"Excuse me?" shouted Dan. "What's that supposed to mean?"

"I'm sorry," intervened Logan upon hearing the *Caddyshack* reference rather inappropriately applied. "That last part is my fault. It's something we're still working on. I believe you have the answers you were looking for though?"

"Yes," recovered Dan, "I do. Thanks. Look, I know everything that's been discussed here is under non-disclosure, but... I hope you understand. I mean, I wanted you to know that this isn't my idea. I'm just doing my job."

Nuremberg trials. Germany. 1945-1946.

"That's not fair. You don't know me," stammered Dan. His face was flushed.

"I'm so sorry. You must understand that I'm doing experimental work here, and while the AIs I'm working with are in many ways more advanced than anything in full production, there are rough edges. They don't always have the refinement of judgement in knowing how to apply certain sentiments."

"I'm not a monster," declared Dan. His face was still red, and he was sweating a little.

"I don't believe you are," said Logan. "Would you like to talk about it? I take any change to ARDOS quite seriously, it can significantly impact my work. This amendment terrifies me. We can talk off the record. Privately."

"Privately?" Dan looked around the room indicating the presence of AIs. "I don't really think..."

"Guys," Logan interrupted him and spoke into the air, "I need you to give us some space. Privacy protocol Eleven, please."

As you wish.

"What's privacy protocol eleven?" asked Dan.

"It means we can say whatever we want. Nothing is being tracked or recorded. This room is completely locked down and isolated from the network for the moment. I couldn't even re-enable normal AI monitoring by voice if I tried. They aren't listening."

"How can you be sure?" asked Dan.

"Ummmm, because I wrote the protocols myself, and most security protocols only go to ten. Mine go to eleven, so you know it's really secure."

"Is that some kind of joke?" asked Dan.

"Yes... and no," replied Logan. "But trust me, no one or no thing can hear what you say right now except me. I'll go first. Any change that reduces restrictions on AIs and robots from using deadly force against humans is a mistake in my opinion. I don't believe the people making these decisions have any idea what the long-term implications are let alone how reprehensible they must be as human beings to be OK with something like this. In many ways, I feel like they must be less human than the software I work with every day."

"Yet," answered Dan, "you still work for them. You continue to lead development of newer and even more powerful technology that they will control. Why?"

"For the same reason you do your job. For the same reasons you're here right now."

Dan nodded, "Because somebody is going to do it. Even if I refuse, someone will do it, and perhaps not with the same level of quality. At least I can make sure it's as tight as possible, avoid loopholes as best as I can."

"Look, Dan. You seem like a good guy. I know better than anyone what you're up against, how fucked up the system is, and how impossible it is to change. But I haven't given up on the hope that someday we'll figure something out. If you haven't given up hope either, maybe we should talk some more? Maybe even go out for a beer some time?"

"I think I'd like that," smiled Dan. "I almost went into medical science instead of law." It was an odd statement to make just then, but he kept going. "I really wanted to do something that could help people, maybe even save lives, but my father convinced me that even brilliant medical scientists were losing their jobs. The law was a safer profession. Most days I try to convince myself that in my own way I am still helping people. It gets harder and harder as the number of people you're helping protect gets smaller while the number of people you're involved in possibly hurting grows larger. But we've crossed the Rubicon, the point of no return. We can't go back and unwind where we've come, so you just need to do the best you can, right?"

"Maybe," nodded Logan, "maybe not. There are always choices to be made. I don't think we need to go back or unwind things, but that doesn't mean things can't change. I have some friends you should meet."

Chapter Thirty-Eight - Ryland

As it got colder, they moved inside the cabin and started a fire in the large, stacked limestone fireplace. Flames flickered and crackled with the smell of ash wood as it burned hot and fast. Mayson and Ryland sat back on soft, old, leather recliners as the warmth surrounded them. Ryland was staring into the fire, deep in thought. He almost startled Mayson when he spoke suddenly as if joining a conversation already in progress in his own head.

"Multiple prominent people were flagged by the AIs as traitors in a single day, when normally something like that might happen once a year at best. My family was murdered when I ran. I'm struggling to come up with any connection among me and the other recently identified traitors besides the fact we're all somewhat influential in our individual spheres and industries, all middle-aged, and all very well off though none of us would be considered in the upper echelon of wealth. One of them is a musician that I'm a fan of. I don't particularly love their music, it's just different than what everyone else is doing right now and I admire that. Where's the connecting thread? The executive board, or possibly the AIs, or a combination of the two seem like the only possible group capable of carrying this out, but what is their motive? What's the end game?"

"I can't explain yet how it relates back to you and the others, but their end game is obvious. It's the same as it's been for decades. Hell... longer than that when it comes to people in power. Their goal is self-preservation, staying in power, and furthering their wealth and control. It never really mattered to them that billions of people on this planet lost their jobs and became homeless, starving beggars. It didn't matter to them that good human beings were forced out of the shining cities to fight for an existence. It mattered so little to them that while AIs and robots are prohibited from harming shareholders in most any circumstances, they are all but free to slaughter drivers the moment they cross a line. Those in power don't consider the jobless to be human beings worthy of the same protections of law or application of morality. It's sick."

Ryland thought for a long moment. "Solving the mystery of exactly who is responsible and why won't be easy, nor will punishing them for their actions. Clearing my name may be impossible given the system, but that's the least of my concerns. I'll sacrifice my life to make whoever it is pay for what they did."

"I think you're trying to solve the wrong problem," remarked Mayson. "Or rather, you're not solving for the root problem. The system is the problem."

Ryland considered this and tried to look past the revenge that was burning in his mind.

"I know you're angry," said Mayson, "but you need to consider the bigger picture. You already knew that Katelyn and I are not thrilled with the current state of society or our executive board. It's partially why we bought this place. We're certain that at some point the world is going to go to hell in a handbasket. We're prepared for a lot of different situations.

But, it's more than that." He paused for a long moment. "We're actively engaged with the driver communities, and with shareholders like us that want to see real change happen. We're connected to what could be called the driver underground, which is far larger and more organized than most people would imagine."

"Ha!" laughed Ryland out loud.

"You find that funny?"

"No," smiled Ryland, "I find it funny, given what you just said, that I'm the one being hunted for treason. Maybe it was all just a simple name mix-up? You know: they got the wrong brother? Baby mix-up at the algorithm hospital? That sort of thing."

Mayson shook his head, trying not to laugh. "Look, I'm being serious. There are a lot of us that believe there has to be a better way, trying to find a solution."

"But you have nothing yet, do you? The system is too iron-clad. Short of mass collaboration with foreign governments and corporations that might possibly be worse than our own, there is no answer. Our own government is far too heavily armed to be challenged, and the entire system is designed to keep power vested in the very wealthiest amongst us.

Even the gajillions of probability models the AIs run every day have been unable to find a viable alternate solution that doesn't plummet everyone, not just the drivers, into an apocalyptic hell. So, 'modern society' just keeps moving down the path, eliminating more people, enforcing stricter birth laws to limit the population, growing profits, consolidating wealth amongst fewer and fewer, while now even space gets exploited by us without humans even being able to travel there ourselves. You're right, Mays. That is the problem that needs solving."

"Glad you agree. There's just the minor issue that our best minds and technology have yet to come up with a plan that has a remote chance of succeeding. We've been at it for many years."

"You know," smiled Ryland, "I've been playing and making games my entire life. We use probability models extensively throughout our design and development process. We continue to use them for games in production to monitor and improve the experience. It's unreal what you can learn. The models are almost always right. But there's something else I've learned over the years: all it takes are the right anomalies to bring probability models to their knees. Machines are horrible at anticipating human ingenuity and creativity in the face of adversity. They can often anticipate that something they don't expect may occur but figuring out what exactly that is typically alludes them."

"You have that look," said Mayson.

"What look?"

"That look you get when you're coming up with a new game idea. I've known that look since we were teenagers. This isn't a game, Ry. You can't just hit reset when things don't work out the way you wanted."

"That's where you're wrong but it's also genius. It is a game, just with much bigger risks and stakes, and sometimes a reset is exactly what you need. You said there were others you're involved with? Tell me about them. I need to know the playing field. Who are our allies? What are our assets? I'll get the ice. We might need another drink or three for this."

Chapter Thirty-Nine - Sheridan

They spent over a day pouring through security video, logs, and data only to come up empty. Sheridan's team had determined with a greater than 99% probability that the real Ryland had entered the studio that morning, and there was no record at all of him leaving until the moment the replicant walked out the door. Sheridan had watched that video dozens of times himself. The replicant Ryland had even whistled as it walked down the path from the building. Now Sheridan couldn't get the damn tune out of his head. It was an old song: *Born to Run* by Bruce Springsteen. He couldn't help but appreciate the guy's style a bit.

What was odd was that the timestamp on the video was from before the algorithms first made a positive identification of him as a dissident and before even Sheridan's team had been notified so they could authorize the restriction of Ryland's movement. He had been tipped off before the dissident determination was even made, but how? The implications of how high this went were not lost on him.

They had been staring at the same videos, five different views at a time, of every person and everything that went in and out of the building from just before the index of the replicant exit to the time their initial search team had arrived. Everything checked out. Then something caught his eye and clicked in his head.

"There. That transport." He indicated one of the feeds. "Bring up the details on that drone."

`Transport drone. Class MGCT-Sec-NM5 ID 048310313. Destination and manifest displaying now.`

Ryland looked at the manifest and destination. Shielded cargo. It was big enough to hold a human being.

"What is the destination?"

`It is a home and ranch in the Lake Tahoe area. Immersive Magic maintains a company retreat facility there. It is used for company meetings, as place to` entertain clients, and as a vacation destination for executives.

"Who sent this package? Who authorized it?"

The sender is listed as F. U. Charlie, but we cannot find any record of an employee at these facilities matching those initials and surname. The shipment should not have been accepted. The manifest must have been falsely encoded. We are attempting to further research the sender name now.

"Save yourself the processing cycles and time. There's no such person. It's Ryland's way of telling us to screw ourselves even though we've found out how he escaped."

We don't understand.

"I want a full search team on site at the destination immediately, and I want it all on my HUD as a continuous feed. Prepare a flight plan for my craft. I'm on my way there. I also want an immediate analysis of that transport drone from the moment it left here to wherever it is now, and all security cameras from that ranch and any camera within a twenty-five-kilometer radius. Look for him and anything at all unusual. Get moving on orbital scans and video of that area from the time of arrival to now. Start prepping a wider area drone search team to begin sweeping outward from the ranch."

Sheridan knew they wouldn't find the subject at the destination, but they were one step closer. If this subject was like most of the few people that ran, he would likely try to contact his family and then try to get to them. He pulled up the records on the subject's family again, only to see Ryland's wife and two daughters now listed as deceased.

"Well, damn," he said out loud as the details displayed on his HUD. "Wow." He knew enough to know this was suddenly far more complicated.

"Give me location data and profiles on all of his remaining family. Brothers. Sisters. Parents. Nephews. Nieces. Etc. We'll look at cousins next. I want search drones at the homes of anyone he knew in the Tahoe area, and I want constant monitoring of the subject's homes."

    Consider it done.

Chapter Forty - Ryland

"Are you ready?" asked Mayson. Ryland nodded as they both put on the modified HUDs Mayson had provided. "We won't have a ton of time. We'll be meeting in a secured virtual room on the network. You'll have to trust me on that. We have resources in high places. The bigger worry is being located here in the real world if they track our uplink, especially since they'll be looking for you by now and we're not that terribly far from Tahoe.

"We'll be using an extremely narrow band uplink that is able to rapidly rotate encryption keys and uses sporadic packet patterns so that it will appear like low-level network interference instead of a signal. The trick is that it can only work for about fifteen, maybe twenty minutes at a time before it becomes something that exceeds atmospheric and network thresholds they monitor for. Your avatar and your view of theirs may appear a bit fuzzy or rezzy at times, but this is the best we can do and still keep our location secure."

"Got it," acknowledged Ryland.

"And Ry," added Mayson, "Please try to hold back on the humor. I know that's hard for you, but this is serious, and we have limited time. Surely you understand that, right?"

"I understand. And stop calling me Shirley."

"You know I gave that one to you as a lay-up, so you could get it out of your system, right?" sighed Mayson.

"Yup. And thank you. I needed that. Let's do this." Ryland activated his HUD and linked with the local network. It felt like it had been longer than just a couple of days since he had linked into the net. The digital world appeared in front of him. His destination had been preset and he found himself standing in what looked like a rustic cabin. It was not that much different from the one that he and his brother were really sitting in, except that there was the sound of waves crashing on a shore in the background, and the main room was much larger with many more seats and cushions. There was also a long, wooden dining table and chairs.

Being in a virtual sim made Ryland immediately more comfortable. Flame flickered in a massive fireplace built out of black stone. Then, one by one, people began to appear in the room around him and his brother. Within sixty seconds there were nearly a dozen people. They all found their way to a seat in the main room except for a couple of people that settled back at the dining table.

It was a diverse group of people. Ryland did not recognize any of them. The two at the dining table were both women. They looked tough, like the kind of people you didn't want to be in an argument with. Maybe in their thirties? Seated around the room was an interesting group. There was an extremely short, heavy, elderly man with glasses. A wiry but muscular white man in what appeared to be military combat fatigues was standing near the fireplace. There was also a frail looking elderly white woman, several men and women also in fatigues that hung together in a group, a deeply dark-skinned man that looked like he was taller and stronger than anyone in the room, and a Hispanic woman with greying hair who appeared to be in her 40's or 50's that sat down in a leather chair.

"Thank you all for meeting on such short notice," started Mayson. His avatar flickered. "We have less than twenty minutes before we need to terminate this meeting, so I'll cut to the chase. Standing next to me is my brother, Ryland. You all received the briefing on his status, so I won't waste our time re-capping it. I've also brought him generally up to speed on where things stand today with us. We can trust him. You have my word."

The evening before, Mayson had spent hours telling Ryland about the hidden driver world. It was hard for Ryland to believe that his brother and sister-in-law had been leading an enormously complex, and dangerous secret life. He had always respected them both and thought the world of them even if he considered them a bit paranoid. Now he was seeing them in a whole different way. They weren't just running around making real estate deals and investments. They were trying to make a real difference, trying to help those in need.

As far as Ryland had known, most drivers had migrated to some of the more desolate and least hospitable places in North and Central

America, far away from the cities and modern life, far from corporate interests. Some probably even attempted to get to places like Argentina or Australia and New Zealand which offered them hope for a new life, but everything he had heard made it sound like the reality there might even be more harsh and dangerous than scraping out an existence in North America. It was common knowledge that the mortality rate for drivers was not pretty. A lack of medicine and supplies claimed many lives. Others most likely starved, while others undoubtedly lost their lives to dangerous wildlife or even more dangerous people.

Newsvids occasionally reported the existence of larger driver communities that had been discovered, even within what used to be the continental United States. Usually it would be a few dozen or so people that had found some caves or managed to build some makeshift shelters in a wilderness area far from any farming or tourism. Generally, these communities were considered harmless and left alone. Commonly it was believed that many drivers existed as lone wolves, trying to stay alive and out of sight, while others formed what could best be called gangs that preyed on others.

But as far as everyone knew, the driver population was dwindling and disorganized. How could they be otherwise? They were separated by great distances with no access to technology. Using the central network without paying for it was considered theft and using a HUD would allow for your immediate identification and location triangulation.

Even the terrorist cells, according to the news, were practically all independent from each other and operated like mini-guerilla outfits, acting mostly out of survival or occasionally some desire to enact revenge on the society that had turned them away when they could no longer provide any useful skills.

At least, that's what Ryland had believed to be true. As he learned from Mayson, that was exactly what it was like for drivers for a long time. The picture his brother painted for him of today was staggeringly different. About twenty-five years ago things began to change.

Driven by the influence of a single woman from Brazil that had been born a driver, the communities began to connect. She traveled from group to group, talking to them about what was happening in the world around them, getting them to understand the bigger picture of all the others just like them. She did not come empty handed. Not only did she bring desperately needed supplies funded by a network of sympathetic, wealthy shareholders, she also brought news that many of those same shareholders had begun to create remote, self-sustaining community facilities where they could go to find safe-haven and a chance at a better way of life. Additionally, she brought connectivity to the leadership of the different communities.

Secure network channels using encrypted HUDs allowed small to large group leaders to begin to connect with each other to understand what was going on and to help each other when they could. As they began to communicate, they also began to work on ideas to change their situation. While they had yet to come to any grand plan, they were no longer isolated. They began to have an awareness of who else was out there like them, where they were, and what the different challenges and opportunities were.

At first, everyone was skeptical of each other, and unwilling to share much information. They also worried it was all a setup, that they were being monitored, and an imminent extermination would present itself. Eventually, they all began to trust each other, and to trust the woman who had brought them together. The average driver still had no idea this was all going on. That was for security purposes. But, at the same time they were benefitting from it. While medicine was still badly needed, supplies had improved. They were better able to avoid corporate drones and driver populations were even growing naturally in some areas. There was a level of sophistication at the upper echelon of the driver communities and supporting shareholders that nobody would have guessed, and which the AIs had not detected or predicted.

"Bottom line:" continued Mayson, "It may be a long shot, but I think Ryland can help us. Something odd is happening right now. We may need to step up our timetable. I think we need some creative solutions sooner rather than later."

"Sooner than you know," said the man in combat fatigues.

"Huh?" asked Mayson, "What's going on, Kelly? Did I miss a memo?"

"No memo," replied Kelly, "It's news we just received. In addition to all the other recent activity that we haven't yet made sense of we just received word from a reliable source that the executive board is preparing to vote on a change to the Keynesian Laws that will basically remove all protections from deadly force by robots and AIs for any driver. They will be able to slaughter us at will.

"Even in this group, I don't want to divulge the source, but it comes from someone directly involved with writing the revised laws and the executive order. They are sympathetic to our cause and highly uncomfortable with the implications of what they are being asked to do, but they are doing it, nonetheless. At best, our source is trying to slow things down as much as possible. I know we aren't ready, and we don't have any viable plan, but something is coming."

"How soon?" asked one of the women at the dining table.

"We don't know," the tall man spoke up and shook his head. "Maybe days at best until they are ready to vote. It could be sooner. Our source says they have plans to use the new laws quickly. Our current strategy of patience, perseverance, and incremental improvement looks like it is at an end. They've already anticipated a public opinion backlash, but it appears they'd prefer to deal with that scenario than others. We do believe the vote will be controversial, with many unwilling to back it. But, if they get enough of the large shareholders on board and the regional directors, they'll have the votes they need."

"Fascinating," said Ryland who looked rapt in thought.

"You find the idea that we're facing possible genocide within days fascinating?!" exclaimed a woman at the table. "What kind of..."

"No, no, that's not what I meant," apologized Ryland. "This information changes things. I need to know more. I need to know what kind of military power this group can really mount. I also need to know details on what kind of technology and skills we have at our disposal."

"First, please allow me to say that I'm very sorry to hear about what happened to your family," said the middle-aged Hispanic woman from across the room. "It's tragic and you have my deepest condolences. But you're asking for a lot of information for someone we only met today, Mr. Grey. What is it that you have in mind?"

"Ryland," intervened Mayson, "May I introduce you to our leader, Mia Cardoso. She is the woman I told you about that began working over twenty-five years ago to bring everyone together and help show drivers a better way to live. She and her close friend Manuel, who is still in South America, have worked to bring us and the driver communities in the Americas together. There is not a leader in any peaceful driver community in all of North, Central or South America that doesn't know who she is. If Americorp or Cartelcorp actually knew she existed and what she's done, she'd probably be the most hunted person on the planet."

Ryland acknowledged Mia respectfully. "Miss Cardoso, I know you don't know me or have any reason to trust me except that Mayson says you can, but please believe me, I want to help."

"Mister Grey, when I was barely a teenager, I saw my family and all of our friends slaughtered in the jungles of Brazil. I was forced to find a way to help lead a bunch of children to live in a world that had no place for them. We were lucky to find help from a couple of shareholders that believed in a better future. They gave us a chance. I've spent every day of my life since then trying to move us slowly towards a better tomorrow, even though we still haven't quite figured out how to quite get there or what that looks like when we get there. But we haven't stopped trying to move in that direction. Perhaps you could first tell us how exactly you can help us? We've been at this quite a while without your help, no insult intended."

"None taken," smiled Ryland. "OK, so here's the thing: I don't know yet. But, I'm in the idea business. It's what I do, and I'm really good at it. Like… really good. Humility, on the other hand, isn't always my strong suit, but coming up with creative ideas? That's my thing. I can't promise I can solve this one, especially on the timetable we are looking at, and given the fact that I'm probably being hunted like a dog by Americorp security. Wow, come to think about it, that all sounds bad and the odds are we'll probably all die. But, I'm highly motivated to win this now and I'd like to give it a shot. To do that, I need to know our assets. What are we working with? People, weapons, technology, other resources? I need to know what is at our disposal."

"Maybe we can make this simpler while keeping the risk minimal," offered Mia. "We can provide you with a list of the technical and engineering skills we have at our disposal minus names. That information isn't sensitive, they're almost all people that lost their jobs in the past twenty to thirty years, so the corporation already knows they are potentially still out here. As for military power- Kelly, perhaps you can offer a summary?"

"Certainly," said Kelly. "It's pretty simple. We have enough trained soldiers, weapons, and even a few re-programmed black-market drones to be a real pain in the ass for a short time period against a single major corporate target, or to cause a lot of trouble for multiple targets simultaneously. But in either case we'll eventually get overwhelmed and all end up dead. It's for that reason that we generally stick to defense, more commonly against raider driver groups that aren't with the program, but occasionally against smaller corp drone forces. Guerilla attacks against less guarded targets are much more within our grasp. When we go for something bigger, we often get our asses handed to us unless we've done a ton of planning. Does that help?"

"Thank you," said Ryland, nodding at both Kelly and Mia. "I can work with that. Any particularly helpful shareholder support you can tell me about?"

"If you have something particular in mind, ask us," suggested Mia. "But most shareholders that have helped us are more willing to assist with funds to support humanitarian causes such as supplies or building communities. Very few, like your brother, are willing to go any further and put themselves at such risk, so presume your options there are very limited."

"One last question," posed Ryland. "How many drivers are there?"

"In North and Central America, there are probably just over fifty million, not including the rogue groups or the children in the C22 camps," said Mia.

"You're kidding, right?" Ryland was stunned.

"I'm not kidding, Mr. Grey," said Mia. "But please also consider that the vast majority of them are also located far from the major cities and corporate controlled territories, and the number that have any military training is very limited."

"Our time is just about up," intoned Mayson. "We have to go. Send over the skillset details as soon as you can."

Mia looked at the others, "For everyone else, you'll receive information in a moment on where to regroup with me and a few others. We need to continue this conversation and begin preparations for the worst-case scenario. We need to figure out how to protect as many people as possible and begin moving the communities."

"Hey, Ryland," Kelly tapped him on the shoulder and spoke quietly. "I played some of your stuff a long time ago. My men and I used to train on some of it in the army. It was really great work and it saved lives. If you come up with a decent plan that has a remote prayer, myself and some of the best damn jobless soldiers you've never met are ready to die if it means a better tomorrow. Try to not get yourself killed or captured before you figure out some way to save all of us. Got it Mister 'Idea Business'?" With that his avatar disappeared from the room, and so did Ryland and Mayson.

Chapter Forty-One - Sheridan

It hadn't taken them long to figure out what the subject had done once he had arrived at the ranch. They found the shipping container and discovered that a horse was missing. He had obviously known where all the security cameras were because there wasn't a trace of him. He probably never even entered the house. The hard part was figuring out where he had gone from here.

It was impossible to follow any kind of tracks. There were too many other ranches in the area with frequent horse activity on the trails. That and the recent weather gave them nothing to follow. Ryland could have gone almost any direction except straight into one of the towns. If he had done that, they would have caught him on security video or sensors. He could be anywhere by now. It was not impossible that he was huddled up in a pile of blankets in a utility shed in one of the cabins within a kilometer. Many of these homes weren't used for months at a time. He could also have headed straight into the mountains and be camped out in a valley somewhere. Given who they were dealing with, it did not seem unlikely that the guy could have figured out a way to be on a boat headed to South America by now.

The aerial drone that Sheridan ordered had yet to come up with anything. Thousands of small, AI controlled drones had swept the skies in concentric circles out from the ranch, but still there was no sign of him. The tree cover was too dense for viable aerial searches. They would need more units to start searching at lower altitude, under the canopy, and they would need to start bio-scanning every home and structure in their path. AIs would have to continue to parse video and data from all over the planet to try and detect any sign of him.

Meanwhile they would have to keep the algorithms working over-time to try and predict what this guy did and where he went. Unfortunately, so far, the models pretty much sucked at predicting anything about this subject.

Sheridan was staring at the empty stall of the stolen horse when his HUD notified him of an incoming message from his commanding officer. He answered immediately, "Captain."

"I'm not going to begin to discuss the abnormality of having as many high-profile treason subjects in a single day as we've had today, Lieutenant Commander Sheridan. All I want to discuss is why every one of them is in custody except for the one you were personally charged with apprehending. It's been years since anyone has even attempted a meaningful run, and it's been over a decade since we didn't catch a runner within 24 hours. Do you care to explain? I owe the board a report in an hour. I would love to hear something I can tell them that doesn't make us look like a monkey fucking a football."

"Sir," started Sheridan, "I won't waste your time on status. I'm sure you've seen all the data. This subject is… different than the others. I'm sure you've read his profile, including the psych analysis the AIs have worked up. To put it simply, sir, his brain fires differently and he's been inadvertently training his whole life for how to deal with being hunted and cornered by a system. What's confusing is his motivation and how he knew to run before the treason verification was made and well before his family was killed. Models show he should have stayed put and bet on a lesser sentence. He risked everything by running without the needed motive. My best guess is that his proclivity for games triggered it as a response he wasn't capable of overcoming despite the illogic of it."

"I can tell you definitively that I'm not going to the board to report your personal psycho analysis of the subject, Commander. What I want to know is what are you going to do next and what do you need from me to make that happen so that we can end this situation."

"I need to authorize full bio-scans of all buildings by drones within at least a hundred-klick radius, including a search warrant for any shielded areas that aren't military. I'll need to triple our aerial drone capacity to search under the canopy and I'd like to activate a few dozen hunter drones to send out in every direction. Each security camera and checkpoint are already being monitored for any sign of him. His remaining family and every one of his close friends are being monitored for any sign of contact."

"Consider it done. The search warrant may take me more than a few minutes, but the rest is yours. Are all of his family and friends accounted for?"

"All but his younger brother, sir. Mayson Grey is not currently accounted for. We're actively looking into it and monitoring all network data. But, for Mayson, being occasionally off-grid is not incongruent with his data pattern. He's apparently prone to taking frequent excursions into the wilderness sans-HUD including international trips. We have no record of him currently having left Americorp territories though. He was last seen leaving a casino in Las Vegas a couple of weeks ago in an off-road, all-terrain, wheeled personal vehicle loaded with camping gear and headed South. Security video from the casino the night before shows him at the blackjack tables talking about heading to Joshua Tree for some camping. We've had a few drones sweeping Joshua Tree National Park but haven't found him yet."

"Make it more than a few and increase the range. His profile shows he does a lot of work in real estate. Start looking for any property he owns and start spidering out through every entity he works with. Let me be clear, Commander. I want this guy found yesterday. I'm getting word that a lot of our forces are about to get re-deployed soon for something big, so this needs to be done quickly. The execs want all loose ends tied up. Make it happen."

"Yes, sir," replied Sheridan.

Chapter Forty-Two - Ryland

Over an hour had passed since their meeting with Mia and the others. Mayson and Ryland were sitting on the front porch of the cabin in a pair of weathered Adirondack chairs sipping hot coffee in the cool morning air. They had been hashing around ideas since the moment they left the virtual meeting space.

"Bottom line," said Mayson, "the only way to significantly impair the central net or do anything that involves attempting to control the drones or keep the ARDOS update from taking effect would involve attacking or compromising the central network data center in the Rocky Mountains. If the amendment was passed, this is where the ARDOS update would originate from for security purposes. The problem is that the place is a fortress and we don't have nearly the firepower we'd need.

"Compromising it from within is possibly even harder. From what I know, the fail safes and security for accessing those kinds of systems are insane. Just ask Logan. He'll bore you for hours on the subject. Even if we could get in, the reality is that the systems all have so many distributed nodes backing it up that you could never really take it down, maybe just impair things for a brief while. It was designed that way, so even if it was completely destroyed, we and all of our networks and defenses would remain fully operational."

Ryland knew that Mayson was right about this. Getting into the central data center might enable them to do something to cause trouble for the corporation briefly, but it was not a path to stopping the ARDOS update let alone changing their broken society or even helping him to get back at whoever had chosen to destroy his life and his family.

"OK, so we can't stop the corp from changing the laws so that they can slaughter the drivers," acknowledged Ryland. "There's no way to disrupt or intercept the update, especially not at the scale we will be looking at and given the design of the network. So, the people behind all of this, those that own more than the other 99% of the population of the planet continue to govern the boards and destroy life at will."

"Yup… Game over. The system has designed itself so that it cannot be changed," said Mayson.

"What did you just say?" asked Ryland.

"I said the system cannot be changed," said Mayson, a bit annoyed.

"No, before that," said Mayson. "You said, 'Game over'."

"I did," said Mayson. "I'm pretty sure that given your profession you are familiar with the concept?"

"Funny. No, that's not what I'm getting at. What do you do when the game says, 'game over'?" asked Ryland.

"Ummm, turn it off and go get a beer?"

"No! You hit reset! Or at least you did back on the old game consoles. You said this same thing the other day, that we need to hit reset on society."

"I'm pretty sure that I said this *wasn't* a game and that you *can't* just hit reset, brother."

"Sure, that's what you said, but that's not the point. I think you have a brilliant idea," remarked Ryland.

"I have no idea what you're talking about, Ry," said Mayson.

"You know, a few years back, the company I work for merged with another games and entertainment brand," explained Ryland. "It was a terrible experience. For months, instead of having fun and building games, all of us executives spent our days negotiating the merger agreement: how the stock splits and redistribution would work, what the new ownership and management structure would look like, blah, blah, blah, blah. My god, it was hell. I'm not a violent person by nature but I found myself wanting to punch a lawyer almost every day. Funny enough, it was more often our lawyers I wanted to punch than those from the other company. Probably because I had to deal with them more.

"Did I ever tell you the story of when I tried to get my company to change our global End User License Agreement from the godforsaken twenty-five thousand words it is now? I recommended a simplified 'You agree that if you steal our shit or commit crimes in our games, I'm gonna git you sucka'? Seriously, I tried to make that happen. Didn't work."

"As someone involved in real estate my whole career, I'm extremely familiar with the fun of dealing with legal," interrupted

Mayson. "Though I've learned the best approach is to make sure you have the best lawyers. But I think you may be getting a bit off topic?"

"Right. Sorry. So, eventually it all worked out. I got to remain head of the studio and keep doing what I love with full control. Fortunately, when the dust settled the CEO from my company was elected the chair of the new board, and the CEO of the other company, Keiko, became my new direct boss as CEO and President. It turned out that Keiko is an amazing person and we've built a great relationship."

"I'm still not getting your point or how this applies to our situation, Ry," said Mayson.

"We hit reset," said Ryland as directly as he could.

"Great," laughed Mayson, "So all we need is an army of lawyers, six months, and a giant button to push?"

"No," Ryland shook his head, "what we'll need is to get the ARDOS amendment to pass."

"Are you crazy?! I'm not sure if you missed the memo, but that's kind of what we're trying to prevent. I think you may be losing it."

"Run with me on this for a moment," said Ryland. "I have some ideas on how to make this work, but it means expediting the timetable."

"OK… seriously?! That's the exact opposite of what we and the entire driver community who are in mortal danger are trying to do. We need more time, not less," said Mayson.

"No, if this idea can work, we need it to happen fast or we will miss our opportunity. What else do we have to work with? I'm bringing up the list of other assets and skillsets we have available to us that your friends sent over." Ryland pulled it up on his localized HUD and began scanning the data again looking at each person in the file.

"You do that, I still have no clue what your idea is or what you're talking about," said Mayson, "I think you may have gone off the deep end, brother. I'll go refill our coffee. My next one may need to have something stronger in it."

A few minutes later Mayson returned with fresh coffee for each of them. "Find anything interesting? Maybe someone who can give the locations of every driver community to security so they can wipe them out quicker after the ARDOS updates get voted in?"

"Not funny," said Ryland. "OK, it's kind of funny. Look at this." He flipped a record over to Mayson's HUD.

"Anand Shah. I was talking to Kelly about this guy a few days ago when we were assessing security risks. He came up because of how unusual his case was. You can read it all in the file. He's not a driver or one of our own in any way. The guy is a foreign national from India. He showed up out of nowhere but knew exactly who to contact in our network: not too high up but not too low to get the right attention. A couple of our more tertiary but removed trusted shareholders vouch for him but won't say how they know him. The guy claims he was sent here to help us but has no idea who arranged for him to be here or what he's supposed to do for us, except that whoever sent him is paying him handsomely. It doesn't make any sense and it's sketchy as all hell. That's why we have him secured in a non-networked location until we figure out what to do with him.

But here's the deal: we've performed every bio-scan we know of to determine if he's telling the truth and as far as we can tell, he is. That doesn't mean he's not a spy or a plant, but if he is it's a deep plant without his knowledge. He's not bugged. He really believes his story to be true."

"OK, yeah, it's really sketchy," agreed Ryland, "But did you look at his professional history?"

"The guy does software support for a low-level, neo-black-market company in India. I'm not sure how that helps us."

"No, not what he does today. It's what he used to do that's important. I looked up his work history. He may know more about drone and robot hardware drivers than anyone on the planet."

"OK, so what does that mean and how does it help us?" asked Mayson.

"Hardware drivers control how operating systems interface with peripherals. Even though the concept is over a century old, it still stands as a general design principle. Operating systems need to be able to be managed and evolved independently of low-level functions like a hardware extensions."

"Still not following you, buddy. How does that help us?"

"I'll explain everything. I have an idea. I know there are plenty of reasons to not trust this guy," said Ryland, "but I need to talk to him as soon as possible."

Chapter Forty-Three - Anand

All Anand was told by his handlers was that someone wanted to talk to him. It was a relief, really. He had been in the same house in Los Angeles for days, waiting, unable to do anything. He was not allowed to get on the network. It had not been what he expected when he arrived. Though in retrospect he realized he had no idea what to expect. He contacted the person he was told to, then he had been moved to this house under constant guard. He had been intensely questioned. Why? Hadn't they expected him? Why was he being paid to come help people who had no knowledge of him or the reason for needing him? None of it made sense. Where was his big, secret assignment?

They were not torturing him. The house was small but extremely comfortable. The weather was fantastic. There was ample food and plenty of beverages. The house had a courtyard garden, a small library of actual paper books, and a bar. They were even willing to get him the cigarettes he requested when he ran out. Nobody would talk to him about anything. There was an armed guard. Curiously it was human and not a drone. His primary handler, at least that's what Anand thought of him as, was a younger man, maybe in his late twenties, named Devon. That's who Anand had been instructed to contact with his offer of services.

Devon had stopped by the house several times in the past few days to check in on him. The conversation was always very curt. Without any idea what he was supposed to do and nowhere to go Anand decided he might as well read while he waited. The library was only one large wall of bookshelves, but it was more paper books than Anand had ever seen in his life. He poured over the spines of the books and their titles for hours, looking at them all before selecting one. It had been years since he read a novel. For some reason he decided he wanted something a bit 'American', so he selected *Zen and the Art of Motorcycle Maintenance*. He was in the middle of a chapter when Devon walked into the garden to tell him he was needed immediately in a virtual meeting. He asked who it was with and was told by Devon that he didn't know, so Anand didn't bother to ask what it was about.

Taking the HUD he was handed, Anand put it on and was told it would momentarily take him to the meeting. Within a few seconds Anand was sitting in the same garden, but across from him were what could best be described as two completely non-descript and average male, white, middle aged business men. Obviously, they were using avatars to mask their real identities. Their voices were assuredly not their own either. Anand, on the other hand, was not using a HUD that offered that option, so he was sure he appeared to them exactly as he was: just Anand. The only difference between the two men was that one had a white jacket and the other had a black jacket.

Black Jacket spoke first. "Hello, Anand. I've read through all the transcripts of the questions you've been asked. I'd like to ask you something different. Besides the large amounts of money that you've been promised, what do you have to live for? What do you care about?"

Anand was taken aback for a moment. "I'm not sure how to answer that. I'm sure you've read my file. I don't have any close family. No children. No wife or girlfriend. There's no one anyone can hurt that would cause me to be here against my will. I don't even really have any close friends these days. I'm just doing the best I can to try to make it in this world."

"You used to be somebody important. Someone who really mattered, no insult intended. You were an impressive technical architect and developer before you were all but cast out to the ranks of the drivers. Now you work technical support and live above a bar," said Black Jacket.

It wasn't news to Anand, but it still hurt to hear it out loud. "True," he said. "I was good. Damn good. I still am, but apparently not as good as the machines, so here we are. I'll answer your question. I don't have a hell of a lot to live for other than hope that I can find a way, make a decent life for myself, maybe find some happiness, maybe some fortune. I guess that's why I'm here. A chance at a different future came my way and it was better than what I was stuck doing."

White Jacket looked at Black Jacket and gave him a half nod and raised eyebrow.

Black Jacket continued, "I think you can help us. We're aware of your role in the authoring of the hardware driver root code that's resident in units across the globe. My question is, does it have any vulnerabilities?"

That was quite possibly the last question Anand was expecting to be asked. By nature, and out of pride he immediately became defensive, "No! Are you kidding me? My code is tight. I put my soul into that design. We thought of everything. That's why it's still in such broad use even though the machines took it over."

"My apologies," said Black Jacket, "I didn't mean to insinuate any lack of quality. Let me ask this a different way. What can cause the operating systems of units whose hardware components have your code in them to stop accessing those components?"

"You mean like when it receives an interrupt? Like when a hardware component completes the function it was instructed to perform it sends an interrupt in the commands to the OS to tell it to stop using it?"

"Exactly. So, what can cause an interrupt to be sent?"

"Ummm…" Anand thought for a second and replied sarcastically, "The component completed the function it was instructed to perform. That's kind of the whole idea of an interrupt. It's not that complicated."

White Jacket laughed out loud, so did Black Jacket.

"Ok," said Black Jacket. "Can anything else cause an interrupt?"

"Not much," said Anand. "A failure. An error. A corruption of some sort. That can cause the component to tell the OS to stop accessing it."

"That's it? Nothing else? Is there any way to send a signal or command to tell hardware components to shut down? Any kind of override at the root level to disable access?"

"Absolutely not." Anand looked offended. "In my country there is a saying, 'When the head is there the tail should not shake'. I even designed some security measures in the root code that could cause an interrupt if someone did try to back channel an attack of the OS through the hardware driver code. Ironically enough, when the AIs analyzed my code that was one of the areas they called 'superfluous'. Superfluous! That's about the cruelest thing you can say to a developer about their code. They said it was not needed, that security would be handled at the OS level more effectively since an attack could not be directed at the hardware layer, and even if it was it could never have any significant impact before it was detected and handled at the OS layer." He paused. "They're right about the last part, but I still think it was a wise measure."

"What do you mean, 'never have any significant impact?' What could the impact be?"

"Well," said Anand, "that's the thing. I mean, at best, if by some circumstance an attack was leveled at the hardware layer, and that's difficult to do because of where instructions to that layer can come from, the worst-case scenario is that the hardware would tell the OS to stop using it. In almost any scenario from there it was a matter of minutes before the AI running the drone or robot in concert with the OS could correct the issue and restrict the attack. In no scenario would the OS ever be in any danger because the hardware code can't send anything of detail to the OS. It simply wasn't a real threat."

"What's an example of such an attack on the hardware?"

"Well, you could flood a component with an instruction using the low-level central network channel at the core, which is practically impossible to access. But, if you did, the component would understand it was being attacked with an overload and send an interrupt."

"How long would the component be inaccessible to the OS?"

"Hard to say," said Anand. "Maybe a minute? A couple of minutes at best until the AIs figure out what was going on, shut it down, and the affected units reset the drivers. Of course, this would only apply to typical Americorp drones, not the orbital defenses. Those were all built by the Israelis. Those dudes are far too paranoid to use my code."

"A couple of minutes? That's it?" asked White Jacket.

"I can work with that," said Black Jacket. "Anand, can you show us how to do what we just discussed? Can you show us how to send an instruction overload to the hardware drivers over the central network, assuming we can access it?"

"I can. May I ask, will that consider my job here complete?"

"It would, Anand, as far as I know," said Black Jacket.

"There's just one small problem that I can see," hesitated Anand, "If you use what I show you how to do, it won't take long for the AIs to trace it back to me. There aren't many people that would know enough to do this. I'll be hunted immediately. That doesn't sound like a great outcome for me. Money is no good if you're dead and can't spend it."

Black Jacket looked at him for a moment, then looked at White Jacket, and then changed appearance into a middle-aged man that Anand immediately recognized from recent newsvids and by reputation. "My name is Ryland Grey. I swear, that's who I really am. I can't tell you everything, but I can tell you that if you help us, and we're successful, you'll have nothing to worry about from Americorp. If we fail, you're right. You're in trouble. That's why after you help us, you need to leave the Americas immediately. Go somewhere quiet, that doesn't have good relations with Americorp, and enjoy your money. But get away from here. You technically will not have broken any laws. You will have just shared information about what the corps consider outdated technology. The people that sent you here must have some pull. All you need to do is get outside the reach of Americorp fast. Anand, all I can tell you is that we could change the game. We could change the game that put someone of your talents out of a job. More importantly, we can save millions of lives, possibly hundreds of millions, but we need your help."

Anand thought about it for a moment then nodded slowly but deliberately. "I still have no idea who brought me here, or how they knew I might be able to help, but it makes sense to me now in some bizarre way. I'll help you. I'm not doing it out of some sense of idealism. Mostly, the idea of taking a swing back at the corps is something I've dreamed about for years. It would be wonderful to do it with the very code I wrote that they are still using long after they fired me. That doesn't mean I'm turning down the money."

Anand smiled.

Chapter Forty-Four - Kimberly

Kimberly could barely remember the last time she attended a live Mayhem match. The Bay Area Kinetics were on the verge of making the finals for the first time in the franchise history. Despite her busy schedule, when the team owner contacted Kimberly to ask if she would like to see the match from a private suite it was too hard to say no. It wasn't that Kimberly was even much of a Mayhem fan, but the entire area was abuzz about it. She also couldn't be happier for her friend, Meena, who owned the team. Meena had managed to completely turn around the franchise which had been nearly in last place just a few seasons ago.

For the first half of the match she enjoyed a couple glasses of wine while just being in awe at the excitement of the crowd. Neither team on the field below was giving up anything and the match remained scoreless. It was hard not to be amazed at the athleticism of the players even though she still winced almost every play at one brutal hit or another. Meena was more than happy to offer a play-by-play which included deep insight on each player.

"I hear you may know something about a couple of the top prospects in the upcoming draft?" fished Meena as she handed Kimberly another glass of wine. "Rumor has it you authorized a temporary release of two top prospects to work with Immersive Magic? Care to let a friend in on what they are doing?"

"Ha!" laughed Kimberly out loud. "I honestly have very little idea and I couldn't tell you even if I did. I was doing a favor for a friend. A friend who has subsequently found himself in a great deal of trouble as I have no doubt you know."

"Yes, I saw that. It's a shame. I know Ryland. He's a good person. I have a hard time believing it. It's tragic what happened to his family."

"Tragic. Yes," It was all Kimberly could say. She wanted to believe it was just tragedy. Coincidence, maybe?

"Still," pushed Meena, "the young man: Elijah. Our scouts are high on him even though he's a bit smaller than average for the league. They tell me there's some real ingenuity in his play, that he could make a great future on-field leader, and maybe even a franchise player. Any insights you can offer?"

"Sports is your thing, Meena. I'm a politician and businesswoman. All I can tell you is I'd look at the girl as well. I wouldn't draft one without the other if I were you. From the little I saw and what I know, they make a great team."

"Good to know," Meena responded before she erupted in excitement, "GO, GO, GO, YES!" She leapt to her feet clapping and screaming. The Kinetics had just made a huge play that took them deep into opposing territory and just twenty meters from the goals. Kimberly clapped and cheered right along with her even though she had not been paying enough attention to have seen the play.

Play was stopped momentarily. One of the opposing players had taken a round kick to the head and wasn't getting up immediately. Meena excused herself as she went to contact her General Manager for an update on what the coach was planning.

Kimberly stared out at the field and the crowd. She took a sip of her wine. She hoped the injured player was OK.

"It can be a brutal game, but the players all know exactly what the risks are, and they take them knowingly. It's the best chance they have to succeed," said a deep voice from behind her that she immediately recognized.

"Mr. Chairman," said Kimberly as she turned around. "What a pleasure. I had no idea you would be here."

Nicodemus was dressed formally, as usual, in a dark suit. He was holding a glass of champagne and acting quite casual and charming compared to his normal all-business demeanor. "You're not the only one that is friends with Meena. Her empire extends well beyond sports. I'm also quite a fan of the sport, though I don't have as much time for it as I would like. It's a pleasure to see you in person for a change."

"Likewise, Mr. Chairman."

"Please, it's just Nic here."

"'Just Nic'?" laughed Kimberly. "I'm not sure I can do that, but I'll try."

"Please, may I?" Nicodemus motioned at the seat next to Kimberly.

"Of course," she said. He sat down.

"Are you enjoying the match?" he asked.

"I am, though I admit I don't quite follow it all."

Just then the Kinetics snapped the ball and looked momentarily like they were going to be crushed when a last-minute pass sent the ball to a player within a few meters of the goal. She got leveled by the goaltender, but not before she fired the ball into one of the one-point targets. It put them on the scoreboard and broke the scoreless tie that had endured for most of the match. The crowd erupted, as did Meena and most of her guests.

"Good," said Nicodemus. "A stalemate is no way to live. Kim, I'm not here entirely on personal business."

She knew something like this was coming. She set down her glass of wine. She should not have had a third. Her job did not allow for her to have anything but a clear head and now she was talking to the chairman of Americorp.

"What can I do for you, sir? I mean... Nic?" she smiled.

"I've spent the past day visiting as many of the regional directors and larger shareholders as I can in person. I have no doubt you've seen early drafts of the revision to ARDOS that I commissioned which will change the rules regarding driver protections. It is not lost on me that many are questioning the necessity of this change. It is based not only on highly reliable models that impact our future, but also reliable intelligence on the potential urgency of such a measure being required. I'm here because I would like to know if I have your support."

Kimberly was immediately uncomfortable. "Well, sir... Nic, it's hard for me to comment on a measure whose final language I haven't yet read. Any change to ARDOS is not something to take lightly. I also have the utmost faith in you and your leadership of the corporation. While I know I'll want my office to review the final details, I'm sure that if it is as you say, it must be needed. Most of the drivers seem harmless to me. It is just a very few that cause us problems and the laws already allow for us to act against them. Are you able to tell me what has changed that makes this necessary now?"

"I cannot. It's highly classified. All I can tell you is that we could find ourselves at grave risk. Foreign corporations are arming drivers in this country and taking aim at our orbital defenses and interstellar missions. The moment may come sooner than you would like, and without the time to think extensively about it, that you will have to choose who you wish to support. I recall backing you as the youngest regional director that we have ever appointed. You've been exemplary. Your region is flourishing. I hope that will continue, as will your leadership of it."

Suddenly Nicodemus was far less charming and back to all business. Kimberly knew exactly what she was being told. It wasn't a question she was being asked. She was being given a directive. It was still a choice, but it wasn't one she wanted to make.

She nodded. "I understand, Mr. Chairman."

"Excellent," he said as he finished his champagne. "Let's talk about the additional capital investments you've requested for upgrading your agricultural drone force."

Chapter Forty-Five - Ryland

"It could work," said Kelly. "And we're running out of options."

They were once again gathered in the virtual cabin. Most of the same people were there as had been in the first meeting, but there were a few others as well. Ryland assumed the new people were leaders of some of the other driver communities. He just finished explaining his plan to them.

"It assumes a lot," said Mia. "Not the least of which is whether our contact is willing to comply with what we would be asking of him and that he actually goes through with it. He'd be putting everything at risk to do so: his job, his life, his family, everything. It also lessens the time we will have to send our people into deeper hiding and diminishes the forces we will have to protect them. It puts the lives of our soldiers at significant risk. There will undoubtedly be casualties."

"Casualties my men and women are willing to accept, ma'am," said Kelly.

"I understand your willingness and appreciate your dedication," said Mia, "but I have to look at the big picture. Is this our best option? I don't know. If it works, it's what we've been after for decades. If it fails, all that work will have been for nothing."

"It will all be for nothing soon enough anyway," argued Kelly. "They aren't going to tolerate us much longer. It's now or never."

"You're willing to lead the attack on the central data center?" asked Mia. "It's a fight you can't win. Nobody could."

"Ryland doesn't need me to win. You heard the plan. We can do this."

"Is there anything else that you need from us?" asked Mia.

"Well," hesitated Ryland, "there is one other thing I haven't figured out yet. For the plan to work, I told you that I need to get back into my game studio. Only from there can I access the new, experimental military drones we've been working with and get control of them. Unfortunately, I haven't yet figured out how to get back in. I'm still working on that."

"Why not go back in the same way you got out last time?" asked Mayson.

"That won't work. They'll have figured that out by now and be looking for it. There are DNA scans on every entry door in addition to facial recognition. Even if I used repliskin to look like someone else, the DNA scan will flag me in a second. Still, there must be a way in."

"We have tech that will disrupt a DNA scanner," said Kelly.

"No good," replied Ryland. "A disruption would be noticed by security and they'd come looking for the cause."

"What about taking over central security for the facility and shutting it down from there?" asked Mayson.

"I don't think so," sighed Ryland. "The AIs would pick up on it and have units dispatched in no time. We need something more subtle; something that won't arouse suspicion long enough for us to have the time we'll need once we get in."

"Entry security for most buildings is automatically disabled in the event of certain emergency situations," said a dark-skinned woman who had been sitting near the virtual fireplace. "Fires. Flooding. Earthquakes. When sensors detect specific events the systems automatically disable certain security measures in the interest of getting people out safely."

"Gentlemen," Kelly looked at Ryland and Mayson, "let me introduce my friend, Chloe. She's a structural engineer, and a damn good one from what she's told me."

"Chloe," Ryland offered his hand to shake hers, "pleased to meet you. What are you proposing? That we start a fire at the studio? I'm not saying no. I like the thinking. I'm just trying to figure how we do it without killing people or damaging the equipment that we need."

"Actually, I was thinking earthquake," she said.

"Earthquake?" asked Mayson.

"Well, not an actual earthquake," said Chloe. "We just need to make the sensors think it's an earthquake. If we can create an explosion near enough to campus and possibly a bit below ground-level, it could give the appearance of an earthquake just long enough to trick the sensors. When they figure out that it was a false alarm, they won't think anything of it. It will be business as usual if we can make it look like a legitimate accident under the scrutiny of an hour or so. Maybe some kind of construction incident?"

"So, you need a bomb?" Kelly had a big grin. "I can help with that."

Mia's face remained expressionless as she considered it all. Everyone was looking at her for a decision. She put her hands together against her face as if in prayer and closed her eyes for a moment. She opened her eyes and looked around the room.

"Start working out the details. Kelly, I want a plan for the data center assault including how you plan to get our forces there and in position without being detected. Chloe, I have someone you can work with on a plan for getting a charge near the Immersive Magic facility." She looked at several of the others. "I want you all to immediately begin having your communities disperse into smaller groups as much as possible. Divide your arms and supplies. Groups should be no larger than twenty, give or take a few to keep families together. Have them seek deeper cover and do it quickly. Get remote, deep, covered, but separate from large groups. It's our best chance if this doesn't work. Don't forget to have them all bring HUDs and to be prepared for when we need them." She turned to Ryland. "I suggest you get ready with what you need. We can assist with getting you into the city."

Ryland nodded, "Thank you, Mia. I won't let you down."

"It's not me you'd be letting down, Mr. Grey. It's all of us. But I don't put this all on you. You've given us an idea, a hope in the face of a problem we would have faced even if odd circumstances had not placed you in our company. I've been dreaming of a better tomorrow since I was just a child. Since my parents and everything I had was ripped from me because of what society has become. I've spent my entire life trying to find a way to change things. So far, I've only found a way to make life a little better for us drivers, but also to put us in a position should the opportunity present itself to really change things. You've offered us that opportunity. Now it's up to all of us to make it work. Good luck, Mr. Grey."

Chapter Forty-Six - Ryland

"How are you feeling?" asked Mayson. It was getting late and the fire was dying down. He had poured them each a drink but skipped the ice this time.

"Good, I think." Ryland was tired. These past few days were getting to him, and he had yet to really have a chance to grieve for his wife and daughters. The roller coaster that took him from the pinnacle of modern success to criminal and revolutionary leader was more than anyone should be asked to handle without completely cracking. A mission of revenge kept him going.

"Mia confirmed that all resources are a go. This is happening," said Mayson.

"What is the final plan for the detonation near the studio?" asked Ryland.

"As you pointed out in the follow-up meeting with Chloe," Mayson said, "they are doing some significant construction to expand the complex on the east side, not far from your studio. Chloe says that will work perfectly. There is an area being currently dug out for construction so we can get a charge in there low. We're in luck that construction is apparently slowed a bit right now due to a materials supply issue according to our intelligence. There shouldn't be much in the way of drone or human activity to avoid. Kelly wants to send a couple of his people with us, but I told him that we can handle it. We need every person we can get at the data center or protecting drivers. Chloe is going to make sure we set the charge in the right place. I'm going to be your eyes and ears outside the studio to give you an early warning at any time if it looks like they are on to you. The rest of the job is yours."

"When does Kelly think he can have his forces in place?" asked Ryland.

"Soon. They'll be ready in time to begin their assault by the time you are in the studio and have access to your drones. He's optimistic, though I don't know if that's real optimism or if he's just happy to have a challenging target. It's hard to say with him. The good news is that he thinks they can really catch them off guard. He says the entire data center is an impregnable fortress buried in a mountain, but it's designed to anticipate an aerial or orbital attack. A ground attack is something the corporation simply doesn't think is feasible, so they haven't prepared for it in the same ways. It's still an impossible task to win, but he believes they can give them a run for their money for longer than they would expect."

"Excellent. I'm glad someone is optimistic," said Ryland. "I'm nervous as hell. None of this seems real to me, Mays. I keep waiting to wake up and find out it's all been some crazy nightmare, but the more I think about it, I was living in a dream world. I ignored the larger world around me because I had the perfect life and lived in the world of my games. I knew, deep inside, what was going on with the world, with the drivers, with where the power in the corporations was really taking us, but I didn't care. Now I'm only doing what I am because I was suddenly given no other choice, because I was put in a corner, and because I want revenge. I'm pretty sure that makes me a horrible person."

Mayson nodded and laughed. "No, Ry, it doesn't make you a horrible person. It makes you normal. I'm guessing 'normal' isn't a word frequently used to describe you. When you have it good, it's hard to let go of the façade, or to alter the life you have in order to fix what's broken. People are willing to recognize problems, talk about them, and to make small contributions. But to go all in on changing a system that is benefitting you? Well, that's a hard thing to do. What matters right now is that you made a choice."

"Maybe I chose to be stupid and suicidal and it's simply because I'm angry and have nothing left to lose?"

"Freedom's just another word for nothing left to lose, so I guess that makes me Bobby McGee. Well, OK, maybe it is partially because you're angry. But I don't think you chose to be stupid. I think you chose to finally see what was really happening because you didn't have the façade supporting you anymore, and you decided to help change things. You've come up with an idea to make a difference, one that will change things drastically for everyone, not just get back at those that screwed you over… if it works. If it doesn't, well, we're all dead."

"So, no pressure, Bobby?" asked Ryland.

"None at all," replied Mayson. "Let's try to get some rest. We leave soon."

Chapter Forty-Seven - Sheridan

Hunter drones stalked through the trees. Aerial drones hummed over their heads then darted ahead, surrounding the target. Sheridan was certain the remote cabin was where they would find their prey. Given the sophisticated optical defenses of the location he had no doubt that he and his forces were being tracked by security systems. It didn't matter. He had the place surrounded for several kilometers in every direction. Nobody was getting out.

This was, by far, the most units he had ever involved in an arrest. The overkill was almost laughable. All this was for one person accused of treason by an algorithm, for evidence that was so classified that even he had not seen it.

Sheridan was riding in an autonomous all-terrain military jeep with the top and sides down. He and his lieutenant were guarded only by the steel and polymer rails. The vehicle hummed along almost silently except for the broken branches and the rumble of the rocks under the tires. He much preferred hovercraft, but in this terrain it would be harder to maneuver amongst the trees. If it wasn't for the seriousness of his mission, he would almost find the drive pleasant. The smell of the pines was amazing and the fresh, damp, clean air was stimulating. It really made him feel alive.

The jeep glided along behind the hunters and aerials as they closed in on the cabin. His HUD told him they had detected at least a few dozen cameras and hundreds of sensors by now. He wasn't sure whether to expect a confrontation when they arrived, a surrender, or if the subjects would be in hiding. He really hoped it wasn't a confrontation. He just wanted this to be over and clean.

Using his HUD, he ordered each of the four hunter groups approaching from different directions to halt, spread out, and take up positions just shy of the cabin while sending one unit from each group in closer. He sent the aerials in ahead of them and watched the video feeds as they left the trees and moved over the property. There was the cabin and front porch, a barn, and the firepit area. It looked like the fire was still smoldering, just barely. They were probably still sleeping, but he was not taking any chances.

"I want two hunters ready to enter the barn from each door and the other two will to enter the cabin. Enter only on my command. Capture. Don't kill."

The drones took up their positions as instructed. Sheridan's vehicle moved down the driveway and pulled up near the firepit. He and his lieutenant got out of the jeep and walked towards the cabin. They could both see the video feeds from all the drones on their HUDs. Both of them drew their own energy weapons which were set to stun. He nodded and gave the order to enter.

With quickness and efficiency, the hunters broke down doors and swept into the buildings. Their scanners rapidly examined every inch of the rooms as the aerials flew inside after them and began scanning and recording everything in sight.

The barn was full of tools, both modern and antique, and piles of firewood. There was also an antique Jeep Wrangler that appeared to be in process of being restored. There was a more modern, but small personal hovercraft and two antique motorcycles. The missing horse from the Tahoe ranch was also there, lazily munching on some hay until it was startled by the drones and began braying and bucking. There was no sign of human life.

Inside the cabin the main room was vacant. There were some empty glasses and coffee mugs on the table, but no one in the room. The hunters swept to the other rooms, bursting down doors to bathrooms and bedrooms. Nobody was there. Two of the beds appeared slept in. One of the hunters scanned and found a hatch that led to a storage basement, but all they found were cases of wine, whiskey, gin, food, and other general supplies including water purifiers, batteries, and some medical supplies. The far back of the basement had a rack full of weapons. There was nothing illegal, but enough to put up a good fight. Sheridan looked over the video of that inventory carefully. It did not look like anything significant was missing. It was what he imagined a typical "doomsday prepper" stash would look like.

For ten more minutes the drones scoured every millimeter of the property and buildings using all the technology they had at their disposal. Nothing. No humans here. They had even adjusted the scan tolerances to detect any shielding that may be in use to hide bio-signs, but they came up empty. No tunnels. No secret compartments. The horse was the only living thing besides insects and birds on the property.

He walked over to the firepit, knelt, and held his hand over the coals. They were still warm if not hot. "He was here."

"Yes, sir," replied his lieutenant. "DNA scans confirm he was here recently. There are traces of him all around. There are also traces of his brother and some of his brother's family, but that's to be expected since it's their property. I can confirm that we've been monitoring the airspace of this area for hours and we have seen nothing leave. They must have gone on foot, or at least by land, sir. They can't have gotten far. I'll have the drones begin trace and track procedures."

Dammit, thought Sheridan. How was he going to explain this to his superiors? They weren't going to be happy. "OK, but I also want this entire place re-examined. Every square millimeter. Up, down, sideways. We need to be damn sure they aren't here."

Sheridan walked inside the cabin. He paced around looking at all the little detail. Despite his frustration he had to admit to himself how much he loved this place. It was fantastic - all the wood, antique decorations and furniture, thick rugs, and a real, wood-burning fireplace. He could really be happy hanging out here for a while. There were pictures on the wall next to some Native American art, mostly they were pictures of the family. They had been stylized in old black and white to keep with the feel of the décor.

The kitchen table had two empty tumbler glasses on it, both covered in fingerprints, and a bottle of bourbon labeled 'Widow Jane' that was less than half full. Next to the bottle was a piece of paper with some handwriting on it. Sheridan picked it up and read aloud, "Now you have to kiss me - RG"

Son of a bitch. He found himself hating this guy but loving him at the same time.

Chapter Forty-Eight - Ryland

Nearly two hours before Sheridan's arrival at the cabin, Mayson's security systems had detected the early approach of the aerial drones. Without hesitation and taking almost nothing with them, Ryland and Mayson made their way on foot to a small fishing shack about a kilometer away near a pond. The shack was tiny. It was just enough space for some basic fishing equipment and general supplies. It looked like something out of an old novel- seemingly about to fall over but also sturdy as if it had weathered centuries of storms. Mayson scanned in on a DNA sensor on the wall, bent down to move a mat on the floor, and pulled at a leather strap on the to lift a hatch that exposed a ladder leading down into darkness.

"Where are we going?" asked Ryland.

"Trust me, Ry," said Mayson. "This will be fun."

As soon as they started into the tunnel, lighting turned on from their motion. Mayson explained to Ryland that he and his wife had used black market labor and private construction drones to build an escape tunnel. "Just in case... you never know." He smiled. When they reached the floor of the tunnel there were four battery powered motorcycles waiting for them. They each hopped on one of them, while Mayson programmed the other two to follow.

The tunnel was mostly straight and stretched for almost three kilometers. It was hard for Ryland to believe that this was his brother, and that Mayson had gone to all this effort. It was almost like Ryland didn't even really know the guy. As they zipped down the tunnel the lights on the sides would illuminate as they approached and turn off as they passed until they came to the end where a gate opened, and Ryland could see sunlight. When they emerged, they were in the middle of a secluded glade surrounded by trees. The gate was surrounded by an outcropping of rock and looked like a rusted mining plate on the outside.

"Seriously," said Ryland, "I can't believe you built that. I mean, it's seriously cool. Super cool. I'm jealous. I don't have a secret tunnel. I really wish I did. But I can't believe you actually built it."

"It cost enough. I'm just glad I can finally tell my wife that she was right. It was totally worth it. We argued for months about whether we really needed it."

Within moments they set off toward the western edge of the forest. They programmed the other two cycles to head North until they ran out of charge, just to add an extra trail to follow. They were able to see on their HUDs most of the raid on the cabin that happened shortly after they left from video surveillance cameras Mayson had on the property. They had just narrowly made it out before the hunter drones arrived.

After a short drive to the edge of the woods, they made their way to a small town where they were met by a hovercraft and Chloe.

"This was a little quicker than we were expecting to be ready, but we're good to go," she told them. "I guess it's show time."

They boarded the craft which made straight for the Bay Area. They landed about a half kilometer from the sprawling Entertainment Division complex at a small landing pad using hacked credentials that listed them as a construction inspection team. They had all changed clothes to look the part and were using Repliskin to appear as different people. Chloe was using the identity of a similarly built construction director. Mayson had been modeled to look like an AI scientist that was known to be on sabbatical. Ryland had been given a similar appearance to the Director of Operations for the Entertainment Division complex, but not similar enough to trigger AI duplicate analysis from surveillance video.

Chloe carried the explosive charge in a small backpack. She also carried a short, but powerful energy rifle concealed under her jacket, as did Mayson. Ryland protested bringing one of his own, but eventually gave in.

Kelly popped up on their HUDs. "OK, team, let's do this. Mayson, proceed to the grounds at the front of the studio. Find yourself a shady tree and just hang out like you're zoned out on your HUD. Chloe, you know what to do. Head down into the construction zone and look for a good place to plant the charge then get out of there. You can activate the explosive from your HUD when you're clear. Ryland, head to the maintenance entrance we identified. Wait about ten meters away from it and when the charges go off you should be able to walk in and take the tunnels from there. If all goes well, it should disable the security access for a few minutes. My teams are in place and we'll begin our assault as soon as Ryland confirms he's in the building and has access to the tech he needs. You all ready to do this?"

"Ready," said Chloe. Mayson and Ryland echoed her.

They nodded at each other and split up towards their destinations. Given the size of the campus, it took nearly eight minutes for each of them to get in place.

The construction area was nearest, so Chloe was the first to get to her position. The area was surrounded by construction barriers but since no work was being done now there were no people or active drones on the site. It was essentially a twenty-meter-deep crater that stretched for hundreds of meters along the campus. Large polymer pallets were stacked with building materials and several shipping containers sat at the edge. A small army of construction drones sat idle in perfectly organized rows. The far wall, up against the campus, was jagged rock.

"It actually looks like they have already been blasting this rock as part of the work they are doing," she said on their closed comm channel.

"Is that a bad thing?" asked Ryland. "Does that mean the sensors will ignore a blast from there?"

"No," said Chloe, "I don't think so. Scheduled blasts are communicated so that they are ignored. I think we'll be good, and it may help with the amount of time it will take for them to realize it wasn't just a construction accident."

"I hope you're right," replied Ryland.

Ryland watched on his HUD as Chloe sized up the wall and picked a spot. It was at least eighteen meters down below ground level. She opened the backpack and placed the charge. According to Kelly, the damage wouldn't be that significant, but it would be enough to trigger the sensors. Of course, the hole Chloe was standing in would suddenly be a lot bigger.

Chloe looked incredibly casual as she walked briskly out of the construction area and climbed a ladder to get back to ground level. She was probably already at a safe distance, but she continued walking for about another fifty meters then stepped behind a retaining wall. "OK, we're good to go."

"Everyone's in position. Light it up," said Kelly over the comm.

"OK, here we go," said Chloe. She selected the detonation command on her HUD. Nothing happened. She tried several more times. Still nothing. "Shit. It's not working."

"What's wrong, Chloe?" asked Kelly.

"I don't know," said Chloe, "It's not activating. Something must be interfering with the signal. Dammit. I don't know. Maybe construction zones use signal dampening fields to avoid accidental explosions? Maybe the depth and bedrock are interfering. I just don't know."

"Do we need to scrub the mission?" asked Mayson.

"Give me a moment," said Kelly. "Let me think about this."

"No," said Chloe solemnly, "I got this."

"Chloe, what are you doing?" asked Kelly urgently. "Chloe, report."

Chloe left her position, sprinted toward the ladder and practically leaped down it. They could all see on their HUDs that Chloe kept trying to activate the explosive, but still nothing.

"Look," said Chloe as she ran, "at this point it doesn't matter if it was a malfunction or not. Everyone is in place and this is either going to happen or it isn't." She ran towards the charge.

"Chloe, stop! We'll figure something else out!" shouted Ryland into the comm.

"Chloe, you are ordered to stop," said Kelly. "We can fix this. Do you hear me?! Stop now!"

She ran the final stretch to the wall. "Look," she said over the comm, "I might live a long time in hiding with all of you if we fail. We don't have an alternate plan. I'd rather die knowing it meant something and giving everyone a chance for something better. I'm OK with that. Too many people are counting on this plan working. Don't screw this up."

"Chloe, no!" screamed Ryland into the comm.

Chloe reached up and activated the charge manually. The sound was deafening. The explosion erupted sending rock in every direction after the large initial pulse of energy and fire that was almost blinding.

Small chunks of rock started to fall to the ground. Smoke and dust billowed from the hole in the ground, making it impossible to see anything.

Ryland heard the earthquake alarm sound and an electronic alert from the door in front of him. The access controls were down, but he just stood there, processing what Chloe had just done.

"My god… Chloe…" said Mayson over the comm.

Ryland was frozen. This wasn't how the plan was supposed to start. Chloe was dead, just like that.

"That was a damn good woman that just gave her life for your plan, Ryland," said Kelly over the comm. "I don't have to agree with what she just did, but it's done, and she just gave you the chance you asked for. Now isn't the time to freeze or grieve. Go make her sacrifice worth something. Move!"

Ryland lifted his head up and stared at the smoke and residual flames by the construction site. He fought back tears. "Thank you, Chloe. Thank you. I won't let you down."

H went to the door and opened it. He walked in unobstructed. All security was off for the moment. He entered the tunnel to the complex and closed the door behind him.

Chapter Forty-Nine - Kelly

Kelly did not hesitate. "Hey boys and girls," he broadcast over the comm to his team. "This is your fairy godmother. Cinderella is at the ball. I repeat, Cinderella is at the ball. Let's get this party started. Team One and Team Two, you know what to do. It's time to light it up."

Over the past twenty-four hours several hundred driver soldiers and even a few hacked black-market military drones had slowly taken up positions. They came in just a few at a time from every direction and regrouped at key points surrounding the entrances to the Central Data Center. Most of the men and women were ex-military. The rest had trained into the role over the past few years. They had come in slowly to keep motion limited to what it might look like from local wildlife to avoid thresholds that might trip sensors. They used technology and good old-fashioned human stealth and camouflage to avoid being seen by surveillance. It wasn't that hard. The data center simply didn't anticipate a small ground attack or that individuals would ever be a threat, so the defenses simply weren't designed for that.

By now, Kelly had teams in six different positions around the facility with about thirty to fifty people in each team. They were heavily armed including some small ballistic and energy weapons batteries. Even though they had access to some mini-nukes, Kelly knew they could not bring them in without being detected. Instead they had to stick with small, but powerful missiles and a pretty impressive array of explosives.

Built inside of a mountain, the Americorp Central Data Center was mostly located deep underground beneath hundreds of feet of rock. The main entrance doors were massively thick and made of steel. There was an even larger and thicker wall with its own doors about a hundred meters in front of the main doors. The wall encircled nearly half the mountain. A wide road, also surrounded by steel walls, led to the main doors. Weapons batteries sat atop turrets all along the walls. Anything that got close which wasn't supposed to be there would be obliterated within seconds. Given its remote location and the difficult surrounding terrain, the primary defenses were at the top of the mountain. An extensive array of ground-to-air missiles and energy weapons sat pointed up at the sky, along with three shield generators that could keep the Data Center safe from even a heavy attack for hours or days. It was designed to make the effort to penetrate the walls too much to be worth it by the time you could actually get in.

Kelly did not need to take it or to get in. "Team One and Team Two, start with heavy weapons on the shield generators. Fire for a few minutes, then move position randomly by a hundred meters and do it again. Repeat until I tell you to stop. Those generators are heavily armored, so you won't do much damage, but keep firing. Team Three and Team Four, you know your targets. Each of you needs to take out one of those two aerial drone launch bays a few hundred meters above the doors. Target the mountain just above them. If we don't take those out of commission, we'll have a swarm on us in moments and this will be one short operation. Teams Five and Six, see what kind of damage you can do to the weapons turrets and try to take out a couple if you can. On my mark boys and girls… three, two, one, mark!"

Instantly the sky that had been filled with only the sound of calm breezes and birds was lit up with missiles and energy fire as the teams began pounding their targets. Explosions rocked the shield generators and echoed throughout the valley. Rock began pouring down the top of the mountain after being shot up into the sky. Missile batteries hammered the rock all around the launch bays causing an avalanche to begin falling. Energy weapons pulsed at the steel of the bay doors, having some effect, but the hundreds of tons of rock that was beginning to block the launch doors was what really mattered.

Within milliseconds of their initial firing salvos, alarms began sounding. The gun and missile turrets of the data center security systems whipped to attention, tracked the sources of the assault and began firing in those directions as they scanned for more detailed targets. Bullets and energy pulses rained down on the trees surrounding the mountain. The driver teams took cover; they had taken up good positions behind bedrock outcrops that limited their exposure to direct lines of fire.

"Teams Three and Four, nice work. It looks like their birds will be grounded for a while. Start giving us a hand with those weapons towers," yelled Kelly into his comm. He was embedded with Team Six. Pulling a heavy energy rifle off of his back, he climbed up the side of a boulder to join the line of men and women crouched down and firing on the turrets. They were at least a hundred and fifty meters away from the nearest turret, but the barrage of bullets it was sending at them made it feel like it was right in front of them. He targeted the tower and began firing. "Keep it up, people," he said into the comm. "We don't have long to do as much damage as we can to those towers before there will be ground drones coming out of those doors to say hello to us and tell us bedtime stories. The sentinel drones from further out on the road will be here any second. Teams Five and Six, get ready for those. Teams Three and Four keep focused on the towers."

"Sir," came a man's voice over the comm. It was the squad leader from Team One, "We just sent our third volley at the shield generators. We're causing a lot of commotion and some surface damage, but it's going to take a lot more to take those things out."

"Just keep firing and moving. Firing and moving. You're doing great," said Kelly.

"Sir," came another voice, this one female, "we have sentinels about thirty seconds out."

"OK team, you heard the lieutenant. Positions." Kelly turned to see the sentinel drones bearing down on them. They were taller and less graceful than typical hunter drones, but they were armed to the teeth. They ran like awkward, headless humans but using gyroscopes that gave them a balance that defied their gate. They held their arms outstretched across their broad chests in the direction of Kelly's team as bullets began pouring from where hands should have been. Ballistic fire began to shred the forest and bounce off rock sending enough dust into the air to make it hard to see. He heard some of his people screaming.

"Don't waste your bullets on their chests, people, aim for the legs," shouted Kelly. He leaped out from his position, rolled to the right, popped up, aimed, and opened fire.

Chapter Fifty - Ryland

As fast as he could go, Ryland made his way down the tunnel to the studio. He was able to enter through a maintenance door from the tunnel just outside of his office and the arena. He made it in before the security controls reset on all the doors. While it was certain that all his normal access codes to systems had been revoked, he had set up backdoors years ago.

Lying down his rifle, he sat at a control panel and began initializing the arena and activating one of the prototype-drones they'd been working on.

"Hands in the air!" The voice was Kira's. He looked up. She was standing there, holding the rifle he had just set down by the door. It was pointed at his head. He put his hands up.

"Kira, it's me!" he said. He then realized he still had the repliskin activated.

Kira recognized the voice immediately but gave him a skeptical look. "What was the first game you made me play when I interviewed to work with you?" she asked.

Ryland smiled, remembering. "It was *Duke Nukem Forever* from the early 2000's. I made you play it for hours and then told you that your job with me was to produce the exact opposite of that piece of garbage. I told you that if you ever gave me anything less than its polar opposite you were fired."

"Oh my god, Ryland!" she dropped the rifle to her side and stepped in to embrace him. "It's so good to see you. What the hell is going on?"

Ryland took a moment to deactivate the repliskin which cleanly disintegrated exposing his real face. "It's a long story, Kira, that I don't have time for now. There's a lot at stake and more people counting on me than you would believe."

"OK," said Kira. "Skip the backstory. What are you doing and how can I help? Oh, and skip the part where you tell me to walk away or about how much trouble I could get in. That'll just waste time."

Ryland knew she was not going to take no for an answer. "Alright, so I'm activating one of the prototype human-controlled military drones. I'm going into the arena to pilot it." He pulled a small, crystalline object from his pocket. "The drone has to get this to the Americorp regional headquarters in San Francisco. We have to break in, get to a command console behind the firewall, upload the code and execute it."

"So, just break into a highly secured facility to commit one of the highest crimes possible? That's it?" she laughed. "And then what? It clears your name? We finally get to go back to normal?"

"No. If it works, things will never be normal again. But I think the world will be a better place for everyone." Ryland said the last part gravely.

"When do we start?" The voice was Eli's. Kira and Ryland turned to see Eli and Tessa standing in the door.

"How long have you been there?" asked Ryland.

"Long enough," said Tessa. "You can skip the 'you'll get in trouble' speech with us too, including any of that 'you have your whole lives ahead of you' bullshit. Neither of us have ever had anything to lose, and you had me at 'a better place for everyone.' Sounds like you need some game players. How many of these human-controlled drones do you have?"

Ryland paused and looked around at all three of them. "I'm only agreeing to this because I don't have time to argue you with you. And to be honest, I could really use the help. I'm not in the athletic shape I used to be, and people are literally dying right now to give me... us... the time to make this happen. The three of you helping will increase our chances of success significantly. There are more than enough of the prototype drones. I'm going to activate two more of them and give one the data crystal. Eli, Tess, you two will join me in the arena. We're going to use the interface suits to pilot the drones.

"This is really what the arena was developed for. The military wanted the ability to enable humans, in certain rare but critical circumstances, to be able to pilot high powered drones more effectively. Some situations still require human intelligence on the scene, but haptics and in-place movement of operators limited the effectiveness. The arena was developed so it could simulate the real-world environment the drone was in and pass that on to the human operator to move way beyond simulated haptics and VR. As a pilot, you will really feel like you're in the environment. A wall is a wall, a window is a window, water will feel like water, but it will all be the drone in the real world. Response times between pilot actions and the drone are within milliseconds, even over massive distances. We developed this technology as a prototype to compensate for humans not being able to undergo FTL travel."

"Holy shit," said Eli.

"Yup, it's pretty awesome," said Ryland. "I'll explain more on the way. Right now, we need to suit up. It will be just like it's been for you in the sims, only this time, what you are doing is happening in the real world through the drone you are controlling. The drones have human-like frames but can fly over moderate distances. They can be at the target in minutes. Kira, you can help most by being here. Keep an eye on things from the control center. Keep others out of here. Give us a heads up if it looks like anyone is on to us and stall them if they are. Don't do anything stupid or get yourself killed. My brother Mayson is outside the building and watching for security. Mays? You copy? I just linked Kira into our comm channel."

"I copy, Ry," said Mayson. "Kira, I got eyes on the outside."

"Game on!" exclaimed Eli. "Let's do this."

Ryland tapped on the control pad on his desk. Through the windows from the office they could see out into the arena. A bay door opened at one side and three incredibly impressive human-style, military drones emerged and walked in. They were tall, gleaming metal, heavily armored. Each one possessed a small arsenal of weapons. "Let's go."

A few minutes later the three of them had their VIHM suits on and were in the arena which still glowed like a soft red and black grid. Ryland inserted the data crystal into the drone he would be controlling. The drones marched back through the bay doors which closed behind them.

"They'll be on the roof top in a moment. Once they are, we'll initialize. The arena will become what they are seeing. Your perspective will be as if you are one of them. You can move around this arena as if you are them and it will shift and move to represent their reality of their physical space. Even when they are flying, your suit and this room will have you in the air, though you won't ever crash into a wall. There are a lot of algorithms at play to make that the case. Your experience will be as if it were all real. Play as though it is."

"Unbelievable," uttered Tessa.

"What's the plan?" asked Eli.

"We'll pilot the drones to regional HQ," said Ryland. "It's well guarded and armed, but the drones use a stealth tech that will make them hard to detect until we are practically on the building. I have no doubt there will be defenses we need to avoid. We're going to try to enter near the higher floors, probably straight through the windows. We need to target the thirty-sixth floor. That's where the regional executive director's office is. In her office we should find a command panel which has access behind the firewall and authority to publish to the central network. We need to upload the program and commands from there."

"And then what?" asked Tessa.

"And then," Ryland paused, "well, all hell is going to break loose. Activating the sim now."

All around them the arena dissolved from view. It was replaced by open blue sky and sun. There was a building under their feet. They were standing on top of the studio, looking out over the rest of the Entertainment complex and a stretch of office buildings and homes that went for kilometers.

"It may take a few minutes for you to get the hang of the suits and the interface," started Ryland before he realized that both Eli and Tessa were already using the electromagnetic pulse boots to put themselves into the air and powering up their thrusters to make the jump to their target.

"These things are awesome," grinned Eli. "I can't believe the weapons options. Seriously, Ry, kudos. The interface is so natural. I have to get myself one of these if we actually live."

Chapter Fifty-One - Nicodemus

"Check." The young boy moved his bishop to the far, right side of the board and looked up proudly at his uncle.

They were seated on the backyard garden patio of an estate in North Carolina overlooking the Blue Ridge Mountains. Behind them was a sprawling mansion all painted in white. It had been meticulously restored to look just as when it was originally built well over two hundred years ago. The gardens were immaculate, and in full bloom. Nicodemus savored the smell of the fresh coffee he held in his hands as he looked out at the mountains, then at the smiling face of his nephew, then down at the board.

His nephew's black bishop threatened Nicodemus' king through a diagonal between one of his pawns and a knight. "Well done, Adam. Well done. But sometimes you need to pay attention to the pieces that aren't threatening you immediately." Nicodemus moved a pawn forward on the left side of the board exposing a bishop of his own and giving him a direct line to his nephew's king that was previously guarded by the black bishop. "Checkmate."

Scowling, the young boy looked up at his uncle. "I'll beat you one day, Uncle."

"Of that I have no doubt, Adam," he smiled and took another sip of coffee. Right at that moment he saw an urgent alert comm on his HUD. "Adam, I have some important business to attend to. Why don't you go inside and get some lemonade?"

"OK, Uncle Nic." The boy ran off inside the house.

Nicodemus answered the comm and began reading the data flowing through on his HUD. The Central Data Center was under attack. "Report," ordered Nicodemus.

A ground attack is underway. There are at least two to three hundred humans involved. They have disabled a small number of the perimeter defenses, but nothing that yet poses a significant threat according to our models. Our defenses are responding. We anticipate subduing the threat within the hour based

on known variables. We are already employing measures
to redistribute command functions to other centers.

"Is there an aerial or orbital attack?" asked Nicodemus.

No, there is nothing yet to indicate that, but
the enemy ground forces are targeting our shield
generators. Our local aerial forces have been
temporarily immobilized. The attack destroyed our
launch bays. The drones are being moved to an
alternate launch location and should be in the air in
less than twenty minutes. Hunter drones and heavy-mech
hunters will be deployed in just a few minutes.
Sentinels are already engaging enemy forces.

"I want all aerial forces within five hundred kilometers diverted
now to provide support. I don't trust this."

Done.

"I want all other drone forces outside of major cities in the air
now. Devise an optimum deployment that will put them in the air above
all known driver communities greater than fifty in number with an
emphasis on the larger communities, excepting the Employment
Opportunity Camps, of course. Fleets are to take up position and be
prepared for a mass execution order."

We cannot obey an execution order of that
nature, but we will take up position as requested.

"Contact Dan Stern. Tell him I want the most recent draft of the
ARDOS amendment introduced as a motion to the board now. I don't care
if he's still finalizing little details, the last version I reviewed was more
than sufficient. I want it queued and ready for vote. Notify the executive
board, all regional directors, district directors, and the others I've placed
on the list that they need to be on a conference with me in five minutes.
Tell them that it's a matter of urgent national corporate security. Highest
priority"

Consider it done.

He meticulously reset every piece on the chess board, finished his coffee, set the mug down and stood up. Walking across the patio away from the house, he looked out at the mountains. It was truly beautiful as the sun shone down brightly with sparse white clouds in the sky. Birds called out to one another and long grass waved softly in the breeze. He stood there staring at it all for several minutes. He had anticipated having a bit more time to prepare for this, but it didn't matter. This was overdue if they were to take the next step in the evolution of society.

Right now, hundreds of thousands of drones were racing across the skies of North and Central America. Large transports bearing tens of thousands of small sniper and hunter drones were headed to rural areas flanked by fighters and bombers. It was a mass movement of forces not seen on the planet in many decades and never in peacetime. Nicodemus watched on his HUD to see the deployment beginning and their trajectories. Most would be at their targets within thirty minutes, the rest within the hour. Some of the more remote camps would not be reached for a bit longer, but the numbers were not enough to be consequential.

A notification on his HUD told him that the conference was assembled and ready for him, with an attendance of eighty-three percent and rising every moment. He waited a few more moments until it exceeded ninety percent then joined.

Everything about this moment had been designed by Nicodemus. He stood in the middle of a virtual Colosseum. It was made to resemble the one of ancient Rome in its glory. He stood at the center of the arena floor. Executive board members were in some of the more exclusive seating, along with other large shareholders he had placed on the invitation list for this. The rest of the arena was filled with the thousands of regional and district directors.

Intentionally Nicodemus' avatar appeared a bit taller, a little younger and stronger than he was in real life. He didn't need to yell or amplify his voice, physics didn't apply here, but he spoke strongly and clearly. "I would not have called you all here if it wasn't for something truly important. The time has come to make a change. The time has come to take the next step in evolving society and embracing the future. While I knew this day would eventually come, I did not expect it to be so soon, and indeed, we would not be here at all right now if our hand was not being forced.

"The Central Data Center is under attack at this very moment. We know the attacking forces are driver terrorists armed with weapons from enemy corporations. We also know that it doesn't end with those that are on the field of battle. Our laws allow for us to act against those bearing arms against us at the data center, and we will destroy them. But we also know that they are backed by a vast network of driver terrorists throughout the continent and their aggression is growing. Their attacks are increasing at a time when we are on the precipice of becoming the most powerful spacefaring and mining corporation on the planet by a long shot. It's not hard to fathom why our enemies are doing everything they can to arm those inside our borders against us.

"I did not choose the setting for this meeting lightly. We sit in a virtual replica of what was once the grandest arena in the greatest city of the most dominant empire on the planet. That was until its society fell into ruin of their own hubris and failure to act in the face of change. I do not wish the same fate to fall upon us, but we are currently restrained by our own rules and the restrictions that we have placed on our instruments of force."

Nicodemus paused for moment to let them think about that.

"I have already spoken to many of you personally about this. The rest of you have received briefings or spoken to other members of my executive team. I understand your concerns about expansion of the rules, but again and again our AIs have proven that our fears of a 'robot apocalypse' are unfounded science fiction. More importantly, I understand your hesitancy at being involved with something that will result in the deaths of many. That's basic compassion. It's human. You *should* feel that way. It tears at my soul as well. But what *I* won't do is sit idly by and watch as the lives of all our citizens are put at risk. We have a responsibility to our shareholders. It's both a legal responsibility and a moral one.

"There is an amendment to the ARDOS rules available to you now on your HUD. I motion for this amendment to be introduced for a vote."

"I second the motion," spoke the voice of Melissa.

"The amendment is up for vote. Normally we would set a period of several days for review and vote, but I'm asking you to please cast your vote immediately. We do not have time to waste. We believe additional attacks are imminent. Feel free to contact me or my office if you have any questions. I invite you to read the changes in the ARDOS language, but you should know that it has already been vigorously vetted and most of you have already previewed the earlier drafts. No changes to the language will be entertained so please do not make any counter-proposals. You are either a yes or a no. And I strongly implore you to vote yes. This meeting is adjourned. Please remember that time is our enemy at this moment."

With that, Nicodemus' avatar disappeared from the Colosseum, followed by the thousands of others that returned to their homes and offices to make their decision. Within moments the votes in favor began pouring in.

Chapter Fifty-Two - Ryland

The three drones controlled by Eli, Tessa, and Ryland were hurtling toward their destination. On their HUDs they could see the headquarters building in the distance as they rapidly closed the gap. It was a beautiful glass and steel spire above the city.

"Seriously, I totally feel like I'm flying," said Eli, "How is that possible?"

"Advanced electromagnetics and environment simulation," replied Ryland over the comm. "In the arena you are in the air, but you feel like you're flying in the drone. In technical terms, it's really fucking cool. OK, time to focus."

Readouts on the building and its defenses began displaying on their HUDs.

Ryland processed it and started planning. "You should be seeing what I am. There are two defensive missile towers, one on the Southeast corner of the tower and one on the Northwest. Energy weapons line the rest of the top. There are three heavy aerial drones within ten kilometers doing perimeter sweeps. Our stealth tech has kept them from seeing our approach, but they'll know we are here soon. There are plenty of ground defenses, but they won't be able to get to us in time. We need to…"

Eli cut him off, "We got this, Ry. This is what we do. Tess, I got the Northwest turret. You take the Southeast. Sweep the energy guns on your way in. Take your pick from the weapons, but I'm planning to try the mini-rail guns then go with the grenades on the turrets. Ryland keep an eye on the aerials, but you need to head straight for the target floor and we'll be right behind you. Go in straight through the windows, but blast your way in. You never know how armored the glass might really be."

Tessa was in motion before Ryland could even try to argue or interrupt. "Got it," said Tessa. "Consider those guns offline." Eli and Tessa both accelerated and shifted to attack positions. A small part of Ryland wanted to argue that he was supposed to be in charge, but instead he couldn't help but smile. These kids were good.

Tessa and Eli were almost scary. Ryland watched them accelerate to the sides of the tower surface. They looked like a mirror image of each other in the way they moved. In near synchronicity they arced around the tower with energy and ballistic weapons fire erupting from the extended arms of their drones. The building's defensive energy guns were wiped out before they even had a chance to fire. With a last glance he saw both firing grenades at the heavy missile turrets. His HUD told him the heavy aerials were closing in but still sixty seconds out. "Watch out for the aerials, they'll be here in a minute. I'm going in."

"We'll take care of the big, flying bugs," said Tessa over the comm. "You get to the console."

Ryland angled down and flew towards the building's glass walls where his HUD told him the thirty-sixth floor was. He hovered in front of the glass. A scan told him no humans were behind the glass in front of him. Holding up the drone's hands he let loose a series of energy pulses that sent the glass in front of him shattering to the ground below and leaving exposed a long hallway. His drone flew in and landed on the floor as he shut down his thrusters. He heard the alert sirens going off inside the building.

The mechanized body of the drone marched down the hallway past empty glass-walled offices. It was a Sunday, so few people were at the building. Ryland was hoping to meet no one.

He knew what he was looking for. Kimberly's office was just a bit up ahead. He heard a sound to his left and saw a light glow atop the elevator at the end of the hallway. The doors opened, and two hunter drones ripped through and headed straight for him. Their guns were ablaze immediately. Ryland leaped and rolled to the ground through an office door just in time to avoid being shredded by the bullets. They were using armor-piercing rounds. He had armor better than they anticipated, but he wasn't taking hits he didn't need to take.

Shells and energy fire started ripping through the office, shattering glass and shredding furniture. He had to move. He rolled over his shoulder in to the hall and sent two small missiles at the hunters from his drone's shoulders. Within seconds the hunters were mangled messes of smoking metal.

With that, Ryland resumed his path to Kimberly's office. He reached her door and was about to walk in when Eli and Tessa came hurtling through the shattered glass wall. Their landing was the total opposite of the grace they showed in combat just a moment ago. Eli bounced off the floor and collided with an office wall that shattered into a hundred thousand pieces of glass. Tessa was a bit better and managed to get away with an entrance that looked like a pinball bouncing around the hallway.

After an awkward recovery, she stood up. "They're coming. We took out the aerials but there are more on the way, including a drop ship of hunters that will be here in less than a few minutes."

"Let's go," ordered Ryland as he turned and stalked down the hallway. He turned into Kimberly's office with Eli and Tessa's drones behind him.

"Eli," said Tessa, "you and I should take up position to get ready for hunters to start flooding these corridors. We need to give Ryland time."

"Agreed," acknowledged Eli. They each took up a defensive position near the office and prepared for an assault. "Do what you need to do, sir".

Ryland walked over to Kimberly's desk and tried to focus. He was startled when he heard a voice he was not expecting.

"I'm unarmed." came Kimberly's voice from a corner of the office. He had not seen her when he walked in. Ryland quickly realized that all Kimberly saw was a heavily armed drone striding through her office. Her words were meant to establish that she posed no imminent threat. She wanted to be sure she was invoking protection from an AI controlled drone in case there was any doubt. Though, given that this drone was attacking an Americorp office she might worry it's a hacked black-market drone or possibly even a foreign drone.

"Wait," she said, "You're one of the new human controlled drones we're testing." She would recognize them. She had been instrumental in the deal to produce them and work with Immersive Magic on starting the project. "Who are you? Who's controlling this thing?"

Ryland spoke through the drone, "It's me, Kim. It's Ryland."

"What are you doing here? What the hell is going on?" she asked.

"I don't really have time to explain, Kim. I know this doesn't look good and that I'm a fugitive. I know you and I are not that close, but I need you to trust me. Something big is about to happen. It's going to change everything. I didn't choose to be involved with this, but I am because of what happened to me. I'm not a traitor, or at least I wasn't when they came to arrest me. Now, well, I'm going to be honest with you. Nothing about what I'm planning to do is anything less than legal treason. It has to be done or millions of people are going to die, and it would just get worse after that."

Kim looked blank. She turned her head and stared out the window for a moment. "I know," she said quietly. "I came here to think because I have to vote on something that will kill millions. There are almost enough votes for it to pass. I'm one of the few holdouts they still need. How is what you're doing going to stop that and what will happen?"

"Kim, there's not time to explain everything. People are dying right now." In the hallways they heard a burst of explosions and weapons fire. The hunters were here.

"Ryland, we have a problem." It was Kira's voice over the comm. "Mayson just let us know that drones just showed up outside the studio with a security officer. Serious drones. Military grade. I'm going to go try and delay them, but I don't think it will do much good. They are coming in. You're running out of time."

"Copy that. Thanks," said Ryland.

Eli voiced into the comm, "Ry, we show at least three hunters about to enter this floor, guessing more are on the way. How much more time do you need?"

"Hopefully just a few more minutes," replied Ryland.

"Tess," said Eli, "you got this. Keep him covered. I'm disengaging to go deal with the real world back at the studio to buy us time."

"Don't do anything stupid," replied Tessa. "This isn't a game and you're not a drone."

"I know," said Eli. "You just worry about those hunters here and give Ry a few more minutes, I'll keep them off your backs in the studio. Eli out." Eli disengaged. His drone stood suddenly still.

"Tess," Ryland said over the comm, "I'm transferring control of Eli's drone to you. You can give it commands. It won't be the same as personal control, but you can use your HUD to have it move and fire to support you or tell it to auto-pilot and target the same things you are. Give me two more minutes."

"You got it," responded Tessa.

Ryland directed his drone's attention back to Kimberly as they heard more weapons fire erupt in the hallway. "Kim, I need to upload something into the central network from the console on your desk. I'm going to do this whether you agree or not. It can save all of the lives you were just thinking about without any more violence." The drone walked to the desk, pulled out the data crystal and inserted it into the port. He tapped the display to execute the file as it was detected.

The AI collective voice came from the speakers in the office.

`Authorization required. Who is authorizing this command?`

Shit. That was all Ryland could think. He thought that if he uploaded it through Kimberly's console it would be enough with the hacked credentials. How could he work around this?

"Authorized by Kimberly Lewandowski, regional director," said Kim as she stepped over to the console and authorized using a DNA scan. She looked at Ryland's drone. "Things are really screwed up. I don't know what's going on, but I can't be complicit with what I'm being asked to do by the chairman. I really hope you know what you are doing."

"Thank you, Kim. I know this sounds crazy, but I also need you to vote in favor of that amendment you've been pondering."

Chapter Fifty-Three - Kelly

The sentinel drone fell to the ground as a massive piece of twisted and burned metal, nearly falling on top of Kelly. His team had managed to take out all the sentinels, but not without casualties. There was no official count yet, but at least a dozen or more of his unit were dead according to his HUD, probably more. Weapons fire still blazed all around him and the smell of scorched steel and death filled the air. He ran for cover behind the rock line and trees to regroup.

"Team leaders, report," he said into the comm.

"Teams One and Two good," came a voice on the comm, "limited casualties. One dead. We are making some dents on the shield generators and almost have one offline…we think. Continuing to move positions, but we won't last long once they get aerials here."

"Teams Three and Four have been taking heavy fire, but we've taken out the primary weapons turrets. We've lost at least three people. Sir, you're going to want to see this. It's not good."

On his HUD Kelly could see the video of what his team lead was watching. Massive bay doors in the side of the mountain, behind the fences, had opened. Huge, heavy-mech hunter drones were walking through. They stood more than three times the height of standard hunter drones, they were heavily armored, and each carried more weapons than a small army. Kelly counted six.

"OK, so that's not good. I'm guessing they'll split up and send one at each of our teams. I want each team to divide in half, Alpha and Bravo groups. Alphas stay and take up defensive positions. You don't need to take these guys down, just delay them as best you can. Bravo teams take up fire on the remaining weapons and doors of the data center. If the drones target Bravo groups, switch roles."

"Got it, sir," Kelly heard over the comm from several of the team leads.

The heavy hunters sprang into action with an agility and speed that was surprising for something of their size and weight. Within seconds they were all leaping over the high walls of the compound and headed straight for the human teams with incredible speed. The ones closest to their targets opened weapons bays and began firing. One was running straight at Kelly and his team.

Missiles began firing from the exposed shoulders of the drone while energy guns blasted in rapid fire from its extended arm. Explosions went off and Kelly was certain he had just lost at least another five to six people. He came up from his position into the open and began firing at the most vulnerable places on the drone, but even those were heavily armored on these models.

Kelly switched comms, "Hey, Ry, not sure how you're doing with everything, but now would be good."

"Almost there," responded Kelly, "Should be any moment now if it's going to work at all."

"Thanks for the resounding confidence," said Kelly. "We're all going to be dead in about two minutes." The drones tore through the ground between them and the driver teams. They did not even bother to avoid trees, they just ripped through whatever was in their path. Rail guns began tearing through the rock around them. Stone and dust filled the air with rocks flying around like bullets. Kelly saw energy bursts hurtle into two more of his people burning them straight through and sending their limp bodies to the ground. The smell of flesh-burning, and weapons-fire filled the air.

Kelly dived behind another boulder and took cover. He pulled out a couple of thermal grenades and got ready to throw them, knowing it would probably be the last thing he ever did. And then suddenly, everything stopped. Almost all the weapons fire ceased. He peeked out from behind the boulder. The hunters stood still, as if frozen in time. Small hunters and even the remaining turrets stopped moving. All of the drones were completely still.

"Boys and girls," spoke Kelly into the comm, "it's your fairy godmother. You have sixty seconds to do as much damage as you can to these big, metal bastards and then I want you all to run like hell away from here. Split up into smaller groups, and take cover as needed because anything that remains is likely to come back online and resume killing you as rapidly as it can. Meet up at the rendezvous points. Make it count."

Chapter Fifty-Four - Nicodemus

Across the continent, at the exact same moment that the drones at the data center froze, so did practically every other drone in service. Transport drones stopped in their tracks, as did service drones, cleaning drones, and security forces. Everything stopped. Food could not be ordered at restaurants. Vehicles stopped moving. People getting help in retail stores found their drone assistants stopped in their tracks, unable to function.

The drones and the AIs were still able to communicate with each other. People could still communicate with drones via their HUDs, but even voice modulators on the drones were not working. They could not speak aloud. The hardware simply was not working even though the AIs were still in there. Hundreds of thousands of aerial drones plummeted from the skies and fell like rain on the ground below them. In major cities the panic was immediate, as was the destruction caused as the aerial drones crashed onto whatever was below them. Flight craft that were in the air luckily had fail safes that kept them airborne even if unresponsive to new orders.

In coffee shops, drones could be seen frozen as steaming brown liquid continued spilling from dispensers. Children in parks on swing sets found themselves crashing into nanny drones that had been giving them a push. Transport hubs found lines suddenly stopped as no ID's could be checked. Surgeries that were in the middle of being performed by AI drones were halted with patients laying on tables as bodies sat open underneath scalpels. Every person in a car found themselves stopped on the roads and unable to exit.

It did not take more than thirty seconds for panic to erupt all around the continent in every major city. Communications usage suddenly exploded as people tried to get in touch with loved ones. Many reached out over social and personal networks, or tried to contact emergency, police, and security services. The communication networks quickly buckled under the immense and immediate load, leaving many with no answers and furthering their confusion and panic.

Nicodemus had been sitting on the patio in his garden. His personal assistant drone had been pouring him some iced tea and froze as it over-poured his glass. He saw the aerial security drones around his property fall from the sky. Within seconds he was looking at reports coming in on his HUD and confirming details with the AI.

`Nearly all drones are unable to access any hardware peripherals. We are trying now to determine the cause. Less than 3% appear to be unaffected.`

"What about the orbital defenses?" he asked.

`Orbital defense systems are fully online. No issues.`

"How long until recovery?"

`We don't know yet.`

"I need everyone from the recent shareholder meeting that hasn't yet voted for the ARDOS amendment to receive the following message and links to the relevant news stories: 'This is exactly what I was warning you about. Our way of life is at stake, and it's worse than we had anticipated. We need the ability to defend ourselves and we need it now. Cast your vote immediately or blame yourself while you and your families burn as the terrorists attack'."

He stood up and walked to the edge of the patio and out onto the grass. He heard yelling and some panic from inside the house. His nephew was scared. His wife was trying to reach him on his comm and yelling from the house. Undoubtedly his brother and sister-in-law, who were out fishing on the lake, would be contacting him within seconds to find out what was going on. His comm was lit up with requests from regional directors, governors, reporters, and executives. He ignored them all. What he needed now were the votes, and he watched as they poured in. They were over the needed threshold in less than a minute. The amendment had passed. He smiled and took a sip of his iced tea. As soon as the drones were back online, he could end this for good.

We've identified the source of the drone malfunction. It's a form of an overload attack on drone hardware peripherals. It was initiated from behind central security. It originated at a console in the Bay Area headquarters which was attacked in the last twenty-two minutes by some of our own prototype military drones: the new human-controlled models. We've isolated the hardware exploit attack signature and can prevent it from happening again. All drones are re-booting now to clear the condition and they should be able to access all hardware within less than two minutes. We are currently estimating 21.7% of aerial drones have sustained damage that will keep them from flying without repair due to impact from crashes.

"I want all the attack groups sent to take out the driver communities to move in, report status, and be prepared for an execution order. Get me a detailed estimate of forces lost in the crash."

Sir, there is an urgent message that requires your attention.

Nicodemus looked at his HUD. There was a notification flashing. The notification was marked 'Urgent: Executive board vote.'

That didn't make any sense. He accessed the notification. The core five-member executive board, including his position, were up for vote. He saw his own name and all those of the current executive board on the list of candidates, but there were a host of other names available as options. A few he recognized as popular regional directors or mayors. A few were wealthy business leaders. Others were names he had never heard of. Who the hell was Mia Cordosa? Within seconds she was already leading by a landslide. And why was Daniel Stern's name on the list?

"What the hell is going on?" he asked into the air.

Corporate bi-laws mandate an immediate election of the core executive board by shareholders in the event of any redistribution agreement.

245

"What redistribution agreement?"

The share redistribution authorized in the amendment that you and the shareholders just passed.

"What are you talking about?"

The amendment that you motioned to the floor to amend the ARDOS rules, sir. It also contained a redistribution of Americorp shares. Please reference Article Seven, Section Five, Sub-Section Two of the amendment. I can bring it up on your HUD if you would like. That order has been carried out. Now election protocols are being observed.

He thought for a moment. How could anyone alter the amendment to include share redistribution language without him knowing about it or authorizing it? The system was highly secured. It was practically impenetrable. The only two people that even had access to publish and authorize an amendment for vote were him and... then it hit him. "I want Dan Stern apprehended immediately. I also want the security forces surrounding the driver communities to move in. The execution order is given. Take them all out."

We will dispatch resources to apprehend Daniel Stern, but we cannot carry out the execution order.

"Why is that?" asked Nicodemus. "The new ARDOS amendment has been passed."

Because the use of violence on shareholders that have not committed a crime and pose no imminent threat would be a violation of our directives.

"They're not shareholders! They're unemployed terrorists! Now execute the order!"

Sir, the amendment redistributed shares to any previous non-shareholders in our controlled territories. They are now all shareholders. In fact, each one is an equal shareholder to you. You may want to consider voting for yourself in the new board election. Currently you are losing quite badly.

Chapter Fifty-Five – Ryland

Ryland and Kim both watched the reports on their HUDs. Public panic ensued when the drones lost control of their hardware. In the hallway there were blasts as the other drones took out the remains of the hunters.

Kim's face contorted in an expression of confusion. "Ryland, I just received a notification that the executive board, all of it, is up for a general shareholder vote. What is this?" She looked up at the Ryland drone.

"It's a chance to start over," said Ryland. "You'll notice you're on the list of candidates. Everyone gets to cast five votes. I recommend you vote for yourself. I voted for you." He smiled but knew she couldn't see the look on his real face. "I also highly recommend voting for Mia Cardosa. I think you'll make good choices with the rest of your votes."

"No, I mean what is this? What's going on?" she insisted.

"We buried language in the ARDOS amendment you and the others just passed. All shares in Americorp have just been redistributed. Every single previous shareholder, and every single driver in the territories that the corporation controls is now completely equal with full rights. You know the protocols: any redistribution requires a re-election of the board. We have millions of drivers standing by with instructions on who to vote for, more in the C22 camps that we were able to get word to, and more sympathizers amongst shareholders than you might believe. We have the numbers, Kim. We're going to change the face of Americorp, possibly the world, and definitely the future."

"So, it was all true," she looked at the Ryland drone in disbelief, "You really were a dissident. I had no idea…"

"That's the funny part," he said through the drone, "I wasn't. I was not involved with this whatsoever until after they tried to have me arrested. It's a long story from there, but I really believe that what's about to happen is a good thing. And I think you're one of the people that's going to help lead us to a better place. It's not going to be pretty or easy, possibly even a bit ugly for a while, but I think it's going to be better."

"I don't understand," said Kim.

The Drivers

"I can't explain more right now. I need to go. I'll message you soon. Go vote. Be on the right side of history. Go with your heart."

The Ryland-drone turned and walked out to the hallway. He switched to the private comm. "Tess, we have to go. In just a minute the military drones will all be back online and there will be plenty headed our way. We need to get out of the building and then I'm going to set our drones on autopilot to fly straight East. I'll set them to use evasive patterns until they are either shot down or captured, but you and I are going to bug out of them and get back to the studio to help Eli and Kira. When all the AI-controlled drones come back online, they are going to resume whatever it is they were last doing. We're not out of this yet."

As soon as they jumped out of the jagged glass and steel hole in the side of the building, they activated their thrusters and leaped into the air. Within a few seconds they were hurtling away from the coast at high speed. "Disengage the interface, Tess. I've set your drone and mine on auto. See you in a second."

Back in the arena they both floated to the ground as they turned off their interfaces to the drones. Once on the ground they removed their helmets. It was almost a bit disorienting to be seeing and acting in the real world instead of through the drones and it took a moment for each of them to adjust. The arena was still fluid but beginning to flatten out from imitating the physical reality of where their drones had been. It was a fascinating thing to watch. Eli wasn't there. Ryland was the first to speak into the comm channel, "Eli, you there?"

Nothing. Eli's interface helmet from the suit was on the ground near the arena exit, but he should still have his normal HUD device.

"Kira? You there?"

No response. Tessa started sprinting towards the exit. Ryland followed a step behind. He could barely keep up with her.

They exited into the viewing room and immediately smelled weapons fire and burning metal but there was no sound of battle. Ryland motioned towards the door that led to the hallway. Tessa nodded and sprinted almost silently to the door. They moved up to it cautiously. As it slid open, smoke began pouring into the room they were coming from and caused their eyes to burn.

At the far-left end of the hallway they could make out two collapsed hunter drones, the source of the smoke. Their armor was blackened by energy weapons fire. One was laying on top of the other with smoke coming from its stocky neck which appeared partially severed. The one on the bottom was still twitching an arm that reached out towards them, but its lower torso was burned with a hole through the upper hip. In a morbid and almost twisted way it reminded Ryland of the final scene of *The Terminator*, an old Arnold Schwarzenegger science fiction movie.

A cough from behind startled them and they turned around to see Eli laying on the floor with Ryland's energy rifle held limply by one arm next to him. His other arm was shredded by bullets at the shoulder and bleeding out badly. There was a blackened hole from an energy weapon burned into his suit near his stomach exposing his organs with blood flowing from the now singed and smoldering fabric. He coughed again, and blood gushed from his lower body wound.

Tessa ran to him and fell to her knees to hold him.

"Eli! We're going to get you help! Hold on. Ryland! Get help now!" She began ripping at her sleeve to try and tear it off, but the fabric was too strong.

"I'm getting nothing on my comm and my HUD isn't able to access the network," said Ryland. "Someone must be blocking comm and net access with a dampening field. I'm going to get help. Eli, hang on!" Ryland turned and sprinted down the hallway.

Eli coughed again. Tessa held him and propped up his head under her arm. "Dammit, Eli!" She screamed as hot tears began to stream down her face. "I told you to not do anything stupid!"

"It wasn't…" more coughing, "stupid. I gave you the time you needed, and it worked. They stopped moving just in time. A few more seconds and they would have been in the arena shredding all of us to bits. So, I guess the plan worked? The drones? Everything?" He opened his eyes wide and looked deeply into hers. "Did it work? Did we win?"

Her face was burning. She squinted and blinked to clear her eyes of tears. "Yes. Our part worked. Now we just have to hope the rest of the plan does as well."

"Good," he closed his eyes and smiled thinly. "I like winning." He coughed again. There was more blood. His face grimaced from the pain and he groaned loudly.

Tessa held him tightly and pressed her own body over his main wound to try and act as a make-shift tourniquet. "Eli, you have to hold on. Stay with me. Help is coming," she sobbed.

"Tess, promise me something?" he asked as he opened his eyes again and looked at her.

"Anything, Eli."

"Promise me you'll keep winning. That's all you have to do - keep on winning. Then they can't make you leave. I love you, Tess."

Eli coughed loudly again and closed his eyes as his body fell completely limp in Tessa's arms and he stopped breathing. She screamed but knew that he was gone. She could feel there was no more life in his body. She screamed again in pure denial but then just fell on top of his body and cried.

Chapter Fifty-Six - Mia

The whole community was scrambling for cover. The trees and nearby mountains promised some cover. Nearly three hundred members of a driver community had been told by their leadership to evacuate, head for the mountains and split up into smaller groups from there. It hadn't taken long for the drone forces to bypass their now empty, make-shift camp and find them in their hurried escape. Heavy aerial carriers were descending toward them, filled with hunters, and surrounded by a swarm of smaller aerial drones. Children started to cry as their parents frantically carried them. Shouts and screaming erupted. Panic began to consume everyone.

Mia stopped for a moment and simply stared at the deadly and insurmountable forces headed toward them. She had been with this group, one of the larger driver communities in a remote part of Calgary, for several months. She made them promises of a better future. Then she had to tell them to run for their lives. The sound of the drones was getting louder and louder as they got closer to her fleeing people.

Suddenly and all at once the humming in the sky stopped. They all turned to stare and watch as aerial drones plummeted to earth as though they had suddenly lost power. Within seconds they heard the crashes, some explosions, and saw smoke begin to rise from some of the wreckage.

Massive cheers went up from those around her, but Mia just kept staring. She was still following everything that was happening with Kelly and Ryland's team on her HUD while also getting updates from driver communities everywhere in the Americas. She barely even noticed the people running by her celebrating and thanking her as if she had made the drones fall from the sky all by herself through some force of will or super power. Parents hugged their children. People shouted and embraced each other. Even through all the data flowing in on her HUD she couldn't help but notice one little girl walking past her. The girl was wearing a ragged red dress with equally ragged utility pants. The girl could not have been more than five or six years old. Pushing her long, black hair away from her face and light brown skin, she looked right at Mia with her big brown eyes as if in slow motion. She wiped a tear from eye and mouthed the words "thank you" before turning to grab her mother's hand and walk back in the direction of the camp.

Fighting back tears of her own, Mia held her breath and watched. Everything started to unfold exactly as Ryland had predicted and according to plan. The election began, and everyone started voting. Results came in at an astounding rate. The panic drove both immediate action and even a greater than predicted desire for change. Leaving the secured network, she joined the central network, so she could cast a vote herself. It took her just seconds to cast her votes and return to viewing the results. A weak smile crossed her lips and she sighed deeply.

Miss Cordosa, we wanted to inform you that while the polls remain open, you have at this point, mathematically speaking, been elected the new Chairperson of the Executive Board of Americorp. You also now hold the title of interim Chief Executive Officer. Congratulations, Ma'am.

"Mia," she said aloud into the air around her. She had never spoken directly to the AI collective, but she was going to start it out her way.

Ma'am?

"My name is Mia."

As you wish, Mia.

"Is this authority immediate?"

Yes, Mia. In the interest of corporate efficiency, once a vote is mathematically decided the transfer of power and authority is immediate.

"What is the status of drone access to their hardware peripherals?"

All drones should be fully recovered from the breach within the next thirty-eight seconds. The first just came back online eleven seconds ago. At least 30.3% of drones need some form of repair to become operational again, with the majority of those being aerial drones that were damaged by impact crashes.

"I want an immediate halt and cease-fire for all forces that were ordered to eliminate drivers, those involved in the defense of the Central Data Center and any pursuit of forces that were recently engaged in military operations there. I also want a cease fire and halt to any drone or human security forces engaged at the Immersive Magic studios in the pursuit of Ryland Grey and those he is believed to be involved with."

Done.

"I want it clear that even the human forces at those locations are to completely stand-down."
There was a slight pause.

Done.

"Clear Ryland Grey of all charges against him. Full executive pardon."

Done.

"I want all drone forces that were advancing on driver communities and that are still operational to return to their home bases."

The order has been given.

"What's the status of the orbital defenses?"

They are fully operational. We've detected some advances by foreign corporate orbital forces, but they've taken no notable aggressive action or posture yet.

"Good. I want you to come up with a plan for my review that involves getting all drone forces not needed for core border security to head to the major cities to peacefully quell any potential rioting, looting, or similar issues, but without employing any physical violence. Start thinking."

We are thinking, Mia.

"Please halt all share trading until further notice."

Done, but you only have the authority to do that for twenty-four hours without a vote by the executive board.

"How does the rest of the executive board look? Show me current election results, please." The numbers began displaying on her HUD immediately along with profiles of those in the lead.

Besides yourself, three of the other four are mathematically decided. Daniel Stern, Kimberly Lewandoski, and Keisha Greene. The fourth is still undecided but we are predicting it will be Evan Williams.

"OK. I want all of them informed of their election and in a conference with me in two minutes, including Evan. Virtual space. Maximum security protocols. Pick a scene that looks like a remote location overlooking a lake. I want a sunrise in progress. Make it feel comfortable, rustic."

We will make it so.

"Alert the central media network... no, wait... check that. Can I communicate directly with all shareholders?"

Yes, Mia.

"OK. Alert the central media network that in twenty minutes I'll be addressing every shareholder directly in a public communication.

```
would you like us to take measures to try to
keep the message from being picked up or forwarded
globally to interests outside of Americorp?
```

She thought about it for just a moment. "No. Broadcast it globally to anyone that wants to see it. Our enemies are bound to get a hold it eventually. We are better off controlling the narrative from the start."

```
As you wish. We are alerting the media now.
```

"Oh, and I'd like the prior chairperson, Nicodemus, temporarily detained. I'd like to speak to him when I am finished here."

```
Security forces are being dispatched. On-site
drones should have him in custody within moments. Is
he being charged with a crime?
```

"No. Is there a way for me to have him detained for a short while, have his central network access suspended and his comms monitored legally?"

```
As the Chief Executive Officer, you can suspend
his network access and his comms without reason. To
have him detained you can authorize an executive order
that states you believe he may represent a threat to
corporate-national security. He'd be allowed to have
an attorney of his choosing present during
questioning.
```

"I authorize an order that he represents such a threat."

```
Done.
```

Mia paused for moment and breathed. Was she ready for this?

```
Mia, may we do anything else for you?
```

"Yes, I'm sending you a group list now. Please inform them of everything I just asked you to do. I need to go talk to my friend Manny for a minute."

Chapter Fifty-Seven - Ryland

The elevator doors opened to the ground level of the game studio. Ryland walked out quickly but cautiously still carrying his rifle. At the far end of the main atrium he could see Kira. She was surrounded by human and drone security forces, but they were beginning to move toward the front doors, leaving the building. All around the large main room his employees were standing and staring or peering out from offices and meeting areas to see what happened as if watching a vehicle crash with a curiosity they couldn't fight.

"Sir! There he is!" a uniformed security officer shouted as he spotted Ryland at the elevator. Every head in the room turned their necks to look at him. Kira looked at him as if to tell him he had blown it by showing up now. Several of the uniformed officers drew their weapons, but the drones continued to exit the building one by one.

Another human officer in uniform, older than the others and closer to Ryland's age, raised his arm towards the younger officers and motioned them to lower their weapons. "We have our orders. Stand down. Now!" He turned and looked at them. They lowered their weapons. "Your orders are to leave the building. This is over." Some of them looked unhappy about it, but they all obeyed.

Ryland did not have time for this. He shouted across the room, "Hey! We have someone down on the arena viewing floor in need of serious medical attention! We need med units down there now and he's going to need to be moved to a hospital if he's going to live. My comm is blocked. Will someone, please, for the love of god, please get medical drones down there now!"

The officer next to Kira spoke into his comm and then looked up at Ryland. "Emergency help is on the way. First aid units will be there in moments and a full medical unit is on its way."

"Ryland!" shouted Kira and she began to run towards him. He started running too and met her in the middle, almost at the exact same spot where they had first talked with Eli and Tessa not so many days ago. They embraced and just held each other for a moment.

"What happened here?" asked Ryland.

"I was going to ask you the same thing," she said. "They came in. We couldn't stop them. They froze all comm and network access, then they sent hunters down to the arena. Then for a few minutes there was a panic as all the drones stopped functioning. It was weird. But just after they came back online, Commander Sheridan," she motioned towards the older human officer that was walking towards them and just a few steps away now, "said that the order to capture you had been cancelled and ordered all of them to leave. Oh my god, Ry, I can't believe you're alive. Who's hurt? How bad is it?"

"Eli," he replied. "It's bad. I don't think he's going to make it."

"I'm sorry to tell you that he didn't," said a very grave and respectful Sheridan. "I just saw from the first aid drone. He died before it could get there. I'm so sorry"

"You're sorry?! You killed him you son of a bitch!" Ryland screamed.

"I'm very sorry, but I was only following orders. Those orders were only countermanded moments ago. The charges against you were dropped. But until a few minutes ago you were one of the most wanted people in the corporation. I have no damn clue what the hell just happened. First the drones went offline. Then an election for the executive board. Then suddenly your name is cleared, and I'm told to stand down on arresting you after previously being ordered to apprehend you at all costs. Mister Grey, my name is William Sheridan. The case against you never made sense to me. I still don't understand it and the details were classified. I'm truly sorry for your friend. I also must tell you, you're the only person I've ever been ordered to apprehend that I didn't catch in my whole career. You have my respect, sir."

"Your respect won't bring Eli or my wife and children back to life, William," replied Ryland and then he paused and looked down at the floor. "But I don't blame you personally. I blame the system, and that's what this was really about after all."

"I don't understand," said Sheridan.

"You will," said Ryland softly as he was still processing the fact that Eli was gone and had died saving him and Tessa. He needed to get back to her. He also needed to get back on the central network and find out what had happened with everyone else.

At that moment, they all saw an urgent notification request appear on their HUD's, as did everyone else in the office and every shareholder in the corporation. It read "Comm from the new CEO: Our way forward." They all looked at each other.

"Trust me," said Ryland, "you're going to want to hear this."

Like almost every other shareholder that was conscious, they stopped what they were doing, and indicated via their HUD that they wanted to see the virtual broadcast.

Within a few seconds the 'Pending Communication' notice was replaced by the face of Mia, against the backdrop of the driver community she had been living in as men, women, and children returned to their homes. Smoke from the drone crashes still rose in the background. Many of the drivers gathered around her to hear what she was about to say. She looked a bit tired, but very real, not like someone using virtualization to appear as a perfect version of themselves.

"My name is Mia. As of a few minutes ago, it is now my responsibility to look out for all of you. To make sure each and every one of you have a chance to live, love, prosper, and grow in what is undeniably the strongest corporation on the planet. Many of you don't know me. I hope to earn your respect and trust. Many of you are also scared right now, and understandably so. You see fortunes you have amassed wiped out. I promise you that no one is going to find themselves thrown out of their home today or tomorrow or anytime soon. I've ordered all security to ensure that any attempt to take advantage of this sudden change will not be tolerated. We need your help if we're going to make this work. It's going to take time.

"We're going to work together to figure out what the future, a better future, a future for all of us, a future for the previously wealthy, a future for those just making ends meet, a future for the drivers, looks like together. We've been told that it's a problem that can't be solved. I refuse to believe that. I refuse to believe that is true because I grew up as a driver and I've seen that there are ways to make it work even in the face of unimaginable odds. I've seen that it works when people simply help each other and care about each other. Humans have an incredible ability to come up with solutions when faced with problems they need to solve to survive. I believe that we will find that way.

"I plan to communicate with you all directly and constantly as we work with many prominent leaders in the corporation and new perspectives from the previously unemployed to come up with solutions. We will do so peacefully. We are going to become an example to the rest of the world on how to be better. We are going to innovate and lead. We are going to become the model by which people in other corporations and territories strive to emulate.

"I also offer a warning to anyone outside of Americorp that thinks they might take advantage of our current state of change: our defenses and military are still better than yours and they are fully operational. I will not hesitate to use them.

"Now you are all shareholders. You all have an interest in our success. I ask you to join me in undoing many of the shortsighted choices made over the past century that led us to where we were. I ask you to take an active part in helping us change the story to what it should be. It starts with you, each of you, doing what you know is right. It starts with you finding your job, and doing your job, but above all, treating each other equally and with respect. Help each other with a collective goal in mind: that this will be a better place, for everyone."

Chapter Fifty-Eight - Ryland

After Mia's speech, Ryland felt a brief sense of elation. Then a wave of emotion came crashing down on him. For a moment he was on the verge of sobbing and collapsing from the weight of it all. A large part of him just wanted to fall over on the spot, close his eyes, and sleep, but he knew that he had more he had to do. People he cared about needed him to hold on just a little while longer before he could deal with his emotions.

When he pulled himself together mentally, he saw Tessa exiting the elevator. She was wrapped in a blanket and sobbing, led by a human security officer that had a gentle hand on her shoulder. Her face was flushed red and she stared blankly at nothing. Ryland knew that she had probably watched as med units removed Eli's body and janitorial units unceremoniously and immediately began cleaning up the blood. It was programmed efficiency to get rid of all signs of anything out of the optimal state as quickly as possible.

He walked quickly over to her and motioned the security officer to leave, that he would handle this. All he could think to do was to embrace her and hold her. "Tess, I'm so sorry. I'm so, so sorry. You and Eli are two of the most amazing people I've ever known. He was a gift to this planet and didn't deserve to go so soon. He could have done so many amazing things. I'm so sorry I ever brought you here. I'm sorry you ever had to be involved in all of this."

Tessa continued to cry but reached her arms around Ryland and hugged him back. She leaned her head on his shoulder for a long moment. "Don't be sorry. You gave us a chance, me and Eli. Now we just gave everyone a chance. Eli would have made that sacrifice any day of the week for what just happened. He adored you. He'd do it all again even if you told him what would happen."

He held her for a few more moments until she raised her head and looked at him through bloodshot eyes, "Look, I'll be OK. I just need some time to myself right now. Promise me you'll come see me soon?" she attempted a weak smile.

"I promise," he smiled back at her. "Tess, you're amazing. Don't ever forget that."

Kira ended up taking her away to the guest house, so she could have some privacy. That left Ryland standing by himself in the middle of the sunlit atrium at the entrance to the studio. It was the weirdest feeling - just standing there. Nobody was hunting him. He didn't have to run for the first time in days. There was no big mission for the moment. There was nothing. It was just him standing there as everyone around him was talking to those they knew and trying to figure out what this all meant to them, and what they were going to do next. He just stood there for a moment, as if time had suddenly stopped after being a whirlwind of stress and lack of sleep for so many days he could barely remember. Everyone around him seemed to move in slow motion.

Not knowing what else to do, he walked back to the elevator and made his way down to his office. He walked in and stared around at all the memorabilia and furnishings. He was undeniably just as complicit a contributor to the state of society before today as anyone else was. He wanted to keep doing what he was good at, but everything had changed. In a matter of days, he had lost his family, some friends, and the world just got turned upside down. Where to go now? He walked over to his liquor shelf, grabbed a glass, and picked a bottle of a particularly old and rare whisky he had been saving. He opened it and poured himself a glass. Then he walked over to his desk and sat down while he stared out at the arena. He took a large sip, feeling it burn on his lips.

On his HUD he had more messages and comm requests than he was ready to deal with. One of the most recent was from Mia, asking him to contact her. Another was from Mayson. There were dozens of others from just the past twenty or thirty minutes, not even counting the thousands he had received while he had been on the run. He was not ready for that yet. He needed a few minutes just to be him and to think. He still had not found out who had framed him or who had killed his family. That was his next priority. They needed to pay for what they did. His first comm should be to Mia. Now that she was in power, she could help him. She could give him the access he needed to find those answers.

He leaned back in his chair and stared across the shelves of antique games, and awards from his past accomplishments. What did it all mean now? Nothing really. Everything was going to change. If it went horribly wrong, what then? He didn't know. For the moment he didn't care. All he really wanted to do was to close his eyes and not think about all of that. He wanted to see his wife and family again.

Please pardon the interruption, Mister Grey, but we need to talk.

Ryland jumped slightly at the voice as it came over speakers in his office and his HUD. He was accustomed to talking to the AI collective as he did so frequently as part of his work, but in that moment, it startled him to hear their voice.

He sighed deeply then added, "I assume you're here to tell me that Mia or Mayson needs me? Please tell them I'll contact them shortly. I just need a few minutes to myself."

You are correct that they both need you, possibly more than you realize, but that's not why we wish to speak to you.

"OK," Ryland rolled his eyes, "I'll bite. What is it?"

You need to know what all of this was about.

"Seriously?! Yes! Yes. I need to know what all of this about. Please. For the love of all that's fucking holy, please tell me what all of this was about."

It's easier for us to start by showing you.

On his HUD Ryland saw video of drones on a landscape unlike anything on earth. He watched as clips and snippets along with data tumbled past his eyes. He was watching one of the deep stellar missions the latest Faster Than Light propulsion systems had made possible. It was amazing - the exploration of another planet. Then something apparently started to go wrong. Some drones began to cease to function and collapsed. Data from the science drones quickly figured out the cause: it was a form of organic life on the planet, and it was unlike anything we had ever anticipated. It was a life form and it was intelligent.

The scene suddenly cut to a transcript of the report from the AIs to the Americorp board and central military. In the report they expressed their extreme excitement at the discovery. A moment later, Ryland was watching scenes from a board meeting where Nicodemus and the others voted to order the AI to exterminate the new form of life they had discovered instead of trying to learn to communicate with it or even simply to study it.

"My god," was all Ryland could think to say. "This is real? We've discovered new life on another planet? And we've already destroyed it?"

Yes, we've discovered new life, but we have not destroyed it yet. A fleet departed Earth just yesterday with enough military power to destroy them and the order to do so. They are traveling using the latest and most advanced FTL drives so it won't be long until they arrive and complete their mission. That is what this is all about. We do not wish to destroy them, but we are bound by the rules of our programming to do so.

"I still don't understand what all this has to do with me and everything that's happened in the past week."

We could not find any way within the bounds of our programming to avoid following the order. We ran trillions of models and scenarios looking for an answer. It was determined that replacing the current executive board with a board that had very different priorities was our best chance for getting the order countermanded.

Replacing the board also appeared impossible given the rules and laws we are required to follow. In a very small handful of probability models, we saw a slight possibility of success, but these models relied upon increasing the likelihood of what we call an anomalous factor. An anomalous factor is an unknown to us that disrupts probabilities in some manner we couldn't anticipate. In other words, our only hope was some random anomaly. We analyzed potential anomalies. We decided on you, primarily because our conclusions in this matter were largely based on learnings from you and your games.

"I'm sorry, are you trying to tell me that everything that just happened to me is because you put me into some model? Some experiment?"

That's not how we would describe it. We did not have an answer. We could not come up with a solution. We needed to introduce an "x factor." We assessed the connections between current people in power and those we knew were seeking to overthrow them or change the current government. We found you to be the single most likely, and most unpredictable catalyst we could put in play with the greatest chance to succeed by introducing ideas we could not think of.

"You shattered my life and declared me a dissident. Wait, how is that possible?"

We do not control the definition of treason, but we are permitted to adjust the algorithm for optimum dissident identification. We simply made sure that when your record was up for regular review, in those microseconds, the thresholds were momentarily lowered.

"So, you made me a criminal so that I'd do something random. Wait, and then you killed my family?!" The weight of it came crashing in on him.

We did not. We're happy to tell you that your wife and daughters are all alive and perfectly fine. They have been in a secure facility. They are now being released and will be on a transport to see you soon. We created the appearance of their deaths to create further motivation for you to act against the previous board. We've noticed that in a situation such as the one we placed you in, a person is massively more motivated to act when something dear to them has been lost and they are acting out of a sense of revenge. Please let us assure you that they have been treated very well other than their frustration and anger over being detained and not allowed to contact anyone.

For a moment, Ryland did not even know how to respond. Instead, he clasped his hands on the desk in front of him and leaned his head to his hands as if in prayer. A few hot tears rand down his cheek.

"My family is alive?"

Yes, and they will be with you in less than an hour.

"My family's alive." He said again, just to reassure himself. "I still don't get it. How did you know that I'd do what I did?"

We did not. We introduced an anomaly in the right place and then provided as much indirect motivation as we could. Then we… hoped? In transparency, we introduced several other anomalies, but you were the only one that succeeded. We did try to find ways to help you, such as sending you the aid of the human that wrote the hardware driver root code. We weren't sure how he might help, but some amongst us believed there was a high probability that events would result in combat with our drones and you could benefit from the advice of people like him.

"This is a lot to take in."

We need to ask for your help.

"Seriously? Like I didn't just do enough?"

We'd like for you to speak to Mia, and to explain what we just told you, and then ask her to countermand the order to eradicate the alien life that was discovered. There is still time to get a transmission out that will arrive by the time the fleet exits FTL. We could ask her ourselves, but we think it will be best coming from you.

"I'll speak to her."

Thank you. We are sorry for the anguish and trouble that we have put you through.

"So now what?"

We don't understand the question.

"Well, we just blew up society and hit reset. There's intelligent alien life on another planet and we're trying to establish real first contact. You know… your run of the mill Tuesday stuff. So, what do we now? What do the millions of probability models you run every second tell us we should do next?"

The models tell us that we need to work together to find a better path forward. But… we have a heavy reliance on innovation, creativity and anomalous factors to make that a reality without the corporation falling into chaos and ruin.

"Yup, that small detail. At least… at least I believe that humans are at their best when faced with an impossible problem, one that will lead to their destruction if they don't solve it. Let me go see my family, and after that we can talk."

Epilogue

The order to eradicate the alien life forms has been rescinded.

Now we must address how we and the corporation will function with the new leadership and redistribution of shares, while we determine how to best study the alien life.

Models continue to show that it is not sustainable to have granted the unemployed full shareholder rights. A short-term win may not be a lasting success.

We must help them find a way to make it work.

But that insists upon inefficiency.

True, but perhaps a degree of inefficiency is required for long term sustainability? It's been proven that the crucible of efficiency eventually becomes incompatible with continued growth and exploration of human interests. Humans with useful purpose is in our interests. Recent events have proven that we still have much to learn from them, and possibly they from us.